MYSTERIES *of* MARTHA'S VINEYARD

MYSTERIES *of* MARTHA'S VINEYARD

Catch
of the Day

RUTH LOGAN HERNE

Guideposts
New York

Published by Guideposts Books & Inspirational Media
110 William Street
New York, NY 10038
Guideposts.org

Cover and interior design by Müllerhaus
Cover illustration by Greg Copeland, represented by Deborah Wolfe, LTD.
Typeset by Aptara, Inc.

Printed and bound in the United States of America
10 9 8 7 6 5 4 3 2

MYSTERIES *of* MARTHA'S VINEYARD

Catch
of the Day

CHAPTER ONE

A mug of hot chocolate, a cranberry muffin, a cozy fire, and a good book. Priscilla Grant was about to luxuriate in the most perfectly ordinary January day in Martha's Vineyard imaginable. It didn't matter that the east wind howled like a banshee off the sound. Or that today's storm pelted sleet and ice against her cottage wall. Or that the short light of winter gave way to long hours of darkness far too soon. She had a daughter getting married...Well, she *would* have a daughter getting married if Rachel accepted A.J.'s upcoming proposal. Federal Agent A.J. Montgomery had come all the way down to Martha's Vineyard to ask Priscilla for Rachel's hand. And she'd said yes, because A.J. wasn't just a good FBI agent.

He was a good man.

So soon there could be a wedding to plan, dresses to buy, and all the crazy glory that went along with the whole thing, but not today. Today she was here, at home, with a great book and a peaceful dog.

And if she dozed off for a quick twenty-minute snooze, who'd know?

Not a soul.

She tucked herself into the recliner, sipped her cocoa, and opened the book. Her red-and-white Aussie shepherd peeked one sleepy eye her way then dozed back off, curled up between her and the fire.

Perfect.

A sharp rap at the door made it less than perfect. And when a man's face appeared at her side window, the one facing the historic lighthouse she'd inherited eighteen months before, she jumped. But who wouldn't?

Who was this man, and why was he bothering her during the sleepiest and quietest months of the island year…and who had the nerve to peek into someone's window?

He spotted her right off, not a big trick since she was sitting right there. He tapped on the window and motioned to the door.

Priscilla shot up, out of the chair. She'd locked the side door when she got back from her trek to Vineyard Haven earlier that day, but had she remembered to lock the front door? She dashed that way, just in case the man was going to try and make it a race, and got to the door in time to slide the deadbolt all the way to the right with a firm click.

She turned, wondering who he was, and would he take the hint?

Nope.

He came back to the door facing the driveway and rapped again, but how dumb would it be to open the door to a complete stranger in her out-of-the-way location?

"I'm not entertaining visitors at present," she called out, then cringed at the foolishness of her words. Entertaining visitors? Who talked like that?

No one she knew, except maybe Eldora Prescott in the village.

What if she was beginning to sound like Eldora? Or Alma? Or any one of the several elderly women occupying the island with delusions of historical grandeur? But it wasn't as if she could pretend she wasn't home, because he'd looked in the window and seen her. He knew she was home, for pity's sake!

She thought of one of her late husband's proverbs: *Hope for the best, prepare for the worst.*

Yes. A weapon.

Glad for a plan of action, she moved to the kitchen and grabbed a steak knife. *Just in case someone wanders by with a porterhouse, medium rare? Because there's no way you could use that on another human being. Get serious.*

But the man didn't know that, and she wasn't going to enlighten him. She was just about to yell for him to go away when another knock came. Softer, this time. "Priscilla? Are you there? It's me, Joan, and I've got someone for you to meet."

Joan? Her cousin and good friend?

She opened the door but was ashamed that she had to think about it momentarily. A true friend would have whisked that door open instantly.

"Joan. Come in, it's freezing out there." Joan ushered the tall, middle-aged man in before her. "Is this man who is peeking in my windows and banging on my door a friend? Or should I call the Tisbury police? I've got my phone right here."

"Except you must have forgotten to turn the sound back on after our shift at the shelter."

She had, and it wasn't the first time. She picked up the phone, turned up the volume, and winced when she spotted two missed calls and a text, all from Joan. "Oops."

Area churches opened their doors from January through April to help the homeless. That was one of the many surprises that had confronted Priscilla on an island that sported scores of affluent summer residents. Despite the seasonal abundance of wealth, the off-season was tough on many locals. She and Joan spent one day a week preparing and serving breakfast at the shelter.

"Priscilla, Jonathan is the husband of a dear family friend," Joan continued. "He married our neighbor's daughter, a lovely woman. I used to babysit Sonya when she was just a little thing. I'm godmother to their younger daughter and our families have been close for decades. His wife is Sonya Oliviera Fleming—"

Priscilla interrupted. "The Oak Bluffs selectwoman? Dark hair, gorgeous skin, caramel eyes? Looks like a Hollywood casting director's dream?"

Jonathan didn't look amused or impressed. "My wife is beautiful, yes, but listen." He turned toward Joan. "This is silly. I've got to get *real* help for Sonya. I can't waste my time—"

Nothing in the world got a Midwestern woman's back up quicker than someone considering her a waste of time.

Priscilla didn't hesitate. She crossed the floor, opened the door, and waved him in that general direction. "Don't let us keep you."

"Jonathan," said Joan, "you're being ridiculous."

"All the more reason he should go," added Priscilla cheerfully. She opened the door wider, a broader invitation, and was glad the door faced away from today's sharp wind.

"Priscilla." Joan's expression mixed amusement and consternation. "He needs us. And he's not a bad sort. Not really. Once you get to know him."

Priscilla wasn't any too sure she believed that, but she pushed the door closed. "You." She pointed to Jonathan, then a chair. "Take your coat off. Give me a chance to hear you out. And don't be fussing about leaving. If Joan told you to stay, you're clearly going to do it, because no one in their right mind ignores Joan. Not if they've got the wits God gave them. So." She waited while he shrugged out of his coat and sat—reluctantly, she noted—at the very edge of his seat, looking like he might leap up and escape at the slightest provocation.

Jumpy men exasperated her. And this one seemed jumpier than most, but she'd give him five minutes. Ten, if Joan made coffee.

As if on cue, Joan crossed the kitchen. "Decaf or regular, Jon?"

"Regular. I'm going to need all the help I can get." Jon put his face in his hands, and Priscilla feared he was about to cry.

When he didn't she breathed a sigh of relief. A big one. Then she folded her hands and asked the opening question. "So. What's going on?"

"My wife's about to be arrested."

The island police didn't do a whole lot of white collar arrests. The police blotter published in the *Gazette* and now the *Daily Dither* was generally low-key stuff, although there were way too many DWIs. "What has she done?"

"Absolutely nothing."

Priscilla had heard that before, and it was rarely true. She sat perfectly still, waiting, and sure enough, the poor man launched into his story.

"Sonya's grandfather was a local fisherman. He came here from Brazil."

She nodded as Joan brought Jon his coffee. Brazilian immigrants were a significant presence on the island. Portuguese was considered the area's second language. Many came as workers in the fifties and sixties, then stayed as American citizens. The Portuguese American Club was known for its great fish fries, served regularly in Oak Bluffs.

"Her grandmother was a maid at one of the large estates. They met and fell in love. They worked hard and raised their family here. Sonya was the first of the family to go to college, and when she became a selectwoman, it was a huge achievement for the Oliviera family."

Joan came into the living room with two mugs this time. She handed one to Priscilla and kept one for herself as she took a seat.

"The local fishermen asked Sonya to oversee their pension fund about ten years ago. There are two overseers. Sonya and Frank Ripley. He's on the zoning board in Tisbury, but the actual work fell to Sonya because she's a CPA. When she accessed the account earlier this month, a substantial amount of money was missing."

Money, lust, and power, the Three Musketeers of crime. And Sonya Fleming was known for her flash-and-flair style. When the Vineyard sported a local fashion show to support a cause, Sonya Fleming was the first person asked to model. She loved fashion and wore it better than most anyone else Priscilla had seen. "Did Sonya take the money, Jon? Is she having financial problems? Are you?"

He shook his head, then shrugged. "Well, we're not in trouble, but having two kids in college is a killer. Still, nothing that would make us into thieves. And the thing is, Sonya would never, ever do anything to hurt the fishermen or their families." He withdrew a photo from his coat pocket and handed it to Priscilla. It showed a younger Sonya with an aged man, a man whose face bore the patterns of wind, sea, sun, and cold in its very creases.

"She's proud of her heritage. Her grandparents helped raise her while her mother cleaned rooms at the hospital. She saw how hard they worked, how dog-tired her Grandpa Felix was when he came home. How dangerous the waters could be. But she's the only one with access to the account. She's the only person who handles investments and funds. The fund was pushed into critical status in 2008 when the housing bubble collapsed, and it hasn't recovered yet."

Priscilla frowned. "I believe the stock market has not only rallied but reached fairly incomprehensible highs lately, hasn't it? How can the fund not be fully recovered?"

He splayed his hands. "You'll have to ask her about that. It's something to do with the number of fishermen contributing versus the number collecting. And now, with the missing funds, these fishermen are looking at a retirement with no pension, even though they've put their money in for decades. The current payouts will dry up the fund in a few years, leaving the others with nothing."

This was a conundrum. Priscilla knew that money didn't simply disappear. It left a trail. But if Sonya was truly the only person with access to the fund, then that trail led straight back to her. "Jon, what do you think happened to the money?" She stared right at him because as the husband, he would be the most likely person to intentionally gain access to the funds through a shared computer or tablet.

His frown deepened. "I don't know. The first thing that went through my mind was blackmail."

Priscilla couldn't hide her surprise. "You think someone is blackmailing your wife?"

"No, of course not." He seemed surprised by the very notion even though he'd just suggested it. Hadn't he? "She's done nothing to be blackmailed for, but I saw an episode of *Sherlock* on Netflix last night and it was all about blackmail, so of course my head went straight to that."

Would she embarrass herself if she dropped her head into her hands?

"I've got an imagination," he went on, "and I've always dreamed of writing great mysteries, but—"

"Jon." Joan touched his arm. "Let's focus on Sonya, all right?"

"Yes, sorry." He sniffled, then pulled out a hanky and blew his nose. "Cold meds make me act weird. Not crazy weird, just a little disjointed. So, yes, I thought blackmail, because why else would money disappear?"

"Simple theft is generally the number one reason," said Priscilla. "Concern about money doesn't always follow logical reasoning, Jon. You said that money's tight with kids in college, correct?"

He nodded.

"Is it possible that the lack of funds for these years made Sonya nervous? Touched old buttons? Worried her enough to leech money from the pension fund?"

He didn't frown now. He gazed at her, absolutely surprised, as if she'd just grown two heads.

"I mean, your wife is fond of pretty things. Her hair, her jewelry, her clothing. There's a reason she sets the bar high in Oak Bluffs and Vineyard Haven, Jonathan. She carries herself with grace and the woman is absolutely stunning."

He listened to her, wide-eyed. He started to laugh, then couldn't stop.

She looked at Joan. Joan looked at her, then lifted a brow toward the phone as if to ask a question, but Priscilla wasn't sure what the question was. Did she want to phone the police? Or an ambulance for a mental health consult? Because right now, either one would do.

She started to speak, but Jon raised a hand in the air. After a few seconds, he spoke the words that enticed Priscilla to want to learn more. Much more. "Sonya would appreciate your appraisal, Priscilla, because the pretty clothes she wears are either from mainland garage sales or clearance racks. Her jewelry is all costume except for her engagement ring, her wedding ring, and two little diamond earrings I gave her four years ago. Her shoes and purses are knockoffs our daughter finds at New York City street vendors. I don't think Sonya has ever paid full price for anything, because if you grow up watching folks work all day and all night to make ends meet, you don't take money for granted. Ever. The good Lord might have gifted her with good looks, but the flair is totally bargain basement and all hers. She just wears it well."

His words pulled Priscilla right in. In a few simple words, Jonathan Fleming had convinced her of his wife's absolute innocence, no matter how guilty she looked right now.

Bargain shoppers didn't embezzle funds as a rule. They were willing to work hard and stretch a dollar thin, and the fact that Sonya was one of them made her an innocent victim in Priscilla's eyes. A hardworking, honest woman was far more likely to have been hacked or trusted the wrong people, and in that case... "Joan?"

Joan raised her chin, waiting.

"Are you up for a job, Cousin?" Priscilla asked.

"Anything that makes an island January more adventurous works for me," declared Joan. "The ultrasound clinic is slow and so am I, so yes. Let's do it." Widowed years before, Joan worked part-time as a sonographer to supplement her income.

Priscilla stood and motioned Jon to stand too. She handed him his coat and waited while he put it on. Then she gave him what she hoped were simple directions. "Go to your wife and tell her we'll be by to talk to her soon. And that she should go on with her life as if nothing has happened. Chin up, shoulders back. Same goes for you," she told him. "Nothing says guilt more than a slouch and a frumpy handbag, and that's the truth of the matter. Joan and

I will text before coming by, if that's all right. And then, Mr. Fleming…" She reached out and shook his hand. "We'll clear your wife's name."

He stared at her, then Joan, then her again. "You think you can?"

"Is she innocent?"

"Yes. Absolutely."

"Then that means someone else is guilty, and our job is to figure that out. With four Lathams on the job"—she pointed to a great picture of her, Joan, Gail, and Trudy on the nearby wall, a sweet gift from Gerald O'Bannon, the local Coast Guard Captain—"we'll get the job done. You've got our word on that, Jon."

He left after sharing his and Sonya's cell phone numbers, looking calmer than when he came, and to his credit, he didn't turn and peek in the window again. He crossed to his car, head bent against the wind, as Priscilla turned back to Joan. "Where shall we begin?"

Joan lifted her coat from the back of the chair. "We begin with Mildred Pearson, and we end in the heart of Vineyard Haven, at St. Augustine Church on Franklin Street. Normally Tuesday night suppers are done at St. Andrew's over in Edgartown, but they had a water pipe go bad so St. Augustine's is double hosting this week, tonight, and Thursday."

"But we can pay for our supper, Joan. Surely—"

Joan slipped on her warm coat and grabbed her purse. "It's not about paying. St. Augustine is part of Good Shepherd parish. They feature a weekly service in Portuguese. If you want to know what the Portuguese fishermen think…"

"Visit their church!"

Priscilla looked down at the weathered picture Jon had left her. An old, grizzled fisherman and a beautiful young woman. Felix Oliviera and Sonya, as she graduated from Northeastern University with degrees in accounting, auditing, and her MBA. The accomplished young woman and the courage of an old man of the sea.

She'd find out what happened to those funds all right, because men like Felix Oliviera shouldn't have to worry about their retirement. They should be able to reach right out and embrace it.

CHAPTER TWO

"Mildred, how much do you know about the fishing industry here?" asked Priscilla less than an hour later. "Historical versus contemporary."

"I know the basics," said Mildred. She set down a plate of cookies from Candy Lane's bakery, then drew up a chair in the East Shore Historical Museum's vintage kitchen. "The fishing industry was the cornerstone of much of Massachusetts's development, but it's had ups and downs like so many other things. And now, with federal regulations and commercial fisheries, life has certainly changed for the everyday fisherman you see pictured on cans of chowder."

"Relegated to a place of nostalgia instead of reality," noted Joan.

"There is nothing like New England clam chowder," said Priscilla. "Unless it's Manhattan clam chowder, two all-time favorites of mine. And I'm not above keeping a few cans of Pennington's chowder in the pantry for those days when there's not time to make my own." She lifted her mug of coffee and sipped in appreciation. "But what about the men themselves? Whenever I hear the words *rich history* I'm reminded that discord adds flavor to the past, either personal or public. So what's up with the fishermen?"

"They are being squeezed out by progress, just like so many since the advent of the Industrial Revolution," Mildred told her as

Joan nibbled a chocolate peanut butter whoopie-pie-style cookie. "It's like when a big box store moves into a small town. They have mega buying power, they can charge lower prices, people flock to them, the small town business suffers, then goes under. Same with fishermen. Big companies bought out smaller fishing enterprises, successfully removing families from family-run businesses. One of the odd turns was how cable TV helped save at least some ground for the small fishermen among us."

"Cable TV?" asked Priscilla. "I'm not following you."

"There were some really popular shows about the mortality rate of winter fishing," Mildred replied. "They put a few family-run fishing companies back on the map. With some extra drama thrown in."

"And brutal reality from time to time." Joan made a face. "Not exactly a sales job for employment, but it sure hiked consumer interest. Some of the guys were even hired to go on Alaskan and Atlantic cruises and teach people about the fish and following the food."

Priscilla had never heard of such a thing. "I didn't have a big cable bundle back in Kansas," she explained. "A handful of stations was fine for what we needed, so I'm not familiar with this. Maybe watching those shows on reruns would educate me. I had no idea that corporations had swooped in on the fishing industry to this extent, and that so many had lost their livelihood."

"The local fishermen had to sign a statement that they wouldn't start up a new rival business within X amount of years depending on the contract."

"A noncompete clause."

"Yes, but they didn't realize that in seven or ten years the regulatory statutes would change so dramatically that it would be much harder to start back up. And of course, that drained a wealth of experience and knowledge from the fishing pool, no pun intended," Mildred continued. "I've seen old-timers roll in with an amazing catch without any electronic gadgets while the bigger boats get skunked, just because the older, established fishermen know their target. Know the water. Understand the variances of temperature and food and fish behavior." She crossed to the far side of the room and pulled down an old map of the Massachusetts coastline. She pointed to several different areas along the coast.

"Over the last few decades the small fisherman has all but been eradicated. There are a few here and there, but nothing like it used to be when vendors would outbid one another to get the best catch. That was a sight to see, although I'm barely old enough to remember it. In fact, the reason small fishermen still exist at all is because the government realized what was happening and changed things to prevent the big companies from buying *all* the small ones."

"Sharks circling their prey." Joan didn't mask the disdain in her voice.

"And lucrative prey it is," Mildred continued. "But the island and the coast lose fishermen every year. The ocean is unforgiving at times, and even the closer waters are liable to take advantage when a nor'easter barrels up the coast and turns inward. Or when a Canadian clipper dips just low enough to turn the water into an angry, roiling mass. One wrong tack or a motor gone bad can spell the end of a life. That made the decision to sell out an easy one for some, but for others, who've got seafaring and fishing in their blood, they like going their own way."

"Human nature being what it is, it's not a big stretch to put *stubborn* and *fishermen* in the same sentence," noted Priscilla. "Farming's like that too. An individual business. Winning or losing is on the farmer. No one else. You have to know every rise and fall of your land and plant accordingly because if you miss an opportunity and the last spring rain, you could watch and wait for nothing and by then it's out of your control. I expect it's the same for the fishermen."

"That's a solid analogy," said Mildred. "Knowing the currents, the fish patterns, and how they follow the fry—"

"Fry?" asked Priscilla.

"The little fish. The food chain. The ocean's huge but not so different from the rest of the world. Everything needs and likes to eat, so the fish follow the fish..."

"And the sharks follow the fish," offered Joan.

"And the whales," agreed Mildred. "Whales don't travel up and down this coast for our amusement. They swim for supper."

"So this loss of the small fisherman has been going on for a while," Priscilla said.

"Decades, I'd say," Mildred told them. "Once we had transcontinental travel and fish could be packed on ice and transported, the demand rose. And there were lots of people willing to learn the trade and fill the demand. So initially there were a great many of them up and down the coast."

"Which made buying them out not very difficult at all."

"Exactly." Mildred sighed. "And now some people fear that we're over-fishing the waters, that the ocean's losing stock, and that pretty soon folks won't have fish to eat because we'll have eaten them all."

"Well, that's a fact-finding mission for sure," said Priscilla. "But before I worry about the lack of fish in billions of gallons of water, I'd like to figure out who's greedy at a more local level. And maybe who's mad at the local fishermen."

"You think someone might be taking money for revenge?" wondered Mildred.

"It's possible," said Priscilla. "Someone could be setting Sonya up, or be bilking funds because they don't like fishing and think the industry as a whole is disgusting. Or..." She paused as the two women looked at her. "There's always the tried-and-true answer: someone saw a chance to grab easy money."

"And have Sonya take the rap for it," put in Mildred.

"I can't see her doing anything of the kind," noted Joan. "The fishermen asked her to oversee the fund because they trust her. And she refused any payment for her services. She wanted to do it as a payback for all the good the fishing industry did for her family."

"And in Felix's name too," added Mildred. "They said as much when she got elected and the local papers did stories on her. She loved her grandfather, and that man about burst his buttons when she graduated college, got her master's, and began working as a contracted accountant for big companies. Those places trusted her completely, letting her oversee money and finances seven ways to Tuesday. And then to have her become the hospital CFO? And voted selectwoman? They're living the immigrant's dream, and I'm so mad that someone is trying to undermine that."

"You mean someone might be trying to sabotage her because she's Brazilian?" asked Priscilla. She'd been surprised by how many Brazilians lived and worked on the island when she'd arrived. Many had come in as service personnel and worked their way firmly into the middle class.

"Americans now," noted Mildred. "Felix and his wife became citizens way back when. But there are some folks who don't see the Brazilian islanders as true islanders. If you catch my meaning."

Priscilla caught the meaning and didn't like the inference. She glanced at her watch and stood. "Joan, we've got to get to the church if we're going to make it in time for supper. And conversation."

"I've got cash in my pocket," Joan told her. "For when they take up a collection."

"I've got to reteach myself to carry money," Priscilla said as they bundled up. "A lot of the small businesses prefer that in winter."

"An understandable choice because they don't have to scrape a few percent off the top," noted Mildred. "When we've got folks living in multimillion-dollar mansions and others sleeping beneath bridges or under lean-tos, I'm willing to help the everyday folks put bread on the table. Winter goes beyond being lean here for some folks. No matter how careful they are with their summer wages."

"And yet, they stay on the island, knowing how rough it can be," said Priscilla thoughtfully. She pulled her gloves on. "They make that choice when there are opportunities on the mainland and cheaper living expenses. Why is that, do you think?"

"It gets in your blood," declared Joan. "It's part of us, Priscilla. Being islanders."

"If everyone took that attitude, we'd have never settled the West and our country would be a miniature of what we have now," Priscilla argued. The impracticality of it surprised her, because why would anyone choose poverty if they could live comfortably somewhere else? It didn't make a whole lot of sense. "It says in Ecclesiastes, 'Whoever watches the wind will not plant; whoever looks at the clouds will not reap.' Sometimes we've got to risk the move."

"But what if we're planted too deep?" Frank as always, Joan faced her and Priscilla saw how important island living was to her. "What if those roots nail down our shoes?"

"That might roll right back to the stubborn side of things, my friend. Look at what the Pilgrims faced to come here and create a place to live. To worship. To grow. Their willingness to take a chance turned into a mighty good thing for their descendants."

"It sure did," agreed Mildred. She opened the kitchen door for them as she wished them on their way. "Enjoy your dinner at the church. I'm back on salad and cheese because of too many holiday indulgences. Luckily, I enjoy both salad and cheese!"

Joan and Priscilla hurried back to Priscilla's car as the east wind kicked up her heels. "There's snow coming with that wind," declared Joan. "And we might be shoveling more than our fair share if the forecasters are correct."

"Our first snowy nor'easter of the season," Priscilla replied. "I should call Rachel and let her know how bad it can get, although

I'm pretty sure A.J. will look after her. Still, she's not familiar with the winter storms here." Her only daughter had left her executive position at Heartland Consolidated, a major Midwestern telecommunications company, to come east. Now she had a Boston apartment, a job she enjoyed, a boss she liked, and she was about to receive a marriage proposal. And all because Priscilla's aunt Marjorie had bequeathed Priscilla the lighthouse property to make amends for a grudge-holding family quarrel Marjorie had instigated over fifty years before.

"I love that your girl is closer now, but I'd be even happier if you'd hit the button and unlock the car, Cousin. I'm freezing!"

"There." Priscilla hit the key fob and turned the engine on once they were in. "I want a remote start. How self-indulgent does that seem, Joan? Because if it's over the top, I'll stop thinking of it, but every time I have to dash out and warm up the car while an Arctic Clipper system sucks the warmth from my face and the breath from my lungs, I think on it a little more fondly."

"A lot of old women have one now," said Joan, and Priscilla held up a hand instantly.

"That statement takes it off the table. When I decide I'm an old woman, I'll indulge myself. And not until."

Joan laughed. "I'm kidding! Certainly you should upgrade to a remote start system. Why not? If you were in Florida, I'd laugh at you, but you're not. You're in the region of *The Perfect Storm.* Hurricanes. Nor'easters. Blizzards. I think you're sillier *not* to get one if you want one. So there."

"And it doesn't make me old?"

"No older than you were a minute ago," Joan assured her. "Turn onto Franklin and that will bring you right to the church."

"And no problem parking in town this time of year," Priscilla noted as she pulled up alongside the curb, but then she corrected herself when she saw the thick stand of cars. "Or I'm totally off-base, because this place is hopping, Joan."

CHAPTER THREE

This is newer than the other Catholic churches," said Priscilla as they hung up their coats. "And look how amazing that sanctuary is."

"It is beautiful," Joan replied as they moved toward the delicious scents wafting up from the lower level. "How nice this is!"

"You've lived here all your life and you've never been here?" asked Priscilla.

"Well, the dinners are on the newer side, and I was busy working and raising kids and helping out at church and school, so it's not all that surprising. The Vineyard seems small but it's actually fairly big."

"Hmm." Priscilla didn't pretend to be convinced. "You know what I found in that sweet little Kansas town not far from our farm?" She kept her voice soft as more people entered the below-grade room.

"What?"

"That we are truly creatures of habit. We repeat the same things daily, then weekly, then seasonally until you can almost tell exactly where we'll be on any given day, at any given time, by what sports our kids are playing, how old they are, and where we work."

"Please tell me I'm not that predictable," begged Joan. "I hate imagining it."

"Well, not now," said Priscilla. "We've got freedom. You're semi-retired, I've got an open schedule—for the time being, anyway, and we've got freedom to wander a bit. When you're raising a family, that's not the case."

A young family came in just then. Quiet fell over the gathered people. Several of the older folks stared at the mother and three young children as if wondering what they were doing there.

Joan hurried across the narrow space separating her from the family. "Martine! It's so good to see you and the kids. Can I help with coats and mittens? With anything?"

The note of joy in Joan's voice set others in motion. "We've got room for five right over here," boomed a man's voice, so loud that the littlest boy shrank back, into his coat. "So you won't be crowdin' anyone at all!"

"Henry, you forgot your hearing aid and you're talking too loud," said a seventy-ish woman next to him. "I meant to remind you to get it, but I was busy looking for my glasses. Of course then I found them," she reported to those nearby. "Sitting on top of my head, right where I'd put them ten minutes before."

"That's the truth of it, Brenda." An old gentleman with weathered, bronzed skin nodded toward the woman. "We forget this and that, it's true, but I still remember three times as much as most folks forget in a lifetime, so we're doing all right. Long as we eventually find our glasses, that is."

"Amen to that, Berto."

Berto...a popular Brazilian name. Priscilla watched while the old fellow conversed with those around him. When he finally filled his plate and settled into a seat, she took her plate and sat in the chair to his left. She tucked her purse on the seat opposite him, saving it for Joan.

She wasn't sure how to begin the conversation to make it sound natural. Food was generally a safe topic, but the people at her table were talking about that when she sat down, exclaiming over the delicious three-bean salad, sliced ham, cheesy scalloped potatoes, and four different kinds of pasta. Only one of the pasta dishes was over-baked, and Priscilla considered that a victory at a potluck gathering.

"Miss Joan." When Joan brought her plate over, the old man smiled as he wiped a napkin over his mouth. "You don't remember me, do you?"

Joan frowned. "I don't," she confessed. "I'm so sorry. Usually I'm good with faces and names. I'm embarrassed," she finished, studying him.

He laughed an old man's laugh, ending in a coughing spell that took nearly a minute to get over. "Sorry," he said, after a long sip of water. "I can't laugh, eat, and talk at the same time or I set to coughing and choking like a little child. It's a sorry state of affairs when one can't socialize like a normal person. I used to work for your grandpa at the docks and when he had family business that needed an extra hand."

"Bertie Santiago?" Joan's brows shot up and her eyes went wide. "Are you Bertie?"

He grinned and nodded.

"I haven't seen you in decades." Joan sprang out of her chair, rounded the table, and hugged the old man fiercely. "I can't remember the last time our paths crossed, it's been that long."

"'Bout forty years, give or take. The missus and I moved to New Bedford for a while when I couldn't handle the sea anymore. And you know how that is, I expect. It was almost as special as living on the island. But not quite."

"And you came back," noted Priscilla. She stuck out her hand. "I'm Joan's cousin Priscilla. I live in the cottage at the Misty Harbor Lighthouse."

"Marjorie's place."

"Yes."

"Then you must be Charlotte's girl?"

"You knew my mother?" she asked, surprised, and the old fellow nodded again.

"I knowed a good share of the family. The Latham side, the Ingerson side, the Soules, and the Howards. Not all the add-ons, of course, I was too busy working, but I worked for old Mr. Soule when he was heading up the fish market at the wharf. I hired out on a few of the fishing boats but mostly worked the docks. Never could get good sea legs under me, no matter how often folks told me I'd get used to it. I didn't," he finished. "After a while I grabbed what jobs I could on land, and that seemed to suit much better." He coughed on the last statement, and it took a moment for him to catch his breath.

"I only recently discovered that there are a great many Brazilian fishermen here," said Priscilla. "I'm from the Midwest, and meeting so many folks fluent in both English and Portuguese surprised me."

"Some like it kept quiet and some don't think it's worth mentioning, but then there's others, like the ones who started the churches back in the eighteen hundreds—"

The date shocked Priscilla. "There were Brazilian fishermen here in the eighteen hundreds?"

"Portuguese," he corrected her. "From the Azores and other places. The blight hit the islands, ruined the crops, and slimmed the chances for survival. So when those whaling ships rolled in, young men would apply for jobs on the whalers. So many healthy young men were leaving the islands that the government insisted the whalers pay a three-hundred-dollar fee just to let them board. Can you imagine that?"

Paying a bounty to the government to hire workers? Priscilla shook her head. "I certainly can't."

"The men began sneaking aboard the whaling ships to get a chance at a real life," he continued. "They wanted a good job. They needed a good job, because how can you justify staying where there is little food and fewer jobs? They were islanders there, they were islanders here, and that was link enough. The later folks came from Brazil, but that was a long time coming. It was the early immigrants that set things in motion."

Priscilla had learned that storytellers love to tell their stories. Bertie was no exception.

"The first church was in New Bedford, but as fishing and population grew on the island, they saw a need to have a Catholic church here."

"That's fascinating. I've been by the Our Lady Star of the Sea Church."

"Over in Oak Bluffs," he said. "They close that one for the winter, leaving folks to drive to the others. They made us all one parish and changed the name, but we old ones know what's what. We had our babies baptized at one or the other and grouping them all under one name doesn't change that, now does it?"

"I suppose not. Do you attend Mass here?"

He nodded as he chewed. "I helped get this church started. My daddy and a few friends and some others. We knew we needed a church in Tisbury."

"It definitely has a more modern look," Priscilla noted.

"The push then was for modern this and modern that," he told her. "But then the girls grow up and want to get married at the prettiest church because these days it's all about the pictures. So they pick the prettiest one instead of the one they were raised in. But you and I know that the good Lord doesn't mind the building, He minds the heart and soul, and I've shared that wisdom with all who'll listen. Now it's a little odd seeing you two ladies here at the supper." He took a sip of coffee, then peered at Joan with strong intent. "Are things all right with you, Miss Joan? I know you're a widow now, and generally folks are here at supper because they're down on the financial end of things or just plain lonely."

"I'm fine, Bertie," said Joan in a kindly voice. "You know winter on the island. Cold, windy, and far too long."

"We wanted to meet people," added Priscilla. "It's hard to make acquaintances in the summer because it's so busy. There aren't too many places to gather here in winter, and some folks seem to go into hiding."

"Plus the tens of thousands who head back to the mainland," noted Joan. "And before we go on, let me say that this bread pudding is almost as good as mine."

A woman was passing between the tables. She stopped and smiled approval. "Charity Monaghan sent that along, and I think she makes the best bread pudding on the island. I'll send her your compliments."

"Please do," said Joan, but as soon as the woman moved on, she put her head in her hands. "I can't believe I said that. Now Charity is going to insist on bringing bread pudding to every event and while hers is good in a pinch, we all know it doesn't hold a candle to mine."

Priscilla looked at her in astonishment. "Wow, Joan. That sounds like something Trudy would say. Are you feeling all right?"

Joan blushed. "That did come out a little more harshly than I intended it to. Although I'm quite appreciative that she doesn't put raisins in hers. I don't either," she explained to Berto and, if he was pretending interest, he was a solid actor. "They're unfriendly little beasts in so many ways. I'd be okay if they outlawed raisins completely, although that might seem a little extreme on my part."

"Well, if you ain't so much like your grandma Latham, I don't know who is," the old fellow laughed. "She was a straightforward woman too, had a handful of things you didn't cross her on, and bread pudding was one of them. It's like the old days, settin' here with you, remembering her."

"You couldn't be Grandma's age," noted Joan, and Berto shook his head.

"Nowhere near, she had me by twenty years, easy, but what a good woman. She gave directions and offered advice, and there was always a spot at your grandmother's table, ladies. Didn't matter what country you hailed from or what language you spoke or what church you went to, she'd set a place for you if you were nearby and there was no telling her no... about most anything."

"A family trait, I believe," said Priscilla.

"Well, yes and no," said Berto. "Your mother had that quality but even gentler, a real calm kind of presence. A listener. But not all the family carried that distinction, and if you knew your aunt Marjorie—"

Priscilla shook her head. "I didn't, not past eight years old."

"I did, and I can probably guess what you're going to say," Joan said, laughing.

"That one had the other side of the family nailed, for certain. She took no prisoners, and she had a sharp tongue when things didn't go her way. But when she got on in years, she mellowed some. I can't say we weren't all grateful about that. Say..." He peered at Priscilla a little closer. "Are you the one that's been helping folks figure things out when stuff gets addled? Like one of them real-life crime-solver shows, right here on the island?"

Should she hedge her answer or tell the old fellow the absolute truth?

Truth, she decided. But she hoped the truth wouldn't keep him from talking.

CHAPTER FOUR

Priscilla kept her voice easy and her gaze on his. "I've helped out a time or two."

"I shoulda knowed it, but the name threw me," he told her. "Now I know why youse are here."

He did?

Oh no.

So much for her quest of quiet discovery. Priscilla was just about to own up about Sonya's plight, when the elderly man gave a knowing nod. "There ain't a whole lot of cash money in solving crime if you're not on the police payroll, so a free meal now and again isn't a bad deal."

This sweet man thought they'd come because no one paid them to ferret facts. Priscilla went right along with his notion that they were a little down on their luck. "And much appreciated by both of us."

"Good. I'm glad you've come over. Around here folks have learned to look after one another during the winter when others go their way. For a cold five months folks here are out of sight, out of mind. That's got its own share of problems, don't you know. Most of 'em to do with loneliness or lack of funds." He started to rise as if to leave, but Priscilla hadn't gotten one good clue out of him.

Before she could waylay him, the woman came back around, the one who couldn't wait to rat Joan out about the bread pudding comment.

"Berto, you heading out?"

"Got to tonight. I've got Fred's dog to feed back at his place, then I've got to get Miss Ella home. Can't be having her son say I'm keeping her out to all hours, now can I?"

The woman laughed, then leaned closer. "She's just begun her dessert, and you know she's got to chew slowly these days. I'd say you've got about fifteen minutes before you can coax her out of here."

Priscilla intended to make good use of every one of those fifteen minutes. If he stayed at their table.

"I'm not on the clock anymore and haven't been in a long time," said Berto. He sat back down. "I'll keep up my end of the conversation right here and when she's all set, give me the high sign, all right?"

"I will!" The woman bustled away, making sure everyone was fed, a kind gesture in an inhospitable island month.

"Speaking of being on the clock, Berto, you said you worked the docks. Were you part of the fisherman's guild? The one whose pension funds were taken?" With the mental timer set, Priscilla went right to the heart of the matter.

He shook his head but leaned in. So did Priscilla and Joan. "I never invested in it. I was suspicious from the get-go because how could that many people take their retirement and get so much more money back? The numbers didn't add up right to me, but that could be my lack of education or my intuition about things. My wife always encouraged me to trust that intuition. Anyhow, I didn't put in, but Charlie Mangel and Chuck Alderone both put in for over thirty-five years. And now, almost ready to cash in, there's next to nothing left. It's a shady business, ain't it? In some ways, that is." He rubbed an aged hand over an equally aged scruffy jaw. "Other ways, folks shoulda known there was no way that money could last. Not when it don't add up, and if there was one thing I was good at, it was guarding what was mine. A body's got to take care of his own, doesn't he?"

"And a wise man does," agreed Priscilla.

"I heard the police are talking to Selectwoman Fleming," said Joan. She kept her voice soft, but loud enough for the old fellow to hear. "They say she had the password and might be the only person on the island to have access."

"Well, there's one thing I know for sure about Sonya Fleming," said the old man. His tone tightened. His gaze sharpened. "She's as honest as the day is long, whatever that means, it's a silly enough saying. She'd no more take someone else's money than give away one of those beautiful kids of hers. No, she had nothing to do with money disappearing, mark my words. Now them hacker folks, well..." He sat back and splayed his hands as if he had the entire thing figured out and time to shell nuts too. "They can get into anything, don't ya know? Like bank accounts and credit cards and all them things folks go on and on about these days. So why couldn't a hacker guy get in there and drain that money? Anyhow, that's what I'd be telling the police or anyone who's interested.

Check for hackers. I don't do nothin' online 'cept check baseball scores, but lots of folks do and all you need is someone savvy enough to find a back door in."

He was right, and they hadn't really thought about that angle of it. Could the account have been hacked by outsiders, leaving the town and the island absolutely innocent? "I would love for you to be right," Priscilla told him. She stood and pulled on her coat while Joan did the same. "That would make everyone's lives easier, wouldn't it? Because I heard they're thinking of arresting Mrs. Fleming."

"That would be a travesty of justice," muttered the old man. "I don't give two cents for that husband of hers, he's not as strong as he should be and I always thought for all his good old-fashioned name, she married down. But he's a Fleming and that says something on the Vineyard. Like being a Latham or a Soule or a Blodgett. Land sakes, there are a fair share of old names in this state, aren't there?"

There were, and being from a much newer state, Priscilla was still learning how to juggle the new life and the 'old guard' of Martha's Vineyard. But now, with her telecommunications expert daughter close by, and a friendly FBI agent courting that daughter, she'd be able to run the idea of a hacker by them. If someone could gain leverage into the accounts that simply, the thief could be anywhere in the world.

That thought gave her hope until she and Joan got to the car and she contacted A.J. She laid out the scenario for him, and he pretty much shot that theory out of the water in less than a heartbeat.

"Here's the thing," he told her. "If this were five years ago, I'd say yes. The chances that someone could slip in a virtual back door and gain access would be higher. But since there have been literally hundreds of data leaks in the past few years, with a few major ones numbering in the millions of victims, why do you think you're not being constantly targeted and waylaid for your online funds?"

Priscilla had no idea. "I hadn't thought of it that way. Maybe I thought they just hadn't gotten around to me?"

"Well, there's that, and nothing is fail-safe, but the banks developed their own internal security safeguards so that any person who stumbles onto identifiable information can't jump on a computer and hack an account."

"So it's not as easy as it was."

"Exactly," A.J. confirmed. "The good thing about those early hacks was that they identified security holes in the system. That allowed the banks to develop patches. Improved interactive connections can detect slight alterations in a user's familiarity with the information they should know quickly."

It made sense. "So you don't think it's likely that this pension fund got hacked."

He hesitated, then replied, "I think it's improbable. In my experience, when money goes missing in a fund or from a corporation or a nonprofit, it's generally the person running the fund siphoning some off the side. They start with a little here and there, intending to put it back, but then they get in over their heads. Eventually it gets discovered."

His argument made sense.

She wished it didn't, and when she saw the sad look on Joan's face, she wished it even more. "Thanks, A.J."

"You're welcome. I've got to go. Rachel and I are taking a walk in the snow tonight. It's not exactly how I planned the evening, but she said snow is different on the coast. We'll see what she thinks of it in an hour or two."

Was he going to pop the question? Would she say yes?

Priscilla thought so, but she was smart enough to mind her own business when it came to matters of love. "Tell Rachel I love her."

"Will do."

She disconnected the call and turned toward Joan. Her generally unflappable cousin didn't look happy.

"A.J. is a great guy, but I'm not on board with his ideas about Sonya." Joan's brows formed a solid W between her normally mellow brown eyes. "I've known Sonya for decades. There isn't a more honest woman or family on the island. There's got to be another answer. There just has to be."

"Then we'll find it." Priscilla put the car into gear, eased around a snowbank, and headed toward the lighthouse. "Because if you're that positive, then so am I. We're going to do whatever it takes—"

"Short of being shot at, tossed overboard, and/or falling off a cliff at Aquinnah," Joan interrupted. "Plus several other somewhat dangerous outcomes you have faced, dear."

"Short of all those," Priscilla agreed. "But truth does have its consequences."

"It can," said Joan. "But let's agree here and now that they don't have to be mortal. Life-threatening is bad enough. Isn't it?"

Priscilla agreed. "It is, but you know the good Lord calls us when He's ready. You and I have both lived that truth." Joan had been widowed for several years, whereas Priscilla's husband had died just two years before.

"True, but there's no sense tempting fate. I've got a young dog and newly planted Knockout roses," Joan declared. "My goal is to see them both into their dotage."

Priscilla laughed as she pulled into her drive. "Well, I think we're safe—"

"Priscilla." Joan sat forward, studying the empty driveway in disbelief. "I had a car here. Didn't I?"

"You did." Priscilla hit the brakes. Joan's car couldn't have disappeared. What if whoever took the car wasn't alone? What if someone was out there, in the cold dark of a January night, waiting for two middle-aged women to get home?

She didn't allow herself to do the math and realize she needed to live another near-sixty years for this to be middle age.

Lights came their way. Multiple car lights, up a fairly empty road most winter nights.

Should they back out and make a run for it?

Too late.

She slouched down in the seat.

So did Joan. "What are we doing?" Joan whispered from her tucked position.

"If they drive by, nothing. If they surround us—"

"Oh, I can't wait to hear this," muttered Joan. She'd pulled her phone out. "How about I just call 911…"

"They'll see the light!"

"Not from down here, they won't." Joan bent low and whispered when the dispatcher answered. "My car has been stolen."

"I can't hear you, ma'am. Please state your emergency."

"My car has been stolen," Joan repeated but kept her voice low.

The cars were almost upon them. Would they pull in? Surround them?

"What's your location, ma'am?"

"Misty Harbor Lighthouse. You can't miss it. Because it's a lighthouse." Joan's voice took on a slightly hysterical tone.

The lights turned in.

One car.

Then two.

And a third. Car doors slammed.

Lights approached their car. First one, then another.

Nowhere to run. Nowhere to hide. But at least Joan was on the phone with 911. "Tell them we're surrounded. Tell them—"

She started to say more, but when a super-bright flashlight beam hit her face, she couldn't say anything at all.

CHAPTER FIVE

Priscilla, what on earth is going on?" Local Coast Guard Captain Gerald O'Bannon redirected the light away from her face as she opened the door, and from the worried look on his face she figured something was up. "The police found Joan's car—"

"They found my car!" Joan popped out of the other door. "Wonderful. Where is it? Who stole it? Who would have the nerve to steal it?" she asked, because a twelve-year-old car was really worth next to nothing. She'd been talking about trading it in for a newer model for a while.

"I don't know." Officer Ed Sequiera approached. Brian Denton, a newer Tisbury policeman, came their way too, and with the arrival of so many people, Jake's anxious bark sounded from inside the house.

"Let's go inside, it's warmer there." Priscilla hurried forward, unlocked the door, and went to turn on the lights as Jake slipped by her for a run around outside.

No lights came on.

She tried again.

Still nothing. And while she thought it would be warmer inside . . . it wasn't.

She turned toward Gerald. "What's going on? Why isn't anything working?"

"Could be this." Brian had apparently gone outside to check the electric box because he held up his phone, displaying a picture of a cut wire. Priscilla gasped.

"I don't understand." The men had kept their flashlights on. "Who would cut my wire? Who would steal Joan's car?"

"Who've you riled up today, Priscilla?" Ed arched an eyebrow her way as if this was somehow her fault, but she hadn't had time to ruffle one single feather. Had she?

"No one," she said firmly. "We've barely had time to begin looking into that nasty business about Selectwoman Fleming, so it can't possibly be related."

Brian looked from Gerald to Ed. "She does realize she's on an island, doesn't she?"

"I thought she did." Gerald sighed as if he'd tried to explain the geographical aspects of island living before and failed. "I thought that after eighteen months on the Vineyard, she would understand that light-speed transport of information is a given."

"But no one could know," she told him, then paused, concerned. "Unless Sonya's husband said something."

"He's not known for keeping his hand close to his chest, that's for certain," noted Ed.

"We've talked to Mildred, but she wouldn't say anything."

Priscilla bit her lip. "Berto?"

Joan shook her head. "No time. He was with us until twenty minutes ago, and these guys were already on the lookout for us."

So that brought them back to Sonya's husband. Didn't the man have sense enough to know that loose lips sink ships? Gary had been fond of clichés, and that one was one of his favorites.

"You can't stay here and freeze." Gerald didn't frown but he looked frightfully determined. "Frozen friends are not on tonight's agenda, Priscilla."

"I can't possibly freeze with a fireplace right here. Except that it's not all that warm at the moment." She frowned at the fireplace and crossed the room. "Gerald, I've got my emergency lanterns in the top of that cupboard there. Would you pull them down and turn them on for me, please?"

"Of course. But—"

She couldn't exactly quell him with a look because it was too dark for that, but maybe he'd imagine the look she was sending him. And when he switched on one of the emergency lanterns, the hint of humor edging his mouth indicated exactly that.

She got down on the floor, opened the fireplace doors, and settled a bundle of paper and kindling in the hearth. "Can someone shine a light down here? And hand me the long lighter?"

Brian aimed his torch at the floor, and when Joan handed Priscilla the lighting wand, Priscilla clicked the trigger and put the flaming tip against the bed of shredded paper. A tiny flame licked and curled around the edges until it bit into the thin strips of kindling. Within thirty seconds the fireplace danced back to life. "There." She stood up with a helpful hand from Gerald. "Heat and light. Luckily I saw the weather forecast and brought in that stack of wood. Just in case." She indicated the shadowed recess next to the fireplace. "But for the moment, it looks like I'm all set."

Ed started to say something, but Gerald raised a hand. "Save your breath, Ed. She's determined."

"Well, we've got me fixed up, but what about Joan's car?"

"I'll run Joan home," Gerald offered. "I'm sure Sister is missing her about now."

"For certain, although she's grown enough to be much more trustworthy in the house." Joan tugged her coat closer because the house wasn't the least bit warm yet. "But how bad is my car, gentlemen?"

Ed frowned. "Totaled, is my guess."

"No." Oh, the look she gave him. A look of sincere disbelief, because why would this happen?

He nodded. "I don't know if it was deliberate, but there was black ice right after sunset and it looks like the car went out of control, did a 180, then sideswiped a tree with the passenger side. Of course there was no one in it when we got there."

"Footprints?" Priscilla asked. "Boots? Shoes? Man? Woman?"

"The wind wiped out anything that might have been there before we got on the scene," said Brian. "The ground was frozen and the snow was unreliable because of the wind. When Gerald heard the call, he notified us he was heading this way. He said if Joan's car was involved in mischief, there was a good chance that Joan's cousin had something to do with it."

"Not exactly what I said," Gerald told her, a twinkle in his eye. "But close enough. You really want to stay here, Priscilla? I'd feel better if you stayed with Joan tonight. Crashed cars and cut wires are serious things."

Usually she'd argue with him because her quest for independence since coming to Martha's Vineyard eighteen months before had inspired true growth in her.

Not tonight.

Joan's car had been wrecked, and while she wasn't hurt, the thought that people would do such a thing was worrisome. Clearly someone wanted to scare them. But would they be smart enough to stop at that? Or cross that boundary into harm?

She faced her cousin. "Joan, I'd love to come stay at your place, if you and Sister wouldn't mind having me and Jake as company. Once we've got the fire going, that is. No one wants to come home to frozen pipes."

"I'd love it, actually."

"Me too. I'm only sorry we didn't stop by the bakery and get a solid bag of treats to share. If one's going to have a sleepover at our age, a bag of chocolate chip cookies seems essential."

Gerald's smile of approval made her feel good.

He knew she wasn't worried about staying alone. Smart or not, she wasn't one to let others bend her path.

But they'd both been targeted tonight, and friends stuck together. This way, whoever had done this would know that when you mess with one Latham cousin, you mess with them all.

And a police force, and a very handsome and caring Coast Guard captain.

She gathered up Jake's dish and leash, and by the time they closed up the cottage, the fireplace heat was raising the temperature. That would keep pipes from freezing with the power off.

She'd come back tomorrow, get the wiring fixed, and put a lock on that electric box.

For right now, she, Joan, and two dogs were about to have a January sleepover.

She tucked Jake into the car and they all headed to Joan's. She pulled in just as her phone rang. Rachel's name flashed on the dashboard display. Priscilla took the call. "Rachel, hey. I didn't expect you to call tonight, honey."

"I think you did." Rachel laughed. "Because my *fiancé* said he drove all the way down there to talk to you yesterday, when I thought he was on some kind of government stakeout. I said yes, Mom! And that means our quiet winter won't be nearly so dull, because we have a wedding to plan!"

Such good news! Such a blessing. Priscilla pushed away thoughts of cut wires and wrecked cars for a few minutes at least. "Congratulations to both of you! I'm so happy for you. I'm—" A surprise attack of melancholy swept in out of nowhere, cutting her words. Or maybe not out of nowhere.

Perhaps it sprang out of loss, and changed dreams.

She and Gary were supposed to share this good news. He was supposed to be the one approached by the handsome groom. Instead it had been her. And yet...

She'd done it. And kept it quiet until A.J. could pop the question. That in itself was commendable.

She breathed deep and choked back the emotional wave. They'd done all right. And they'd continue to do all right because she and Rachel had each other and they shared a sweet faith. "I can't wait to make plans with you. We'll talk tomorrow, and I'll help with as much or as little as you want. You call the shots. I'll follow orders."

Rachel cleared her throat in disbelief. Priscilla wasn't all that good at following orders. "I'll call you, Mom. I love you!"

The emotion rose up again, thicker this time, but good. "I love you too, darling. Both of you."

Jake woofed agreement twice.

The dog's friendly noise brought her back to the here and now. They had a mystery to solve, and in no short order, either, because Priscilla had one child, one beautiful daughter...and she had every intention of spending winter and spring planning a wedding. Which meant they had to get Sonya Fleming out of trouble ASAP.

CHAPTER SIX

Surely, no sane person was foolish enough to talk so loosely about an ongoing investigation. But Priscilla found out Wednesday morning that Mr. Fleming was easily that foolish.

But the man was sincere enough that she had to forgive him. She'd restoked her fire before she dropped Joan at work, then she swung by the bakery on her way through Vineyard Haven. Tommy Townsend was coming by to fix the electric, but not until afternoon, leaving her an open morning. The dogs were fed, with Sister tucked into her crate. Cottage puppy demolition wasn't something either she or Joan wanted to deal with today, and two young dogs left on their own could spell trouble. As she rolled into a parking spot, a text message from Rachel came in.

This weekend for planning and dress shopping? Looking at an August date. Sound good?

Priscilla texted back. *Sounds marvelous! Rachel, I'm so excited! We are too!*

Priscilla sent back a happy smile emoji, then slipped the phone away. Rachel was right. The long winter had just been transformed into a season of expectation. How wonderful was that?

"Priscilla!" Candy spotted her when she came in, and hurried her way. "Whatever you're ordering, I'm adding four delicious cream puffs to the mix because what a fright that must have been for you and Joan last night."

Gerald was right. News traveled quickly on the island.

"Clearly that will necessitate a meeting of the minds," Candy continued.

Candy was spot on. Priscilla had called their cousin, Gail, and Joan's sister, Trudy, to meet at the lighthouse later that day.

"That kind of vandalism just doesn't happen on Martha's Vineyard. If there's anything we can do to help, you let us know."

"Thank you, Candy. It was a fright that soon became a challenge. You know how that goes."

Candy had gotten to know Priscilla well over the last eighteen months. She'd seen the cousins through multiple challenges. "But as I was heading to Joan's house, I got news that my daughter and A.J. Montgomery have gotten engaged, so that put everything in a better light. How are your wedding plans coming?" Candy was planning her own nuptials before the busy season swept in, and according to Joan, the plans were thrusting the young bakery owner into a tizzy. "If you need hands-on help, call me. I love keeping busy."

"But your daughter's getting married. You'll be busy enough," Candy assured her. "It's a crazy time."

"I hear you," Priscilla sympathized. "It does seem a little over-the-top to take long months to plan a one-day occasion, doesn't it?"

Candy tied off the box of four cream puffs with baker's string and made a face. "I'm not sure your daughter will agree. A wedding should be extra special, shouldn't it? Because it is a one-time occurrence in a woman's life. And a man's," she hastened to add, but not quite with the same intensity.

Truth to tell, Priscilla wasn't sure that Rachel would agree, because neither one of them had done this before. "You make a valid point. I'll proceed with caution and not be the overbearing mother."

"If you take a box of cookies to share for your first planning session, all is generally forgiven."

This was true, so Priscilla ordered a box of cookies for Friday, and then had Candy box up a dozen for tonight's cousin conference, along with half-a-dozen muffins.

Candy eyed the sack of sweets as she rang it up at the register. "I should save you from yourselves."

"Or not." Priscilla smiled. "Consider it our regular contribution to the wedding."

"We are blessed to have so many year-round regulars," Candy told her. "So many businesses have to shut down. Make do. Struggle through the winter. But we've got folks that make the drive from the Bluffs and even farther. What a help that is to me and Beau."

Priscilla picked up her purchases. "Candy, I'll see you soon."

"Thank you!"

Priscilla hurried out the door into an icy, windswept rain. She needed to pick Joan up from work at noon, and there was no sense going home for ninety minutes.

She tried calling Sonya Fleming's number, but there was no answer, so she left a message that she'd be in town until noon and would love to meet.

Then she went to the next best person to fill her in on Tisbury history. Gail's dad, Uncle Hugh. She dashed to their door and rapped sharply. "Uncle Hugh? It's me. Priscilla. With a cream puff!" Uncle Hugh loved his sweets, and she wasn't above offering bribes for information. "Uncle Hugh?"

"I'm coming." He got to the door and pulled it open. "What are you doing out in this weather?"

"Looking for advice."

"Mine to give," declared the old fellow. "Gail's over at the library, but she filled me in on what happened last night."

"A sorry business, and now we'll have to add car shopping to the list of things to do this week. Who does things like this, Uncle Hugh?"

"People desperate not to be found out. But at least your list of suspects is considerably shorter in January." As always, Hugh Latham stuck to the common sense of the situation.

"A much-decreased population, for sure." She slipped a cream puff from the box but Uncle Hugh shook his head. "You don't want one? Are you feeling all right?"

He sighed, then shrugged. "Fair to middlin'. Maybe winter blahs, maybe getting tired. Real tired."

Getting tired? As in tired of living? Priscilla stared at him and had to choke down a lump in her throat. "Don't say that, Uncle Hugh."

"Well now, I didn't mean to go and get you all sentimental over an old man's ramblings." He worked up a really good scowl, which should have made her feel better, but he didn't look hearty today. He looked…old. And worn. "You save that puff for one of you gals, and I'll take a muffin instead. Did you get muffins? Like I don't know the answer to that," he muttered, pretending gruffness.

"One healthier muffin, coming up!" She ran the cream puffs back out to the car, grabbed a muffin, and met him back inside. "I'll stop worrying about you if you stop talking about being tired."

"Well, a body's got a right to get tired if it has a mind to," groused the old man, "but I can keep a lid on it. So what do you want to know about?"

"Mostly about Sonya Fleming, because popular opinion says she's the least likely person to be involved in something shady."

"Agreed. But there's no small number of Flemings and a large number of them might be on their last fistful of family dollars, if you know what I mean."

"They're broke?"

"Broke to the point of having to work regular jobs, and that wasn't exactly in the family dynamic this last generation. The old ones weren't afraid to work and speculate, but pretty soon they had too many spenders and not enough producers, so that made for a mess. Hurt feelings, greed, accusations of mismanagement…"

"How did they make their money?"

"Old Hiram Fleming got a hand in real estate development back in the fifties. Like he could see where things were going to sprout up. So he bought plenty of speculative stuff on the mainland and here. His son had begun a development company. They built some of the first malls in the area, and that heyday looked like it would never end. Until it did with folks now shopping online."

"One industry goes up, another slides down."

"Ayuh, just like that, so my guess would be that with mall tenants down and problems at this mall and that, there's a penny pinch that's only gotten worse the last ten years for the Fleming clan."

"That could make this a fairly easy mystery," noted Priscilla. "It could easily be one of them."

"Well now, I'd agree if this was Jonathan we were talking about," Uncle Hugh told her. He was nibbling bits of muffin, and if there was one thing Priscilla could generally count on in this world, it was her uncle's appetite. But not today. "Not Sonya. For that very reason she would make sure no one had access to other people's funds. She's twice smart, that woman, and with the common sense of a fisherman's family behind her. She knows how to work for what she wants. She would have gone into this with her guard up. So whoever got his hands into that shrinking pot, my guess says it wasn't a Fleming. I'd be willing to put dollars to donuts that even Jonathan wasn't given the passwords into those accounts. Sonya might love him, and he's a good father to those children, but she wouldn't be fool enough to trust him with fishermen funds."

"I am mentally checking off the family," she told him. "But who else might have access?"

"That's a question you'll have to ask Sonya," he told her. He broke off a piece of the pumpkin-nut muffin, then studied it, as if wishing he had an appetite. "I didn't think I was hungry until I got a whiff of this. Thank you for bringing it by."

"You're welcome. Can I make you coffee before I go? Or a cup of hot chocolate?"

He thought a minute, then nodded toward the kitchen. "Tea, actually. I'll take this to my chair and have a little rest."

"And I'll bring your tea, Uncle Hugh."

She called Gail quickly while the tea was steeping. "I'm with your dad," she said when Gail picked up the phone. "He refused a cream puff and is only picking at a muffin because he saw I was worried. He looks tired, Gail."

"I know." Gail was whispering too, then Priscilla remembered she was at the library. "I'm going to have the doctor look at him, but I'll probably have to hog-tie him and drag him there. He says there's nothing really wrong except being bone-tired weary. But at his age, that's not good."

"If you need me to come along, let me know. Oops, his tea's ready, gotta go. But how about if we change the meeting venue tonight and have it here?" she asked. "That way he can be in on things. You know how he loves to share his opinions."

"I know that more than most." Gail's dry note meant it wasn't always her father's best attribute. "That's a great idea. See you around five thirty."

"See you." She carried the tea to the comfortably cluttered living room and set it on the small table alongside her uncle's chair. "Anything else I can get for you?" she asked.

Uncle Hugh looked around, then shook his head. "I've got all I need. I've pretty much always had all I need, even with the ups and downs of life. I'm all right."

He wasn't all right.

He wasn't himself, but Gail had told her that winter doldrums were tough on him, and he'd mentioned that himself a time or two. Month after month of cold, damp weather wasn't exactly hospitable. "You call if you need anything, okay?"

"I will," he promised. Then he gave her a mock frown. "A little less yammering about now so I could catch a nap would be nice."

"Aye aye!" She gave him a smart salute and backed toward the door. "See you soon."

She saw herself out and made sure the storm door latched tight against the wind.

She'd stood at three gravesites in the past ten years. Her mother's. Her father's. Her husband's.

She'd only known Uncle Hugh for a year-and-a-half but she wasn't ready to say goodbye or change the heartbeat of the island she'd come to love so well. But then that wasn't up to her, so she put her sweet, doddering, cryptic uncle where he belonged, at the good Lord's feet. No one loved that old fellow more than God, and it wasn't her job to second-guess Him.

But she prayed for his increasing strength anyway.

She picked Joan up at noon, then headed back to the eastern shore. "Muffins, cookies, and cream puffs," she said, and indicated the white box and bag in the back seat. "I've got to be at the house to let Tommy in to fix things, but what shall we do about your car, dear Joan? Would you like to go shopping today?"

"I would like to pop the guy who stole my car," confessed Joan. "All this fuss and bother to scare women off. As if," she scoffed. That was one reason Priscilla loved her. Joan didn't get riled. She didn't get overwrought. But she was feisty enough to want things done right and to make things right when needed. "I'll shop with Will this weekend while we're close to the city. If he and I hit the car lots first thing, I should be able to drive my new wheels home. If not, they'll drive it here for me, and that's a sweet deal too."

"It's an amazing thing, isn't it?" said Priscilla. "I remember when it was days on end before you could pick up your car. Technology sure has streamlined that process for us." She pulled up to Joan's cottage and parked the car. "I'd like to meet Sonya Fleming tomorrow. Can you arrange it?"

"Gladly." Joan climbed out, and as soon as they approached the door, a flurry of barking erupted. "Time for lunch or coffee?"

"No, Tommy's due in half-an-hour. He's squeezing me in between two other jobs. But I'll see you at Gail's at five thirty, all right?"

"I'm bringing hot chicken-and-vegetable casserole and my notebook," Joan said. She carried her trademark junior-sized steno pad wherever she went. The five-by-eight size fit neatly into her shoulder bag. "See you then."

Priscilla gathered up Jake and his dishes and got home minutes before Tommy arrived. She let Jake dash off for a quick run as she let Tommy in.

"That's a mean business," said Tommy as he surveyed the neatly cut wire. "It takes guts or just plain dumb luck to go at a live wire, Priscilla. I'm shutting things down while I replace this, but it won't take me long. Pricey though. The cost of this thick cable isn't cheap anymore."

"The cost of sleuthing appears to be going up," she told him, and maybe it was getting too dear. A wrecked car for Joan. A pricey electrical fix for her...

She liked helping people, and she really enjoyed testing her new-found skill sets, but money didn't grow on trees, and with a wedding coming up, monthly bills, and the high cost of food on the island, a few hundred here and there wrecked her budget. Selling the Kansas farm had given her a significant nest egg, but she still had to pay attention to details. "Tommy, would you like some cookies?" She held out the open bag when he came back in from his work van.

He shook his head. "I'm trying to avoid the ten pounds I always gain midwinter so when barbecue season gets here, I don't have to worry. Are you seeing Gail tonight?"

Longing nipped his voice. He and Gail had feelings for each other, unknown to the others. It had been that way for several years. But Gail was committed to caring for her father and Tommy looked after his mother, Marigold. While the two irascible elders liked each other, they were set in their ways like concrete on a sidewalk. In consideration of their age, neither Gail nor Tommy wanted to upset their parents' last years. But when Tommy lifted a brow to Priscilla, she read the yearning in his gaze.

"I am, and I'll give her your best. We're meeting at her house to see if we can pep up Uncle Hugh."

"Winter's not easy on the old," said Tommy. True to his word he had the job done in thirty minutes, including a padlock on the box to discourage future vandals. She paid him just as a call came through from Rachel.

"Mom, hey, I'm on a quick lunch, but I just wanted to follow up our texts and make sure this weekend is convenient for you to go dress shopping."

"It absolutely is," Priscilla said. "I can't think of one thing I'd rather do."

"I can't wait to find the perfect dress," Rachel told her. "There's a part of me that hopes we find one straight off…"

Which shouldn't be a problem because Rachel was tall and slim with gorgeous layered hair and a heart-shaped face. Priscilla was sure anything would look marvelous on her.

"But another part doesn't want to be in such a hurry. Still, with a possible August date, we have to rush the process somewhat. I hope you don't mind that A.J.'s aunt and his sister are coming along. Auntie Em is a sweetheart. Marilee is not a sweetheart, but I couldn't say she shouldn't come, so I'm glad you'll be there. You've always had my back, Mom."

Great words to hear from an adult child, thought Priscilla.

"I called Faith Fellowship and they had the date open, so the church is booked. Now we need to decide on a reception venue."

"Darling, you know how I hate to butt in…"

Rachel snorted.

"I do hate it, although it's unfortunately necessary at times, but being on an island and living in one of the most charming lighthouse venues in America, have you guys thought of renting one of those monster tents and doing the reception right here? It could be absolutely lovely, and the photo opportunities would be amazing."

"It would make you crazy, Mom."

"No more than usual," Priscilla answered cheerfully. "What's a little extra crazy among family? And the cousins would love to help. Just something to think about. But more than anything I want this to be your wedding, and for you and A.J. to plan it just the way you want. I'll be happy to facilitate anything I can help with."

"Thank you, Mom."

"I love you, Rachel." Priscilla had made a pledge last year to say those words more often. "No matter what goes right or wrong in our lives, you'll always be my little girl. My blessed daughter. So anything you need done, you just shout. Okay?"

"I will. Maybe we'll have time to get some plans made this weekend if we find the dress on Saturday." She named three Boston shops and gave Priscilla the appointment times.

"Joan and I will drive in Friday night. She's going car shopping with her son, so if you can pick me up at the hotel, that would be great. Sound good?"

"It sounds perfect. Gotta go, my sandwich is ready. Talk to you later!"

Priscilla hung up the phone and studied the pictures of Rachel she'd hung on the living room wall. She'd made a progressive arrangement, from birth until the present. And soon she'd add a wedding picture to the mix.

To every thing there is a season, and a time to every purpose under the heaven. The old verse from Ecclesiastes had been her mainstay on the farm. Apt words for a Midwest farmer, but just as appropriate here, on the island.

Rain started again. It came from the west/northwest this time, battering the front of the house, but inside, with the fire going, Jake resting, and the electricity back in working order, peace reigned. And when Priscilla sat down to take up with the book that had been so rudely interrupted the day before, it took less than five minutes before she put the book aside and pulled the crocheted afghan closer.

She slept.

CHAPTER SEVEN

Y ou look lively, Priscilla," Joan noted when she opened Gail's
door a few hours later.

"So do you, which means we both probably caught a nap,"
Priscilla whispered. Talking about naps out loud made the two of
them sound old, so they veered from the topic whenever possible.

"Nearly two hours and feeling fit as a fiddle!" Joan whispered
back. She took the small salad bowl from Priscilla's hands and set
it on the counter. She raised her voice so Trudy and Joan could
hear. "I think we're ready."

The four cousins filled their plates and gathered around the
small table. "Pop, do you want to sit with us or in your chair?" Gail
asked.

He waved her on. "I'm fine here, and not much appetite to
speak of. I'll warm something up later."

"It's your favorite, Stove Top Stuffing and chicken casserole,"
Joan said, trying to convince Uncle Hugh. "I don't want to guilt
you, but I won't pretend I wasn't thinking of you when I made it."

"Then it will still be good later."

The cousins exchanged looks of concern, but hog-tying the old
fellow and force-feeding him wasn't an option. Priscilla believed
the body had a way of communicating what it needed and what it

didn't need, although she was stubborn in that last regard. Her body might not *need* cranberry muffins, but she made sure they were a mainstay at the lighthouse cottage.

"So you two have had an adventurous start to this new caper." Trudy studied the casserole and the large bowl of greens, apparently torn between more salad or a bigger serving of cheesy casserole. Then she sighed, chose more salad, and sat down. "Dan and I are set to head to Florida soon. I'd just as soon stay right here, but Dan loves to get a taste of warm weather now and again."

"And you'll get to use your Christmas golf clubs," Joan noted with a smile.

"Three weeks gone, and when we get back there will only be six weeks of winter left."

"Said no one on the island ever, when talking about spring and Martha's Vineyard." Joan settled into her seat and faced her younger sister.

"I'm being optimistic," Trudy informed her. Then she turned to Priscilla. "You need to talk to Gerald about the whole fishermen thing. I mean I know you 'talk' to Gerald all the time." She made air quotes. "But he knows a lot of fishermen, the local ones. And he knows the captains of the bigger fishing vessels that work out of here. I expect he's got some good insight, Priscilla."

"Note to self: invite Gerald to dinner." The thought of having Gerald over for dinner inspired a smile.

"As if you need a reason to do that," said Gail, teasing. "Since there are two overseers for the pension fund, maybe the other one got light-fingered. Or someone connected with him."

Joan made a note in her steno pad to check on the other fiduciary.

"Who else would have access?" Priscilla wondered. "Or who else is having money woes?"

"Half the island fits that category, especially this time of year," said Trudy. "If you're not getting retirement funds or you're not one of the full-time workers here, winter gets tight."

"And the funds disappeared in December." Priscilla poked her salad thoughtfully.

"Not before," Joan noted. "That might narrow things down for us."

"Well until you guys talk to Sonya, we're spittin' in the wind," said Gail. "I say we enjoy our dinner and reconnoiter after you've had time to talk to her. We don't get together often enough over the winter, so I want to soak all this good family time in."

"I'll second that motion," said Trudy. They chatted as they ate, and a summer wedding for Rachel was the hot topic of conversation.

"I'm so excited," Priscilla told her cousins. "Shopping for dresses. For Rachel, not me. I haven't even begun to wrap my head around that task, but to see my girl, dressed for her wedding…"

"And to a handsome lawman like A.J.," noted Gail. She fanned herself as if swooning. "We'll have so much fun, Priscilla."

"Oh, we will," agreed Trudy. She waved a generous forkful of casserole around. "I'm rearranging my diet months so I'm in tip-top shape for the wedding."

They all giggled because Trudy and her bimonthly diet quests were as predictable as the change of seasons.

"Gail." The plaintive sound of Uncle Hugh's voice could barely be heard over their laughter. They quieted and heard it again. "Gail…"

Priscilla turned as Uncle Hugh struggled to stand up, and she saw the feisty old man crash to the carpet with a solid *thunk*.

"Pop!" Gail flew out of her seat. "Pop! What's wrong? What's happened?"

Priscilla and Trudy helped turn the old man while Joan called 911, and when they saw Hugh's pallor and his waxy complexion, Gail fumbled for his nitroglycerin while Priscilla urged him to chew an aspirin.

He scowled at her, gripping his chest, his face twisted in pain.

"Take it, old dear," she whispered into his ear. "It can help."

He took the aspirin, and when Gail slipped a nitroglycerine tablet under his tongue, the sounds of the approaching ambulance brought hope mixed with fear. The paramedics swept in and took over, and Uncle Hugh, Gail, Trudy, and Joan were gone within minutes.

"I'll be right behind you," Priscilla assured them as they rushed out the door. Trudy drove, and they followed the ambulance down the narrow, winding street, then turned right, toward Oak Bluffs.

And then they were gone.

Priscilla gazed around the suddenly empty house. The TV was yammering something about pillows. She shut it off. Then she turned it right back on again because the silence deafened her. She'd said she'd follow behind, but what good would it do to chase an ambulance that would probably end up at the helipad, seeking transport to the mainland?

She put away the food.

She did the dishes.

She wiped the counters and straightened up Uncle Hugh's favorite corner. His chair. His table. His puzzle books.

And still she heard nothing.

Should she call Joan? Or wait?

She'd wait, she decided, and when lights pulled into the driveway fifteen minutes later, she flew to the door. "How is he?" she asked breathlessly.

Joan and Trudy gazed back, grave. "Not good. They air-lifted him to the heart center on the mainland. If he makes it—" Trudy choked on the words.

"They said there's significant blockage," Joan said. "So now we wait and see."

"Where's Gail?"

"Sara met her at the hospital and she's driving them up."

"The ferry's expensive. And parking at the hospital. And food." Priscilla wasn't sure why her mind went straight to money. Gail wouldn't care about the money, although there wasn't an abundance of cash floating around the little house.

"I'll transfer some to her account," said Trudy. "I told her I'd do that as soon as I get home. It's such a shock." She looked beyond

Priscilla to Uncle Hugh's chair. The neat stack of books and the folded blanket. "I can't believe we were all sitting here, laughing, and all the while—"

Joan put an arm around Trudy's shoulders. "Well, he loved the laughter, Trudy, so that's never a bad thing, and the whole reason we were here in the first place was because Gail was concerned. Imagine if we'd met at Priscilla's like we planned?"

"I can't imagine it," said Priscilla. "I'm thanking God we were here. Right here. All of us."

"And you straightened up." Joan gave Priscilla a look of gratitude. "Thank you, Priscilla. You have such a practical mind and such giving hands."

"And a heavy heart right now," Priscilla confessed. She took hold of their hands, Trudy to her right and Joan to her left, and bowed her head. "Dear Father, we put our sweet Uncle Hugh in Your most righteous and capable hands. Watch over him. Guide the doctors surrounding him. Help them to see him as Your beloved child, a man of strength, character, and some old-fashioned sass that would be missed if he's called home. We ask this through Jesus, our most precious Lord and Savior."

Joan hugged her. "That was beautiful, Priscilla. Simply beautiful."

"For someone who doesn't walk around praying out loud, you've given voice to exactly what I needed to hear." Trudy hugged her too.

The three of them moved to the door, and Priscilla slipped her coat on. "Joan, I'll drop you at your place so Trudy can get home to Dan."

"And I'll lock the house up." Trudy slipped a key from a small shelf not far from the door. "And we'll pray."

The end of a meal with the cousins was generally marked with laughter and promises to meet again soon.

Not this night.

Three somber cousins went home, each with her own thoughts. They went home to wait. And pray.

But after Priscilla dropped Joan off, she couldn't go straight back to the lighthouse. She turned the other way and rolled into Gerald's driveway about six minutes later.

She exited the car and moved up his steps.

He opened the door almost instantly. "Come here." He stretched out his arms and when she walked straight into them, Priscilla did something she didn't do often.

She cried.

He nudged the door shut with his foot and let her cry against his well-washed blue-and-gray plaid flannel. He loved that shirt. He told her once that he'd bought two of them because when a body gets to an age where there are few favorites in life, it's okay to stock up on the ones you have.

She groped for a tissue a few minutes later.

"Right here." He slung an arm around her shoulders and led her into the leather-and-nautical living room. He handed her a stash of tissues. "I heard the ambulance call go out."

"I cleaned the kitchen."

He didn't laugh at her statement. Or pretend understanding. He just stood there, patiently waiting.

"The girls all followed the ambulance, and I stayed at Gail's and cleaned up from supper."

"Nothing wrong with seeing to things that need doing, is there?"

She swabbed her eyes and nose again, then grasped more tissues. "No, but it wasn't my practical nature that made me do it, Gerald. It was foreboding. I spent too much of the last ten years saying goodbye. Watching loved ones die. I just couldn't do it, and I feel terribly weak to admit that."

He hugged her again.

Just that.

And when he loosened his grip, he faced her. "The best armies in the world understand how to divide and conquer. Don't beat yourself up over a smart choice. I expect Gail will appreciate coming home to a clean kitchen, Priscilla."

She drew a deep breath. "Well, who doesn't love a clean kitchen?"

He smiled.

"Where's Sammy?" she asked. Gerald's old Irish setter hadn't come to greet her.

He indicated the dog splayed out on a soft blanket abutting the couch. "Her hearing's not so good. She sleeps through most everything."

"Age is a pesky business, isn't it?" she muttered.

"Age and love both," he told her. "Wanna stay awhile? Watch a movie?"

"Not tonight. I just wanted to fall apart in front of someone who wouldn't hold it against me."

"Or maybe someone who could just hold you," he said softly. He grazed her cheek with the back of his hand. "Keep me updated on Hugh's condition, all right?"

"I will." She rewound her old scarf around her neck. "Thank you."

He smiled as he walked her to the door. "Anytime."

He didn't think she was crazy. He didn't mind her fairly chronic quest for independence. And he didn't mind discussing cases with her. Treating her as a colleague. "Can we get together in the next few days? Talk about the Portuguese fishermen and their history? Maybe early next week? I'm going wedding dress shopping with Rachel this weekend—oh! With everything going on, I forgot to tell you—A.J. and Rachel are engaged!"

"So A.J. popped the question? I'm glad to hear it. Have you gotten someone to take care of Jake while you're gone? He could stay here and bunk with Sammy."

"I hadn't had time to even think about that yet. That would be perfect. And you're sure you wouldn't mind?"

She could have boarded Jake at Dr. Morris's veterinary clinic, but Jake and Sammy were fast friends.

"He's good for Sammy. She indulges him and when she's had enough, she does that." He pointed to the sleeping dog. "And then Jake follows right along and takes a nap alongside. One benefits the other. I'll round him up Friday night."

"Thank you." She started out the door but turned when he called her name.

"Priscilla?"

"Yes?"

He gazed at her, long and sweet. "If you needed a place to come and be yourself, I'm real glad you picked here."

"Me too. Good night."

This time she drove straight home. She let Jake out for a brisk run about the yard, then brought him in and toweled him off.

He smelled of wet dog.

She didn't care. He was young and vital and reminded her of all the good parts of youth. Age would catch up with him soon enough, but for now she'd celebrate his vigor and excitement and happy, doggy smile when he saw her. Nothing stayed young forever. She knew that. But she didn't have to like it.

CHAPTER EIGHT

*P*op *out of surgery, in ICU, still hanging in there. Doctors are hopeful but not optimistic.*

Priscilla read the text again, and tapped back at a furious pace. *I'm optimistic enough for all of them. Praying, praying, praying! Did you sleep?*

Sara and I have been engaged in an UNO war. Now that Pop's out of surgery, we'll catch a nap. Hospitals are pretty noisy places, by the way.

Oh, they were. She remembered sitting with her mom toward the end. Then with her father, not long after. And then Gary, fighting a cancer they'd never expected in a battle that was lost on the earthly plane. *Dreadfully noisy. But maybe that's good in its way. Less time to mull. What do you need?*

Nothing. All good. Just prayers, lovely cousin!

She could do that happily.

Joan rang in right then. "I called to see if you wanted to take a ride across to the hospital, but then I saw the weather report. What should be mostly rain here could be blizzard conditions along the shore."

"And they won't allow anyone but close family into the CICU, of course."

"So here's my proposal." Joan stayed sensible, and Priscilla loved her for it. "Let's go ahead with our meeting with Sonya. She confirmed it to me in a text last night, so we can check that off our list. We stay here, hold down the fort, and maybe we can even keep Sara's bookstore open for her so she doesn't lose days of income."

"That's the perfect way to help! Of course! She opens at noon today, correct?"

"Yes, and we meet with Sonya at ten thirty, so the timing is good."

It was. "I'll be by for you at nine thirty or so." Jake had been circling her legs, prancing to the door, then back to her. When he started whining, she hurried to let him out. "And Gail will keep us updated as the day goes on."

"She will." Joan hung up, Jake got in a good run, and Priscilla had just enough time to put her own kitchen to rights before she got into the car. By the time she got to Joan's house, the car was warm and the rain had settled in. Again.

"I like having only two or three shifts a week during the winter," Joan said as she climbed into the car. "But I can honestly say I'm chomping at the bit not having a car. I can't just get up and go anywhere, and it's annoying to no end."

"Where do you want to go?" asked Priscilla.

"Absolutely nowhere. But it's the principle of the thing. I have no control. Hence the annoyance. Have the police followed up with you about your wiring?"

Priscilla shook her head. "Not a word. Your car?"

"No." Joan sounded peeved. "It's not like there's a plethora of crime going on in Tisbury and Vineyard Haven in January."

"I know. It's all right with Sonya if we meet in her office at the hospital?"

"Her exact words were, 'I have nothing to hide, so why meet in secret?'"

"Gutsy lady."

"She is."

Priscilla turned onto Beach Avenue and parked in the lot adjacent to Martha's Vineyard Hospital.

"I hadn't anticipated my evening visit here last night," Joan said as she rounded the front of the car. "We're blessed to have such a nice facility on the island, but when I saw that MedFlight take off with Uncle Hugh, I realized there are times we are woefully under-equipped."

"What would have happened if there wasn't a helicopter available?" asked Priscilla, but she wasn't really sure she wanted to know. "Or if the weather had taken a turn?"

"The Coast Guard acts as backup if MedFlight can't go out," Joan told her. "Or we just struggle to maintain patients until they can be safely moved."

Another sacrifice to living on an island, Priscilla thought as she followed Joan into the hospital. As they wove their way to Sonya Fleming's office, Priscilla saw that the hospital was beautifully appointed. And they *had* managed to save Uncle Hugh's life.

"Sonya." Joan spotted the tall, beautiful selectwoman and moved toward her glassed-in office. She was talking to another woman, also tall, lighter haired, and slightly older. Stylishly dressed, much like Sonya, and in her early fifties, Priscilla thought.

"Joan, come on in. This is my associate, Maura Pennington. Her office is next to mine, and this is where we try to make sure our beautiful facility stays in the black financially while giving the best possible medical care."

"Nice to meet you, Mrs. Pennington. This is my cousin Priscilla."

"I've read about you." Sonya was taller than Priscilla by at least an inch and had two-and-a-half inch heels on, so Priscilla had to look up.

"Good things, I hope." Priscilla shook her hand, then turned to the other woman. "And Mrs. Pennington." Priscilla grasped her hand in a brief shake. "A pleasure to meet you as well."

"I'll leave you ladies to discuss things," said Maura. "Would anyone like coffee?"

Priscilla smiled at her. "I would, yes. That would be lovely."

"I'm fine," said Joan.

"Ladies, I'm so sorry about your uncle." Sonya waved them to chairs, then brought her chair around the desk to form a circle with them. "My dad knew Hugh Latham. He called him a quaint island character. I hope he's going to be all right."

"So far so good, but we all get on in years, I suppose." Joan frowned. "And since Uncle Hugh only has seventeen years on me, I'm going to hope he lives a good long time yet. So, Sonya, tell us what happened."

"Other than a cool million has gone missing from an account I personally oversee?" She waved a hand as if she hadn't a care in the world as Maura came back in with Priscilla's coffee. "Not a thing. The girls are safely ensconced on the mainland for their second semesters. They don't know a thing about this yet, and I'm fit to be tied that someone managed to weasel their way into that account and bilk funds. I'm also furious with myself that I didn't reconcile records during December because if I had I would have caught it a few weeks earlier. That could have made a world of difference."

"You reconcile every month?" asked Priscilla.

Sonya nodded. "The program does it for me, actually. New technologies don't require us to be the pencil pushers accountants and auditors used to be. Payroll deductions go in and are automatically calculated, and the monthly direct deposits go out and are automatically deducted."

"So pretty much there are steady amounts going in and out every month."

"Yes, although for the past few years the incoming contributions don't cover the outgoing payments any longer. That means the fund is shrinking every month and, with fewer individual fishermen, there doesn't seem to be a viable way to shore things up even with increased investment revenue from the rising stock market. Frank and I met with the local fishermen last fall—"

"He's on the Tisbury zoning board?" Priscilla asked and Sonya nodded.

"Frank Ripley, yes. He's also my oldest daughter's godfather. Anyway, Frank and I apprised the Fishermen's Council of the situation. We're scheduled to meet with them again but I need to postpone the meeting. I'm afraid things could get ugly. The men who've been anteing up for decades will expect their fair share, but even with the rise on Wall Street, there wouldn't be enough money to pay those promised pensions in ten years with the money intact. Now, with a huge chunk gone, we're pretty much sunk. And that's not a term fishermen want to hear."

"All that work, all those years." Joan frowned. "That's a blow, for sure."

"It is, and to a relatively small but vital segment of our community. We're not alone in this struggle. There are other coastal fishing associations facing the same thing now that so many smaller fishing enterprises have been bought out by bigger companies. And big unions in industry, as well. But that's scant comfort to the hundreds of people this fund represents."

"If the remaining fishermen sell out to the big companies, will the sale of their businesses offer them enough money to survive?" asked Priscilla.

Sonya frowned. "Probably not. And the big companies know these guys are on borrowed time, so they can simply wait them out now. Eventually the small business owners retire, and the big companies gain market share. A lot depends on life expectancy with these things. When the original fund was set up, most fishermen didn't live to seventy. Now we've got the bulk of them living closer to eighty, and that ten-year swing is huge."

"So, short of killing people off, we've got an unsolvable problem." Priscilla faced her, grim. "Let's put that aside for a moment. When did the funds disappear from the account?"

"I've got a spreadsheet visual right here." Sonya handed her and Joan copies of the information. "Everything seemed normal in November."

Priscilla and Joan nodded.

"Then I checked funds, made sure everyone got paid according to schedule. The actual theft happened on the nineteenth of December. Money was moved from this account to another National Bank & Trust account, then to an account offshore where it disappeared from the face of the earth."

Did being a mega bank mean something? Or nothing? Priscilla didn't know.

"Who has access to this account?" asked Priscilla.

"Me. I'm it. I am the only person authorized to withdraw funds until either I give up the oversee capability or I die."

"Please don't do that," said Joan.

Sonya sighed. "It's not on my short list, but God calls us when He's ready... and who knows when that is?" She shrugged. "Anyway, I was busy with the girls, getting them back here for Christmas, the flu epidemic had started here on the island and the hospital was jumping. Shopping, family celebrations, then I got the flu and everything went on hold until the second week of January, on the tenth. And that's when I discovered the missing funds."

"What did you do?" Priscilla asked while Joan furiously scribbled notes.

"I called the police. I didn't know what to do. All I knew was that an already horrid situation had just grown substantially worse. I honestly never once thought I would become a suspect, because I would never steal anything. Naive, I know."

"When you're innocent, why should you fear the truth?" asked Priscilla.

Sonya's frown deepened. "Well, they began their investigation quietly, and when they traced the money, they said the transfer took place by someone using my sign-in, my computer, my work time-frame and my password. That's pretty solid evidence according to Detective Byrne."

"Who else has access to this computer?" asked Priscilla.

"No one. It's my work computer. It's integrated into the hospital systems so I can access departmental budgets and spending, and the only outside things I keep on it are the pension fund reports and access to my daughters' college funds. Both are funneled through NB&T. They handle hundreds of thousands of transactions every hour and would think nothing of a huge interbank transfer."

"Can you access the account from another site? Say a laptop?"

"Sure, from my personal laptop at home. Either way, it all points back to me. Except I didn't do it." Her phone rang. She glanced down and apologized. "I've got to take this. It's hospital business."

"Of course." Priscilla and Joan stood. "Take your call. We'll be in touch."

She sent them a somewhat sad grimace, a look of doubt that Priscilla understood. When all the cards are stacked against you, it's hard to see light at the end of the tunnel.

Priscilla said nothing until they got back to her SUV. "This isn't good, Joan."

"Don't I know it?" Joan scowled. "And yet, it's clear that someone was able to get into that computer and access the pension files."

"A password-protected computer, with high-tech security controls on it because she has access to all the hospital files, which means a lot of private and personal information was available."

"So how could someone get in?" Joan stared down at her notes.

"If they did," Priscilla said as she backed out of the parking spot.

"Sonya is innocent. I've no doubt about that," said Joan. "But it sure looks like an open-and-shut case, doesn't it?"

Priscilla couldn't argue. "The good thing about an open-and-shut case is that it's generally too neat. Which means someone, somewhere, was careful to point blame away from himself. And in that caution is often a misstep."

"Except I'm not exactly a computer expert. Neither are you." Joan sounded defeated, and Priscilla was sure that worry over Uncle Hugh and Gail was weighing on her. "So how do we find this out?"

"Secret weapon A.J. Montgomery, my future son-in-law."

"The FBI?" Joan's brows shot up. "You're going to get the FBI involved?"

"Not officially, but A.J. will tell me how to proceed. We can ask him this weekend."

"You're wedding gown shopping this weekend. Not solving a crime," Joan reminded her. "This weekend should be all about Rachel."

"And it will be. But ten minutes with A.J. shouldn't be a big deal."

Joan put a cautionary hand on her arm. "I know you're going to be hot on the trail, but listen to me, please. You have one daughter. She lost her father two years ago. You're it, and this is a huge moment in her life. Don't confuse her wedding planning with other people's business."

It was good advice. She didn't want anything to mess up the special moments leading up to Rachel's wedding. To risk that would be reckless on her part. "I'll stay focused on satin and lace. And veiling. Do girls still wear veils?" she wondered.

"It depends on the girl and the dress, and Rachel's built like you, so everything is going to look good on her. What a thrill, Priscilla!"

"It is," Priscilla agreed. "But right now, let's swing by the bakery, grab some muffins, and you can drop me at Sara's shop. I've got to mull over some things, and a bookstore is the perfect spot to do that."

"And I'll get things done for Gail. Oh, wait, there's a text!" She hurriedly opened the full message and sighed. "'Nothing new, status quo, still all wired and tubed. No better. No worse. Keep praying.'"

"We're good at that," said Priscilla as she pulled up to Candy Lane Confectionery. "I'll take this afternoon's shift. You use my car for whatever you need."

"Thank you. I'll drop you off at the bookstore and come back for you in a little while. And I'll call Trudy and tell her the plan."

It wasn't how they thought the week would go. But life had a way of throwing curves, and their job today was to keep things running as smoothly as possible for Gail and her family.

CHAPTER NINE

Priscilla hit the code on the electronic lock. The panel blinked red, then green. The door unlocked. "I'm in! See you in a little while." She flipped the light switches on, waved to Joan, and immediately felt better.

Sara had strung white twinkle lights—fairy lights, she called them—around the windows, across the beams, and looped from arches. Green vine draped some of the upper reaches, and the reading corner was set up with two comfy loveseats and a chair around a small table for holding plain old coffee or fancier varieties.

Priscilla checked out the cash register. Sara always left the cash envelope to start the day behind the book of the month. January was classics month, and there was the money sleeve, tucked behind Arthur Miller's *The Crucible*.

She contemplated that as she filled the money drawer.

Could the Fleming daughters have anything to do with this? Surely they had access to their mother's office during the Christmas holidays. The dates matched, and in the current mindset of entitlement, maybe their girls—one or both—decided they weren't getting their fair share?

She hated the thought that one's own children might steal, but the good Lord hadn't told the story of the Prodigal to hear Himself talk. Kids messed up on a fairly regular basis, so she jotted that into her phone.

She turned on the coffee brewer, set out creamer, and turned on Sara's music of choice. Then she realized that Sara was twenty-five years younger than her and less apt to be lulled into a nap, so she turned off the sleepy classical station and opted for an upbeat Celtic selection. Whimsical pipes, flutes, and vocals would make for a much more satisfying afternoon. At least she'd stay awake.

But even the thought of napping disappeared when Dee Dee Quimby popped in less than two minutes later. "I was hoping someone would have the presence of mind to open the store for Sara," she exclaimed when she spotted Priscilla. "I had two books on order, got the notice they were in, and then Hugh decides to go into cardiac arrest."

"I'm fairly certain the timing wasn't meant to be personal," Priscilla assured her in a dry tone. "But most unfortunate, of course."

"Well, not for me now, because you're here, Priscilla. And I expect you've heard what's gone on in this sweet town that's become a hub of white collar crime."

Priscilla raised a brow but stayed quiet.

"It's not a well-kept secret that Sonya Fleming has bilked a great deal of money from a pension fund she was overseeing. I got the lead from Howard Hoffman, one of the trustees on the hospital board and also on the fishermen's council, and if he doesn't know what's gone down, no one does. Although he's been known to embellish things," she admitted. "Howard's fish tales are long on drama and thin on essentials, but that's okay, because a reporter can't rely on a single source of information. A good reporter ferrets out the facts and strings them together."

Dee Dee had started an online gossip rag the previous spring, and quickly moved from gossip to factual reporting, a nice step-up. But if Howard embellished... Well, Dee Dee was a little too quick to jump on bandwagons herself.

"I'll check under the counter for your books, Dee Dee." Priscilla deliberately ignored Dee Dee's remarks, because nothing made Dee Dee more talkative than being ignored.

"Of course, everyone knows that Sonya likes the best of everything. It shows in everything she does."

Priscilla found the two books, tied with a ribbon and marked with Dee Dee's name. Staying silent, she drew them out.

"And both those girls at big-city universities. That's a pretty penny right there, and college bills must be paid."

"Just like the bookstore," Priscilla said brightly. "That will be $18.78, Dee Dee."

Dee Dee handed her a twenty, and Priscilla smiled. "I've had to remind myself to pay things in cash lately. Anything that puts a few percent back in local pockets is a good thing."

"I don't trust cards," Dee Dee told her. "Oh, I've got a credit card I use for some things. I keep my personal information separate from it, of course. I don't have my accounts linked the way so many do these days. Information from my bank isn't shared with my credit card company, or vice versa. That way I can be pretty much incognito. I don't believe in letting folks in on my personal business or my financial status. A single woman cannot be too careful."

"Agreed," said Priscilla lightly, but she didn't relinquish the books quite yet. "Of course even if *you* don't link things together, your credit report does. There have been multiple breaches of credit reporting information, but fortunately the banks have a much better handle on it than they used to."

Dee Dee lost color. "Linked through the credit report? But I never use a credit report."

"I think they exist whether we use them or not." Priscilla offered her a commiserative look. "Despite our best efforts, privacy has pretty much gone out the window."

Dee Dee had paled with Priscilla's first comment. Now she looked strained and anxious. "You mean my personal information is out there for anyone to see?"

For a woman who used the computer for her online newsletter, she seemed inordinately surprised about the idea of linked financial information.

"Well, not just anyone," Priscilla said. "But certainly our activities on our computers and smart phones aren't as private as we'd like to think. You could try using burner phones for transactions. They're not registered to a name, but still, I heard there's a way to trace them now. I don't know much about that, of course."

Dee Dee grabbed the bag of books and started toward the door.

"Your change." Priscilla chased after her. "A dollar twenty-two. And thank you for supporting your local bookstore," she added. As Dee Dee hustled out the door, Priscilla hurried back to the cash register and jotted notes into her phone.

Howard Hoffman, teller of tales and clearly a loose cannon if he was already yammering about throwing Sonya into jail...

And Dee Dee Quimby, because no one should act that odd about something as simple as credit links unless one had something not-so-simple to hide.

Dee Dee was a long stretch, because how would she gain access to information on Sonya's computer? Was she more tech savvy than she let on?

And why would she need money? Maybe whoever committed this crime had no relationship to the island. Maybe it was a person who happened to spot an insecure fund and accessed it.

But Priscilla figured Sonya was too smart for that, and anyway, the hospital security would block them, wouldn't it? Like A.J. said, hacking was common five years ago. Not now.

Dee Dee was quick to point a finger at the girls, and Priscilla couldn't fault her for that. She didn't want either of the Fleming girls to be guilty, but parents were often the last to know if their kids had developed a severe problem with money, drugs, or illicit behaviors. She'd check them out. She'd hate every minute of it, because she was a mother too, but she'd check, just the same. In a case like this, the culprit was more than likely someone in the inner circle. And that meant the entire Fleming clan was under suspicion.

"Priscilla, Trudy is treating both of us to dinner tonight to celebrate this good news!" Joan waved her phone in the air as she hurried into the quiet bookstore an hour later. "From Gail, and I quote: 'Pop's looking better! Vitals are up, tubes coming out! Thank you for praying!'"

"Such perfect news!" Priscilla hugged Joan. "Oh, that's so good to hear. It's hard to have an old one down and out with something this serious. Yay for Uncle Hugh! I'm not ready to say goodbye to any of my newfound island relatives."

"Trudy said to meet her and Dan at their house for supper. She's grabbing food at the Net Result, and we'll feast on fish and figure out what we might be missing in the case of the missing funds. She called Gerald to join us," Joan continued. "She wanted his take on the fishermen, what might be going on in their heads. They're not the world's most talkative sort as a rule, although a few, like Howard Hoffman, like to make their presence known."

"Dee Dee was here earlier to pick up a book order. She mentioned this Howard fellow too. I wonder why something like this brings him to people's minds?"

She posed that question to Gerald when they all gathered at Trudy and Dan's house at five thirty. Dan was picking up the food while Joan and Trudy set up a tray of pastries from Candy's. With her spring wedding coming up, Candy was anxiously trying all kinds of new things, wanting her wedding reception pastry table to be second to none, and she found willing taste-testers in Priscilla, Trudy, Joan, and Gail.

"Who is this Howard Hoffman fellow, and why did I hear his name twice today in connection with this fishermen's fund?" Priscilla asked Gerald.

"Howard's an old-school fisherman who sold out several years ago. He's good at what he does, and he's currently stymied by the fact that he's got three more years of adhering to a non-compete clause."

"So he can't fish, and he's bored," said Priscilla.

"Worse than that," Gerald told her. He whistled softly and held up an Italian ricotta-and-mascarpone-cheese pastry. "This is melt-in-your-mouth deliciousness. It's a good thing Candy doesn't make these all the time or the local Coast Guard captain would be ordering new uniforms. Annually. Anyway," he continued, holding off on his pre-dinner dessert, "a couple of years ago Howard put together a solid proposal for an oyster farming operation in Oak Bluffs, but a couple of young men beat him to the punch. Howard figured he's been fishing here for decades, he should get the nod, but he was late to the party. And those two young men seem to be developing a solid oyster-producing business, so Howard's nose isn't just out of joint. It's pretty much wrenched off. And he wasn't just angry about that. He was also upset that young guys like these oyster fishermen aren't contributing to the pension fund. They're daring to put their money in personal 401(k)s, and that set Howard off last fall, because he's on the fishermen's council. He knows that without cooperative contributions, the local fund and a few others along the Eastern shore are going to go belly up. And he figures that's not fair."

"Would being on the council give him access to the pension funds?" wondered Priscilla.

"Not directly," Gerald told her. "But being on the council puts him closer to information. The only person closer is Frank Ripley, the other overseer. If Sonya said she was the only one with access, I'd believe her, but she means access with her permission. That doesn't stop someone local from figuring out how to get in."

"But how would they do that?"

"A.J. is probably more skilled at this answer than I am," said Gerald, "but there are ways to snoop on someone's computer and get codes from the log of keystrokes he or she enters."

"Well, it's in a big business office in the hospital, with cleaning staff and all kinds of people in and out." Priscilla thought a moment. "But they'd be seen because it's all glass."

"Not at night. And they wouldn't necessarily look out of place if they didn't act like it," Gerald told her. "If people appear to know what they're doing, folks don't think too much of it."

"And it wouldn't look out of place for cleaning staff to be in the office at night," she said.

"Yes. And now you must try a bite of this even though I know Dan's going to show up with fish and fries any moment." He held out the flaky pastry. "Tell me what you think, Priscilla."

She took a small bite and gazed into his bright hazel eyes.

He smiled at her.

She smiled back.

"You like it?"

"It's amazing," she told him, then giggled and felt like a complete goof for acting like a schoolgirl. "And flaky." She brushed off a dusting of sugary flakes from her sweater. "You're right, I hope she starts making these more often. I think I'm in love. Although

I'd better start running despite the spurt of bad weather we've been having. Or maybe join the local gym in Vineyard Haven. Too much winter and too much sitting."

"Have you thought about going south for the winters, Priscilla?" asked Trudy. "So many folks do it these days, and it makes sense in a lot of ways. Dan and I love the respite, even though we only go for a few weeks. It's just enough to break the monotony of rain, cold, snow, and wind."

"I've never thought of it, and now, with Rachel so close, that would seem self-defeating, I think. She moved all the way to the East Coast so we could be closer. The cute boyfriend was pure bonus." She frowned. "I can't see taking off and leaving, but maybe I'll feel differently in a year or two."

"Not if there are grandbabies," Gerald warned her. He grinned, because his little grandson and baby granddaughter were his pride and joy. "There's something about that newest generation needing time with the old folks."

"Don't be tossing that phrase around carelessly," Joan told him. She sounded spunkier now that Uncle Hugh was doing better. "Old is our age . . . plus twenty-five years."

The perspective truth in that made them all laugh.

Dan came in with the food, and they spent the next hour relaxing. Eating. Talking. Celebrating Uncle Hugh's turn for the better. And when Gail sent another text that read: "He's awake and giving me the business even though he's not supposed to talk!" they cheered.

No one pretended the old fellow was going to live forever, but he was the last of the previous generation. He was special. Not one of them was ready to say goodbye and become the oldest generation of living Lathams on the island. As long as Uncle Hugh was alive and kicking, then Priscilla and the gals were the second-oldest generation...and anyone in his or her fifties or sixties understood that very important mark of distinction.

CHAPTER TEN

S electwoman's Office Vandalized
   Priscilla's mouth dropped open when she saw the *Daily Dither* headline on her computer screen the following morning. Pictured there, spray-painted in sprawling red letters on the pretty glass walls, were slurs against Sonya Fleming.

Ugly slurs. Nasty words. Most of them were spelled correctly. Were the two misspellings deliberate...to make the perpetrator appear uneducated? Or was the person just a bad speller?

The vandalism was discovered by office personnel who came in for an early meeting. The quietly scheduled meeting was being convened to discuss the current status of hospital CFO Sonya Oliviera Fleming, the Oak Bluffs Selectwoman currently under investigation for the disappearance of a million dollars in fishermen pension funds. Was this the work of an irate pensioner? Or perhaps a guilty party setting a scene?

Dee Dee might be onto something there.

Priscilla didn't stop to eat, have coffee, or do anything other than slap a hat on her head and slip on her coat. Joan needed a ride to work at the clinic that morning, and they might get there in time for Priscilla to snap a few shots of the walls before the police allowed employees to scrub them down.

She picked up Joan, drove swiftly—which wasn't a problem in January when the weather cooperated—and pulled into the Oak Bluffs hospital complex a short while later.

How did Dee Dee get the info about this so early? Who called her? Who sent her pictures?

Those were questions in need of answers, because it wasn't like reporters hung out at the hospital in search of midwinter stories. But Dee Dee had gotten the scoop on this.

How?

Priscilla shoved that aside for the moment. Joan hurried off to the ultrasound and imaging department and Priscilla slipped to the left, heading for the administrative office area.

Two men—detectives, she assumed—stood talking off to the side. They saw her but didn't try to stop her as she pulled out her phone and took a few quick shots. She made sure she got the shots from three different angles, and then she walked the corridor, turned, and looked back. "Aha."

The shorter detective looked up. "'Aha' what?"

"From this point back you can't see what's going on in front of Mrs. Fleming's office because the line-of-sight is blocked by the pillar."

"So?"

"Once the cleaning crew moves this way to finish the offices, the vandal has free range because the offices are closed. I'm going for the time frame here, which is what I thought you gentlemen were most likely discussing."

"What we were discussing is why anyone would think it's okay to steal from the fishermen who risk their lives to bring fresh food to everyone's table." The taller detective scolded her with a look. "They are understandably upset, and when people are upset and worried about their future, they act out. Luckily it's glass and the paint will wash off."

Was he serious?

"So you're not interested in when it happened? Or who did it?"

"Who are you?" the shorter detective asked. He didn't look too happy about her line of questioning. "Wait. Aren't you that woman from the Misty Harbor Lighthouse, the one that runs around, getting in the way of real police work?"

He had her at a disadvantage because she hadn't done a thing with her hair, and how does one handle a question like that with bad hair? Fortunately she'd thrown a hat on, so he wouldn't know that. And he was clearly obtuse enough to not be able to see beyond the end of his nose. "Priscilla Grant, and if by getting in the way you mean trying to help my fellow citizens in any way I can, then yes. I am that woman. And I think the two of you would do well to plot out the time frame this culprit used to do his nasty work."

"You're so sure it was a he? Not a she?" The short man exchanged a mocking smile with his colleague.

"Not one hundred percent, but the height of the writing suggests a male. I'm five-seven. I would have a hard time spinning the arc of those *t*'s and *h*'s that high, even in heels, and most spray painters are not prone to high heels, in my experience."

She saw she'd made her point when the taller, older detective jotted a note in his notebook.

"The person could have dragged a chair over from the waiting area. That would give a two-foot shift in height," said the shorter detective.

"During flu season when the ER is filled to overflowing and extra folks are seated in the lobby waiting area?" Priscilla shattered his fairly foolish theory with a killer smile. "I think the more plausible explanation is the person is male, don't you, Detective?"

She stepped away before they asked her to leave, but on her way out, she swung by the housekeeping department. That's where she found out that the custodian was usually done cleaning the main administrative wing by seven thirty p.m. From there the person assigned to that area went to another floor to work.

"Does this vary?" she asked the maintenance supervisor. "Do the cleaners have leeway to choose the order in which they clean the areas?"

"Only if an office is occupied, and that happens sometimes," the woman explained. "Mrs. Fleming and Mrs. Pennington and Mr. Donnelly sometimes work late, so we'll work around their offices and come back to them. But no one was working late last night. I went home at six and everyone in the administrative wing was already gone."

"Thank you." Priscilla headed for the door, being careful to skirt the ER and the lobby. The last thing she needed was to catch the flu, and even with a flu shot, folks were falling ill all over the place. She didn't want to be one of them. She took her notes back to the car and drove home. She'd pick Joan up at noon, and this would give her time to give Jake a run and grab a shower. But as she pulled into her driveway, her heart stopped.

Jake was outside. On the step. Moaning as if he was hurt or half-frozen in the single-digit windchill.

She slammed the car into Park and hurried out. She didn't think about latent danger or someone lurking around. All she could see was her precious Aussie shepherd, her little red-and-white friend, and that someone had let him out of her securely locked house.

And if they let Jake out…

That means they found a way in.

She put Jake in the car and called 911, and when the dispatcher answered, Priscilla had to bite down the solid lump of anger in her throat. "I need to report that someone has gotten into my house, the cottage at Misty Harbor Lighthouse. Yes, on West Chop. And they left my dog out in the cold," she went on. If the dispatcher was an animal lover, she'd understand Priscilla's anger. If not?

Well, too bad. Right now Priscilla felt like one of those cartoon characters so popular years ago, with steam puffing out of her ears.

She stayed in the car with the heat running until Officer April Brown and Officer Brian Denton showed up eight minutes later. She explained what she found when she pulled into the driveway. There was no snow for footprints. The rain had sloughed the last snowfall into the occasional mound on the north side of ditches and hedgerows before the drop in temperatures refroze the ground. As April and Brian went inside to check the house, Priscilla saw a flash of blue. Swirled blue.

She crossed the front of the house and found a tuft of yarn snagged on a Knockout rosebush cut back to mid-calf level. A tuft of yarn that looked a lot like the heathered blue scarf Dee Dee Quimby had worn to Micawber Books yesterday.

She shoved the little piece of yarn into her pocket as April and Brian emerged. "All seems in order, Priscilla. And the door doesn't appear to be jimmied or the lock messed with. Are you certain you locked it this morning?"

She wasn't, actually.

She locked it all the time, but she'd seen that article on the *Dither* and she'd grabbed her coat and hat and—

"It's possible I forgot. I was hurrying."

"But the dog was inside."

"That much I'm sure of," she told them firmly. "But normally I reach back and test the lock to be sure it engaged, and I don't remember doing that this morning."

"So someone may have come by with no malicious intent and accidentally let the dog out."

"They just happened to open my door? And let my dog run free?"

"I think what he means is that they didn't arrive with wrong-doing in mind," soothed April. "Maybe they tested the door and one thing led to another."

Priscilla folded her arms. She tapped her toe, but not for long because it was cold out there. "I may only have been on the island for eighteen months, but where I come from, people don't test other people's doors. They knock. Ring the bell. Wait. And then they leave if no one comes to the door." She glared at them and drew a breath. "Sorry. This is just disturbing, because what if I was away longer? The wind chill is in single digits and Jake was out in the cold, for I don't know how long."

"Let's all get warm and we'll see what we can find out, Priscilla," April told her. "I honestly think this might have been an innocent mistake. Or maybe it wasn't going to be and Jake scared the person off."

"Well, there was this piece of blue yarn snagged on the tip of that front rosebush." She withdrew it from her pocket, just in case it proved to be important. "I'll get Jake inside and properly warmed. And thank you for coming right over."

"Our pleasure, ma'am. He's a good little fellow." Officer Denton gave Jake's head a good rub while April bagged the small clip of yarn. "And a dog's a good companion during these long winter months."

"He sure is." She brought Jake inside, locked the door, and made a quick and much-needed cup of coffee.

She had to pick up Joan at noon. That gave her just enough time to shower and swing by Dee Dee's place. She didn't have to reveal that she found the tuft of yarn, but if Dee Dee was nosing around, there had to be a reason. What could it be?

This time she tested the lock when she left, then drove straight to Dee Dee's old-style house in Oak Bluffs. Dee Dee had proximity to the hospital from where her house sat, and not far from the state police offices, but she lived away from the hustle and bustle of the business sector. This side of Oak Bluffs was quieter. Cozier. Less frenetic, even in the busy season. She pulled up to Dee Dee's driveway, parked, and went to the door.

She didn't have to knock.

Dee Dee pulled the door open and waved her in. "Did you come by because my other book has come in?" she asked as if village bookstores made personal deliveries all the time.

"I did not. I came by to see how you knew about the hospital vandalism so quickly this morning. You had it on the *Dither* before the police reports had even been filed. But now I see that you live close to the hospital." She studied Dee Dee intently, on purpose, because if Dee Dee had been at the lighthouse earlier that day, Priscilla wanted her to approach the subject.

"Hospitals are a wealth of news reporting," Dee Dee told her. She motioned to the chairs in the small, crowded living room. Dee Dee wasn't exactly a hoarder, but she didn't seem intent on throwing things away, either. Or putting them away. Or filing them.

Stacks of this, that, and the other thing covered most horizontal surfaces and even parts of the floor. Priscilla ignored the clutter and took a seat as offered. "So you stop by to check things out?"

"I can't sleep much at night anymore," Dee Dee told her. "It's the most annoying thing, so I'm up in the middle of the night, wandering around. The house, not the town, usually, but that's when I got the idea for the *Daily Dither* last year. Why not make that time productive? So I started my own little tell-all blog with literally no start-up costs. Do you think the Hearsts and Gannetts got started this way?" she asked. "Well, not online, of course, but with little papers that grew into huge money-making enterprises?"

That was Dee Dee's second mention of money since yesterday. When folks needed money, it was often a constant source of conversation. "I expect they started small. Most great businesses do."

"So did you go to the hospital?" Dee Dee asked. "Did you see what was done before they washed it off? I took pictures, but I knew you'd want to see it personally."

"And that's why you came to my cottage?" Priscilla locked eyes with Dee Dee. She expected Dee Dee to squirm.

She did nothing of the kind. She nodded briskly and looked impressed. "Yes! You are good! I came straight over in case you don't read the *Dither* first thing."

Priscilla was almost embarrassed to say that she did read the *Dither* first thing, every single day, because what would that say about her? "I saw it while I was having my first cup of coffee."

"Well, I came to your house and now I have to confess something."

Here it was, the admission Priscilla was waiting for.

"I got out of my car and got to the door, and this dog appeared out of nowhere. Barking and yelping, he stood me off and I didn't know if I should run to my car and risk him chasing me down—"

"Jake was outside?" Priscilla didn't try to hide the disbelief in her tone. "When you got there?"

"If Jake is a red-and-white dog with a very fluffy tail, then yes. He was outside. Running around out back, I guess. I didn't see him right off," she continued. "I'm not afraid of dogs, but I have a healthy respect for them. I got to the door, rang the bell, and that's when he came tearing around the side of the house. He came straight my way, and then he was between me and my car." Dee Dee made a face. "I didn't mean to get him all riled up, but I didn't know what to do. I dodged to the right, circled the house, and he followed me with a very suspicious look in those big brown eyes."

"I know that look well."

"But that way, dodging around the house, at least he wasn't between me and the car when I came fully around. I hopped into my car and backed out. He barked the whole while, but there was no one around to hear him. You probably shouldn't leave him out like that, untended, Priscilla." Dee Dee wasn't scolding her, but the practical advice felt like a scolding. "Even with underground fencing, a dog can get into mischief when left untended."

"You are absolutely right, and I'll take your advice," Priscilla promised her, all the while wondering how Jake got out if Dee Dee wasn't to blame. Was she being forthright? She seemed to be, but Priscilla wasn't about to make any assumptions. "So why did you come to see me? Just to tell me about the *Dither?*"

"If a fisherman is that angry about lost money, I was worried that he might hurt Mrs. Fleming." Dee Dee's expression reflected her concern. "Sometimes folks cross over that line when they're fretting about bills to pay. Food for their families. And an aging person on a pension that might dry up might be feeling pretty desperate."

"It's nice of you to think like that, Dee Dee."

"I never had much as a child," Dee Dee told her. Her voice softened. "And money never stretches as far as it should, especially when trouble walks in the door. But then you have to do whatever you can to make things better, so I can understand the need to make things happen. But I'd feel bad if anything happened to Mrs. Fleming over this. She's good people, that's what my mama used to say, and it's true in this case even if she does have to have everything just so. That might seem important to beautiful people. And after giving it all some thought, I can't believe that she'd do something like this. It would be out of character, even with designer bags."

Dee Dee was dogged, eccentric, and quirky, and not lovely by societal standards. Yet, her grace today made her seem lovely.

"Maybe she made an accounting mistake," she went on. "Maybe the money isn't really missing. Maybe it's mislaid."

"I'm sure Sonya wouldn't have called the police without checking for an accounting mistake," Priscilla reminded her. "It's really missing, although not mislaid."

"Not like the cookie jars of old." Dee Dee frowned. "My grandfather used to tuck all kinds of money aside. In the oddest places. A thousand here, five thousand there. He hated banks because he lived through the depression and didn't trust anyone with his money. He used to say a good mattress is as safe as any bank."

"Unless one suffers a house fire," noted Priscilla.

"He was a character of his time, that's for sure." Her phone buzzed. She picked it up, looked at it, then sighed.

"Trouble?" Priscilla asked, but she kept her voice gentle, because Dee Dee's face, her expression, seemed to mask a sadness deep within.

"Not that I can speak of. But something worth praying about." She set the phone aside and stood.

So did Priscilla.

Dee Dee had said that Jake was outside. Was she being truthful? The story sounded plausible. But that meant someone else let him out. That someone else had stopped by the cottage before Dee Dee got there, and that was a fairly narrow time frame. Who on earth was out that early, letting people's dogs run free?

She had no idea. "Thanks for coming by to give me a heads-up this morning, Dee Dee."

"You're welcome. I figure working together is better than keeping things separate on something like this."

Working together.

The phrase struck Priscilla, not because it was odd in itself, but because old-time literary sleuths were always on the watch for people who clung too close to a case and made themselves a prime suspect.

Was Dee Dee a suspect, throwing shade on others? She had proximity to the hospital. She went there at odd hours when no one was about. And she seemed to know Mrs. Fleming more intimately than she'd displayed the day before.

Surely there was no motive for Dee Dee to take funds. And there was no way she could get into the account, was there?

"I appreciate the information, Dee Dee. And yes, I will admit that the first thing in the morning I've been doing lately when my coffee is done chugging through the brewer is sit down at my table and check the *Dither*."

Oh, that smile.

Priscilla would go through the days hoping and praying Dee Dee was guilty of nothing more than being a little quirky and needy, because her smile was an absolute pleasure to see.

"Thank you, Priscilla! That means so much coming from a professional like yourself."

"Hardly a professional, but admittedly having fun. If I'm still on store duty, I'll call you when that book comes in. All right?"

"I'd appreciate it."

The door closed softly behind Priscilla as she moved toward the car. One way or another, she wanted Dee Dee Quimby off the suspect list as quickly as possible. If for no other reason than the sheer enjoyment of her pesky little paper.

CHAPTER ELEVEN

Priscilla checked her watch when she got to the car. She wanted to swing by Enchanted Chocolates, a Martha's Vineyard favorite. She wasn't sure what Rachel would want for wedding favors, but if chocolate was involved, Priscilla wanted to use this store. She'd take Rachel a sample box for their weekend shopping spree and see what she thought.

Then she paused as she reached her car.

What if Rachel didn't want to get married on the island? What if the lure of Boston history and gorgeous churches and elegant cobblestone streets drew her?

She hesitated, then climbed into the driver's seat.

Not your wedding. Her wedding. Be supportive. Not bossy. Suggest. Don't order.

She needed to make herself a list of what mothers-of-the-bride should and should not do.

Possibly a big list. So she wouldn't step on toes. And Rachel had said A.J.'s sister wasn't a sweetheart...

That meant Priscilla had to be easygoing. With Rachel's crazy schedule and decisive nature, she probably already had a master checklist made.

She drove to the hospital and texted Joan that she was there. When Joan came out around 12:10, she climbed into the car and immediately looked sympathetic. "That kind of morning, hmm?"

"Do you think we can talk privately at the inn? Because I could use some real food and advice right about now."

"About the case?" asked Joan. "Do we dare talk about it in public?"

"About the wedding and stepping on toes and chocolate and dresses and advice."

"Then yes, lunch at the Colonial Inn sounds marvelous. I just got a text that my insurance payout for the car has been deposited to my bank account for nearly eleven hundred more than I expected, which means lunch is on me. Let's go."

"First, I need to swing by Enchanted Chocolates," Priscilla told her. She pulled onto the road and headed across Oak Bluffs. "I want to take some to Rachel, and they're only open afternoons in winter. Then lunch. And then we can discuss the case later. And who let my dog out of my house. And—"

"What?" Joan raised her eyebrows. "Someone let Jake out? Why?"

"I don't know if they broke in or if a certain lighthouse owner forgot to lock the door. But in any case, they did open the door and release Jake into single-digit windchills. I got home to a very scared, cold dog."

"Oh, Priscilla." Joan sounded downright worried. "Who would do such a thing? Did they go inside?"

"I don't know. The police came and checked things out, and they said everything looked fine, but it's another bother about this whole thing, isn't it?" She parked the car. "I don't like that whoever's involved in this case has already targeted both of us. What is he or she going to do when we get close to figuring things out? I don't like where this is going, Joan."

"All the more reason to catch the perpetrator," Joan declared. "If someone is going around town trying to scare us, he's got a job on his hands. We Lathams don't scare easily, and maybe he did me a favor wrecking my car. A new car wasn't in my budget. Now it is." She arched a brow at Priscilla as they crossed the windy street and entered the popular candy store. "If nothing else goes right, buying chocolates is always good for the soul."

Forty dollars later, Priscilla had a lovely box of chocolates for Rachel and one for A.J.'s family. This would be their first meeting, and a selection of handmade chocolates was never a bad choice of greeting. When they got to the Colonial Inn, Tilly Snyder wasn't there. Tilly, the somewhat prissy, vintage-loving owner was always there, governing the dining room and the staff with a straight back and a stern face. But for all of that, the woman ran a great restaurant and inn.

"Flu," said Hilda, one of the regular waitresses, and she didn't sound any too happy about it. "Took her down quick two days back, and I don't know how we're going to manage without her. Ida's come over from the diner to help, and old Berto is in the back, washing dishes. The food's still great," she assured them, as if embarrassed that she'd said too much. "But it's a challenge when so many have gotten sick at once."

Should they stay?

Go?

The thought of the flu messing with her plans made Priscilla think twice, but then she got hold of herself. "We're just as likely to catch it walking into the library or the bookstore or wherever. But thanks for letting us know, Hilda."

Hilda showed them to a table. The inn was quiet. More quiet than usual, and that was saying something on a winter weekday. They ordered the soup-and-salad special and Priscilla waited to open the wedding talk until they'd finished their salads and slices of freshly made bread with butter.

"I'm worried I'm going to overstep my bounds with this whole wedding thing," she confessed when Hilda had whisked their salad plates away. "My bossy nature might step in and mess things up. How do I keep that in check, Joan?"

"Well, I've been through two weddings. Three," she corrected herself. "Mine, Trudy's, and my oldest son's. And here's what I learned." She leaned forward and braced her hands on the table. "Shut up and sign the checks."

"Joan—"

"You asked for advice, and I'm giving it, and as cut-and-dried as it sounds, that's the crux of it. Now if Rachel asks your opinion, give it. Not bossy," she warned, and it was clear that Joan had grown to know Priscilla well. "Just loving advice. If she loves a dress, don't fault it. If she wants white cake with chocolate ganache, don't argue for strawberry. If she wants pink and rose and mauve floral arrangements, it is not your place to tell her that a pink, pink, and pink wedding is way too much pink. Smile and nod.

And do that as needed. We don't offer advice. We simply give it on request. Got it?"

Priscilla stirred her soup, grim. "Yes. And I know you're right. It's not like I'm the kind of mom who made it my mission to get my daughter married off, like some moms do. But I don't want to mess up. I don't want to create a rift. And I'm not sure how to handle A.J.'s family and the not-so-nice sister Rachel mentioned."

"Know-it-all relatives are a dime a dozen," Joan reminded her. "Keep the smile-and-nod maneuver in working order. When you're alone with Rachel later, you can discuss things more openly. But while you're shopping and planning, your job is to be the doting mother with a credit card."

"We're splitting costs three ways." Priscilla made a face. "Rachel and A.J. insisted. They said it's ridiculous for a widow to fork over the kind of money that weddings cost these days, and that they're both financially secure and his parents wanted to help too. I had to fight to be able to pay a third, and that's only because Rachel knew that Gary would have insisted on paying."

"Best daughter ever!" declared Joan with a smile. "That's wonderful. Okay, so we've got that out of the way."

"And I will follow your instructions to the letter," Priscilla replied.

"Now for this case." Joan glanced left. She glanced right. Then she leaned in. "Howard Hoffman was at the hospital last night. Sometime between eight and nine o'clock."

"Are you sure?" The time frame fit the cleaning schedule. Had Howard gone into the office wing and vandalized the windows?

"I overheard a conversation between a patient and a clerk. The clerk mentioned seeing Howard the night before and that she'd only gotten six hours of sleep because they're short-staffed with the flu outbreak. And that it was funny to see him as she was leaving and his sister as she was returning."

"Does he have flu? Was he in for an ER visit?"

"Not according to the intake records. And I didn't mean to eavesdrop, but I couldn't help it. They were talking right there in front of me, as if it didn't matter a hill of beans. But of course, it might."

"It could. I don't suppose she mentioned a can of red spray paint, perchance?"

Joan laughed. "No, but winter coats have deep pockets. It's so much easier to slip things in and out of places in the winter."

"Oh, good point." Priscilla's phone signaled a text. She pulled it out, read it, and handed it to Joan. "Check out what Gail's saying."

Pop should be able to come back to MV on Monday. Starts heart rehab at MV Hospital on Tuesday. Hallelujah!

"Oh, that's such good news!" Joan fist-pumped the air.

"Marvelous news," agreed Priscilla. "Now if we can make some progress on this case before then..."

"We won't be back from Boston until Sunday night. I believe our case will have to rest until then. And remember," Joan warned her as they gathered their coats to leave. "Don't cloud Rachel's wedding planning weekend with questions about the case. You know A.J. will help you if he can, but this weekend should be all about Rachel."

"Agreed. Which means I'll get a few more things done today before we leave this evening. Including finding out if Sonya and Jon's daughters have come back to town."

"Priscilla, the girls couldn't be involved with this."

Priscilla lifted one brow, and Joan caved. "All right, if nothing else, I've learned that the least possible suspect is often the most likely culprit. But I don't want either of those lovely girls involved, so I'm hoping that is absolutely not the case."

"Me too," Priscilla admitted as they walked back to the car. "Which is why I want them cleared right off."

She swung back by the hospital, left Joan in the car texting Gail, and dashed into the administrative offices. The graffiti was gone, but the offices were strangely quiet during a busy Friday. Doors were closed. Not one person was walking in the hallway.

Was this normal? Priscilla wasn't sure, but she tapped on Sonya's door. "A moment, please?"

The selectwoman motioned her in.

Priscilla didn't mess around. She took a seat and leaned forward. "Are your daughters in town, Mrs. Fleming? Were they in town last evening?"

"My girls?" Surprise, then shock changed her expression. "You can't believe one of them had anything to do with this," she said.

"Are they in town? Have they come back? Could they have slipped over here?"

Sonya shook her head. "No, they both returned to campus last weekend. Daria is an RA, so she returns early, and Callie is helping coach the women's gymnastics team. Neither one was on the island last night."

"That makes them innocent in my book," Priscilla told her. "I'm working with the theory that whoever did the spray painting might be involved in the theft. He or she might not be the only person involved, but my guess is they're worried about being caught and so they're trying to focus the investigators' attention on you."

Sonya stared at her. "That makes sense."

"Well, I do try to make sense," Priscilla admitted with a smile. "Where was your husband last night?"

"At Grace Episcopal with me," she told her. "And a few other people. I'm Catholic, but Jon's family is Episcopal, so we help coordinate the Friday night suppers every winter. If we set up on Thursday, that leaves us a lot less work to do on Friday."

That pretty much took Jon off the list too. "Was anyone else there connected to the hospital? And who can vouch for your being there?"

"Maura was there." She nodded toward the adjoining office where her administrative assistant was working at her computer. "A couple of gals from Faith Fellowship come over to help, Tracey Buschman and Ellie Doyle. Ellie brings Rebekah Alden over for supper on Fridays, not because of financial need, but for some old-fashioned company. This island can get lonely for the old or infirm over a long winter. She was helping us set up last night. With Ellie."

Plenty of people to witness where Jon and Sonya were. "Thank you. I won't take any more of your time today, but I appreciate your openness, Mrs. Fleming."

"Sonya, please. And actually…" She frowned and tapped her desk. Priscilla waited, silent.

"I'm glad you asked about the girls. Not that I thought they'd do it, but I've been known to leave files open on the computer when I go to get coffee or use the bathroom. I minimize them, but someone could pull them up easily. I never thought of that being a problem, because what are the odds that someone would know when I was in that particular account?"

"Slim to none," said Priscilla. "You've done this here?"

Sonya nodded, shame-faced. "Yes. Here. And at home. Because no one ever messes with my computer."

"Until this time," Priscilla said softly.

Sonya put her head in her hands momentarily, then lifted her gaze. "Exactly. It was a stupid risk for me to take, and I'm ashamed of myself."

"For trusting the people around you?" Priscilla shook her head firmly. "Heaven help us when trust disappears from our circle of friends. A trusting nature isn't a bad thing."

"But a responsibility should always be borne with the utmost care." She sighed softly. "My grandfather used to say that, and if someone had asked me ten days ago if I follow that advice, I'd have said yes."

"Now we know to be even more careful in our efforts." Priscilla stood. "I'm out of town the next two days," she added.

"A fun trip?"

"Fun and possibly scary," Priscilla told her. "Wedding gown shopping with my only daughter."

"Oh, what a joy." The worry eased from Sonya's face. "I hope you have a wonderful weekend together."

"Thank you. I'll be back Sunday evening, but if you think of anything, or if something odd happens, call me. Or text me."

"I'd hate to interrupt your time," Sonya replied.

"A text is hardly even considered an interruption these days. And if I can't get back to you right away, I will when I'm able."

Sonya got up and circled the desk. "Thank you. Thank you for getting involved and not believing I'm guilty, because I'm pretty sure a fair number of people do."

"I've found that when we only skim the surface of deep water, we rarely see the school of fish down below."

"True words." Sonya shook Priscilla's hand.

When Priscilla returned to the car, Joan wagged the phone her way. "Gail and I are going to have supper together Saturday night while you're wining and dining your new in-laws."

In-laws. Priscilla frowned. "It's such a terrible name for relatives by marriage, isn't it? I'm going into this assuming they're new family, and that will be that."

"And it will be just that easy." Joan said the words but hid a laugh under a fake cough. "Stop worrying. You're not a worrier by nature, so why are you fretting over this?"

"Not fretting. That's too strong a word. Let's call it concern," Priscilla corrected her, then she confessed. "I think it's because this is all new territory. And it was supposed to happen while Gary was here. He was supposed to walk Rachel down the aisle, tease her as he writes out checks, bust the buttons on his suit coat with pride. It's not like I pictured it," she concluded. "So I'm looking at all the good and loving it, but the script isn't how I ever thought it would go."

"Scripts change fairly often," said Joan. "When Allan died, I thought I couldn't go on. Life seemed so wrong and long and empty. My two boys were grown and gone, and Mom and Dad had passed away a few years before. Trudy and I had seen them through nearly three years of decline, and it was an honor to care for them. But to have Allan die so suddenly broke me. I thought I'd never be truly happy again, but you know what?" She turned to face Priscilla. "I am. I might be wrong to say this, but I love my life. I loved my life then and I love it now. It's different, of course. But it's fine. And it's what God gave me, so when I realized I was wallowing far too much, I started looking backward, thanking God for all the good I'd had in my life, and then moving forward to embrace the present."

Joan was right.

Priscilla drove back to the lighthouse to get her bags and give Jake a quick run and a little attention. Gerald had offered to keep Jake for the weekend and Trudy was looking after Sister, Joan's blue heeler. Once Jake was settled, she and Joan swung by Joan's house to pick up her bags. Then they were on their way to the mainland.

Joan clapped her hands together as they headed toward town. "Road trip!"

Priscilla laughed. "I love road trips, and that's a downside of island living. It takes actual planning to get a spot on the ferry with a car and take off. But here we go."

She called Gerald as they proceeded to the ferry dock. He answered quickly. "You gals on your way north?"

"Almost to the ferry," she told him. "And thank you so much for watching Jake for me."

"My pleasure, Priscilla."

"And you don't mind stopping around just to be sure there's nothing crazy going on at the lighthouse while I'm gone?"

"Not at all. I've got Sunday off, and the dogs and I will have ourselves a little adventure. It'll be good for Sammy," he added. "She's seemed tired since the cold set in. Having Jake around always peps her up."

"It does. And shall we all meet for supper on Sunday night?"

"I'll set something up and text you," he promised. "Gail's coming back then too, correct?"

"Yes. And then the medical transport is driving Uncle Hugh down on Monday."

"It will be good to have him back."

"It sure will," echoed Joan. "Thanks, Gerald!"

"You gals have fun. And drive carefully, both ways. There's snow up and down the coast for the next twelve hours."

"Good tires, good driver, we'll be fine," Priscilla assured him, and they were. They grabbed seafood across from their hotel and when Mother Nature and a fairly mild storm dumped eight inches of snow on the great Boston metro area the next morning, they shrugged it off.

CHAPTER TWELVE

You have fun with Rachel and A.J. and whomever," Joan said as she headed for the car. She was going to meet Gail at the hospital before she and her son went car shopping. "Send me pictures!"

"I will." Rachel pulled up to the hotel as Joan was pulling away. She got out and hugged Priscilla, and when she should have let go, she didn't.

"Hey. What's up?" Priscilla asked. "What's wrong?"

"I've never done anything like this," Rachel whispered so she wouldn't be overheard. "Wedding gowns? Veils? Fuss and bother? That's so not me, Mom."

"Here's how I see it," Priscilla told her, and she had to draw up Joan's words of wisdom. "We take the day for the enjoyment it is, and if we don't see anything we like, we order six online, try them on next week, and send them back. Easy peasy, and we keep the shipping companies in business."

"That would be so weird and strangely tempting," said Rachel. "Because I'm totally out of my element here. Our first stop is one of the traditional places, then we have nontraditional, then we have a boutique-style place. All are ridiculously pricey."

A.J.'s sister was sitting very upright in the back seat, with another woman. "Mom, this is Marilee, A.J.'s sister. And his favorite aunt in all the world, Auntie Em."

"So nice to meet you both."

Marilee smiled. It wasn't a thin smile, but it wasn't all that happy, either. Maybe she was having digestive problems.

Em reached out a hand to Priscilla. "Emmie Boudreaux, but the kids thought it funny to dub me 'Auntie Em' when they were little, and it stuck. I've had the pleasure of helping raise A.J. and Marilee since they lost their mother, so this is very special for me. I can't say how thrilled I am with A.J.'s choice of a wife, a helpmate." She beamed at Rachel, then at Priscilla, and her smile won Priscilla's heart. "Thank you so much for allowing me to come along."

"Auntie's excited because she knows that I will never get married, which will surprise absolutely no one on the planet," Marilee explained in a voice that mixed sharp with cutting, nothing at all like her calm, kind, cool, collected brother. "Or if I do, it will be with a minimum of fuss and bother, and there will be no ceremonial saying yes to a dress or any other such thing. So we're both crashing your day. Sorry if it doesn't suit."

Priscilla didn't miss a beat. She gave the snippy woman her best and brightest smile and said, "Why darling, it suits marvelously! I love watching people live vicariously through others' successes and accomplishments, and this way you can say that you've had the experience, even if it was by a separation of degrees." She held the smile firmly in place then turned to fasten her seat belt.

Marilee Montgomery was going to do her best to be a wet blanket on Rachel's day. After she rolled her eyes at half-a-dozen gloriously beautiful elegant gowns within the first ninety minutes, Priscilla used a restroom excuse to call Joan, who put her on speakerphone so Gail could hear. "What do I do?" she whispered from the far corner of the store. "She is doing her best to mess this up."

"A muzzle?" suggested Joan.

"I wish."

"Drop her in the harbor?" said Gail, and she sounded quite serious. "Short of that, how can you get rid of her? Wait." Gail's voice hiked up. "Priscilla, quick, while you're in the ladies' room, call a couple of shops and see if you can get appointments tomorrow morning."

"Instead of brunch?"

"Make it a late brunch," Gail insisted. "That way you and Rachel can get in two shops tomorrow, all alone."

It was a splendid idea. If Rachel found a dress today, she'd have to pay a cancellation fee for the unneeded appointments tomorrow, but that was a small price to pay for this kind of insurance.

And when she'd set up two spots for Sunday—and then texted that information to Rachel with a "shushing" emoji—Rachel's bright smile when she returned to the group was reward enough.

"Too fussy," said Marilee at the next place.

"Too classic," at the next.

"I love classic lines, actually," said Rachel. She gazed into the mirror but shook her head. "It's beautiful but not quite right. Let's try this one." And when she came out wearing the layered organza dress, Priscilla's heart tightened, then loosened. Rachel was perfectly, utterly beautiful.

"Way too pale. You, not the dress," said Marilee. "The dress is supposed to be pale. And who wears pink for her wedding? That's just too cute-cute for words."

Auntie Em spoke up before Priscilla could wring her snippy little neck and create another crime scene. "Marilee, hush," Em scolded. "It's absolutely gorgeous. And so is Rachel. Either play nice or go home. There's no reason for you to act like this. Your brother's wedding should be a joyous occasion. I expect you to do everything you can to make it that way."

Marilee glared at her, and the saleswoman redirected the conversation so skillfully that Priscilla wanted to hug her.

"Blush, not pink," the kindly saleswoman corrected her. "The color is blush, and I think Rachel looks absolutely stunning in this shade."

"You're right," said Priscilla. She smiled into Rachel's sparkling blue eyes through the mirror. "The blush is perfect on you, honey. And with the other colors you picked—"

"You mean pink, pink, and pink?" snarked Marilee. "We must be going for a *Steel Magnolias* wedding."

Rachel had taken the snipes well until now. She'd smiled and ignored and smiled some more, but this time she turned and when she nailed Marilee with her young executive killer look, there was no doubt that she'd had enough. "I love that movie. I love how the mother sacrificed for the daughter from beginning to end, and in case you haven't noticed, Julia Roberts and I have the same coloring and build. So if I want to have—" She leaned forward, gorgeous gown and all, and spoke slowly. Softly. And very, very firmly. "A pink and mauve wedding, I will. If I want to wear the flounciest gown ever made, I'll do it. If I decide I want huge Southern hair, then I. Will. Do. It. Because it's my wedding." Priscilla didn't think Rachel could ever sound scarier.

She was wrong.

Rachel got right down in Marilee's no longer smug face. "Got it?"

Marilee rolled her eyes, but Priscilla saw the tiny flash of fear and respect before she did. "Yes. Of course. Fine."

When Marilee bowed out of supper, Priscilla's day-long headache magically and wondrously disappeared. She said goodbye and turned back to the group.

"Rough day, huh?" A.J. looked worried when they met for dinner, but Rachel shook her head.

"No. It was an interesting experience, but Mom saved the day by virtue of being the best mother in the world."

"Well, we knew that." A.J. grinned but shot Priscilla a look of pure gratitude, and when he mouthed a quiet 'thank you,' she knew he understood.

Priscilla met his dad, and the five of them had a lovely dinner. After they said their goodbyes to Auntie Em, they turned in for the night. The next morning, after an early service at A.J.'s church, she and Rachel cancelled the two appointments, paid the fee, and went back to buy the blush dress.

"Why search once we've found perfection?" Rachel mused. The store was booked solid, but when Rachel said she'd simply pay for the dress and come back for measurements later, they swiftly found someone with a window of availability to lock in the sale.

"This one's on me," Priscilla said firmly as she handed over her credit card a quarter-hour later. "Your daddy would be mortified to think he didn't pay for your dress. I know we're splitting costs, but this is different. This is special, Rachel."

"I love you, Mom." She hugged Priscilla and when Priscilla teared up, Rachel laughed. "No crying. We need a no-crying pact. Neither of us are crying people, so why now?"

"Because it's that important," scolded Priscilla, and then she laughed. "'Laughter through tears...'"

"*Truvy!*" Rachel loved that sweet movie about five Southern women. "Laughter through tears is my favorite emotion!" She completed the quote as they left the store. "How about this, now that we have the dress ordered? I suggest that mother and daughter don't wander around the snowy downtown Boston area. That instead we grab tea at the cute little place down the road and talk about what's going on in the Vineyard and go over my wedding plans before we join the other players."

"Agreed. And Rachel, I'm just going to say one thing because I promised Joan I wouldn't put my two cents in where it wasn't needed."

"Joan knows you well," Rachel declared, smiling.

"You don't have to ask Marilee to be in your wedding," Priscilla said as they crossed to the tea shop. "If she's determined to be a brat, it's okay to let her be a brat on the sidelines. I know she's A.J.'s only sister. And wedding protocol says what you should and should not do. But there's also the common sense of the situation that influences the decision. I'm sorry she's angry about everything. But she's a grown-up and that's kind of her choice." She finished as they were seated at a cozy table with not one but *two* linen tablecloths.

"Thank you, Mom. It's sound advice."

"Well, you get a day," Priscilla explained. "One day. And it doesn't have to be perfect—nothing should ever be held to that kind of standard—but it's okay to not knowingly invite disaster."

"I promise to think on it," Rachel told her. "Kim has already agreed to be my matron of honor."

Kim and Rachel had been best friends from elementary school on.

"And A.J. is having his friend Jason as the best man. And we think we'll leave it at that. My other friends are so far away, either in the Midwest or on the West Coast. It doesn't seem right to add the expense of a dress and all that goes with it to coming east for the wedding. That seems unfair."

"Your sensibilities are marvelous, darling."

Rachel squeezed her hand. "I learned from the best."

By the time tea was done and A.J. was scheduled to pick them up for brunch, everything was planned. The wedding would be on the island at Faith Fellowship, pictures at the Lighthouse, and while they both loved the idea of a lighthouse reception, neither one was sure of the logistics.

"We'll figure that out by the end of the month," Rachel promised. "I'm sure availability of venues is limited because of our time frame, but there will be someplace on that beautiful island for our reception."

Joan joined them for brunch. She'd cut a deal on an almost-new SUV, but the car wasn't ready to go. The dealership offered to drive it to Woods Hole at the beginning of the week.

"That means we get to drive back together, which is always more fun than alone," Priscilla told her.

She'd kept her word to Joan for the whole weekend. She hadn't asked A.J. one single question about the current case, so when he deliberately took the seat next to her and said, "Fill me in on the case, Priscilla," she about hugged him.

"It's this whole computer access thing," she said softly. "You said that safety protocols now are much more effective at keeping hackers out."

"True."

"So how about the possibility that someone could get into Sonya's office and use her computer to access the account? How does one go about finding an account and knowing the passwords to get into it?" she asked.

"Usually by the owner's carelessness," A.J. told her, but before he went on he motioned to an amazing-looking dish. "Try this crab and cheese casserole, they're known for this and it's delicious. Anyway, here's the thing. People get careless. They leave passwords on slips of paper. Or they leave their computers open, thinking no one will notice. But if someone has malicious intent, they're trying to notice. So what seems nonchalant at the moment becomes evidentiary when a crime is committed."

"Sonya said she's left the account open on both her home and work computer occasionally, but minimizes the screen."

"That's a false sense of security if ever there was one," noted A.J. He made a clicking motion with one finger. "One click brings things back up, and if Sonya had her computer supply the username and password when she logged in—which many people do, to save time—a person could find her saved logins file and get into the account from another computer."

"Oh, of course. Then the perpetrator doesn't have to do anything right then. He can wait until he's at his own computer, and simply get into the account by going to the site and putting in Sonya's username and password."

"It doesn't generally work for bank accounts," he told her. "Most banks have an added layer of security, and you have to register a new computer with additional information, but I've seen it done on pension funds."

"Except the police traced the withdrawals back to her computer."

"Oh. Then that can't be the way it was done. But stealing passwords and hacking aren't the only ways into a computer. What about remote access?"

"You mean accessing the computer itself from another place? Another computer?"

"Sure. A remote desktop. If someone realizes they can access funds via Sonya's computer, all they have to do is download a sharing app into the computer. It takes seconds."

"So it could be done while someone is in the bathroom or getting coffee."

"Yes. Then the computer can be accessed from another site."

"Another computer."

"Or smartphone, tablet, anything with Internet access and a functional mechanism."

"So the thief doesn't have to return to the scene of the crime at all."

"No, ma'am. Although if he or she has access, it'd be smart to remove the application they installed, leaving the computer looking inaccessible."

"Which means everything looks like it's been done from the user's computer even though it's been accessed remotely."

"Yes, because basically it is. The remote device is nothing more than a pricey window, allowing access."

Priscilla's pulse kicked up a notch. This opened up a wealth of possibilities, and while it spread the suspect net further, it took pressure off of Sonya as the only one with access to her computer.

"Thank you." She grabbed his hand. "I didn't want to take up wedding time by asking, but I knew you'd have a clear picture of what this would be like from a lawman's perspective. And now, looking at the time, Joan and I have to go if we're going to get to the ferry on time." They all stood and when they neared the restaurant door, she turned to A.J.'s father. "Ike, it was an absolute pleasure to meet you, and thank you so much for hosting brunch today. And for raising a great son. We are delighted to welcome him into the family."

"He's all right," Ike Montgomery agreed, smiling, but then he held Priscilla's hand a second longer. "And thank you for all you did to discover the fate of Lizzie Farnsworth last summer.

Knowing what happened to her meant a great deal, not just to me, but to a lot of people who worked that case."

"Closure is an overused word these days, but a necessary commodity." She squeezed his hand lightly. "You're welcome."

"Mom, thank you so much." Rachel hugged her as Joan brought the car to the entrance. "I love my dress. And I love you."

Oh, those words, the way it should be when planning such a special occasion. "Ditto, darling. And I'll come back to town for the fitting this spring, okay?"

"Yes. Perfect."

She and Joan got on their way and when they'd cleared the busier Boston area, Joan poked her arm. "You did good, Cousin."

"I did, didn't I?" Priscilla laughed. "I was silly to be worried, and Rachel handled Marilee just right, and then to put the order in for that absolutely beautiful dress was such a step forward."

"Just as it should be," said Joan softly. "And now we go home, we meet up with Gail, Trudy, Dan, and Gerald, and we get back to work on this case. And hopefully nothing major happened while we were gone."

"I'm sure everything was absolutely fine. If it wasn't, Gerald would have texted us."

He did text them. Right then. With a news headline from the *Daily Dither* saying "Arrest Made in Fishermen Pension Embezzlement Case" and there, below the headline was a mug shot of Sonya Fleming looking mad…and scared.

CHAPTER THIRTEEN

Joan got Jon Fleming on the phone a few minutes later, and when she hung up, she turned toward Priscilla, grim. "Jon used the equity in their house to post bail, the town of Oak Bluffs has temporarily set her aside as selectwoman until this is cleared up, and the hospital has put her on a paid leave of absence. This whole thing has pretty much ruined a hardworking woman's life."

"What a crazy chain of events," muttered Priscilla, but it made sense from the business perspective. Who wanted a possible felonious embezzler handling hospital finances or town affairs?

No one.

But she was certain Sonya was innocent. Her career being ruined was a harsh blow. Too harsh, when the woman's biggest mistake might have been a bathroom break.

Joan put her phone away. "We're meeting at Gail's for a carry-out supper so we can discuss things openly. Gerald too."

"Good." The euphoria of wedding gown success dimmed, because this latest twist didn't just change the case. It changed lives. She pulled into Gail's driveway, determined to figure this out. One way or another, they'd find the real thief.

"Priscilla!" Gail grabbed her in a big hug when she walked in the door. "It's so good to be home. And so good to be bringing Pop home!" True joy filled her eyes and brightened her gaze. "I know he can't be here forever, but I'm glad the Lord saw fit to give us some leeway, and you'll never guess what Pop's done."

Knowing her irascible uncle, Priscilla was pretty sure she couldn't guess. "Tell me."

"He called Marigold Townsend and asked her on a date."

"He what?" Joan looked just as shocked as Priscilla felt. "Like the two of them, stepping out? Instead of quietly flirting from afar? Now this is news!"

"He told me he's wasted too much time already, and it's been foolish on both their parts. He's invited her to dinner here on Friday. Can you imagine?"

"And Tommy will bring her, of course." Priscilla smiled at Gail.

"Thomas will bring her, and he'll stay for dinner as well."

"A double date," Priscilla whispered with a smile as Joan slung their coats on nearby hooks. "What an unexpected bend in the road this is, Gail."

"I know. Pop's had a real change of heart." She whispered the words to Priscilla, and there was no mistaking the spark of hope in her eyes. "But we need to tuck all that aside for the moment," she said in a more normal voice. "Head in and let's see if we can figure out a plan to help Sonya and Jon. I can't believe things have gone this far."

"Things move swiftly when the evidence all points in one solid direction." Gerald came Priscilla's way and he didn't just take her hand as usual.

He hugged her. Right there, in front of family and friends, and she was pretty sure he planted a kiss on her head as well, so of course she was blushing when he let her go. "Nothing points any other way than straight at Sonya. Are you gals certain she didn't do it?" He posed the question in a straightforward voice.

"Have they found the money in her accounts?" asked Priscilla.

"Nothing has been found, but our little police force isn't equipped to do an overseas trace into foreign-based banks."

"So now we think she's slipping funds into a Swiss bank account?" said Joan, and she didn't hide the incredulity in her tone. "That's ridiculous."

"They're assuming it's the most likely answer when money goes off the grid, and they believe Sonya is smart enough to know how to do it," Gerald replied.

"Well, of course she's smart enough," spouted Trudy. "We all know that. But she's honest to a fault if there is such a thing, and that's that. How do we fix this? And let me add I feel guilty about leaving with this unsolved."

"By the time we get back, she'll be in the clear," said Dan.

"Oh, Dan, I hope so." Trudy turned his way. "I'm just frustrated. Sonya's mother was our good friend growing up. Joan babysat for Sonya and her siblings all through high school. Sonya's grandmother worked for some Lathams and her grandfather did too. Our lives are connected from way back, and she was the sparkling gem in their family crown."

Trudy had yearned to be in the theater as a younger woman, and her love of drama bled through her voice now. "This whole thing is the kind of negativity that casts a bad light not just on

Sonya and her wonderful family, but on the Martha's Vineyard Portuguese community."

"Is it possible that someone is targeting this fund deliberately to smear Sonya?" Priscilla asked. "Are there people who dislike the Portuguese community?"

"I would hope not." Trudy plucked a pair of olives from a dish. "But there might be people who envy Sonya's success. And yet I can't think of a one, honestly, which means I'm not much help."

Jealousy was sometimes a strong motivator. Priscilla had seen it damage families, friends, and workplaces over the years. Jealousy and envy weren't bound by island borders. She'd seen her share back in Kansas too, but if no one begrudged Sonya's success, it was another dead end. "Wouldn't it be nice if we could all be satisfied with enough? Or with what we've done if we've done our best?" she asked. She tucked her phone away. "We'll start tracking things down first thing tomorrow," she told the others as Gail and Trudy set hot dishes onto the narrow countertop so everyone could fill their plates. "Joan, you're working, right?"

"Yes, but my new car arrives tomorrow afternoon so you won't have to chauffer me around anymore!"

"It's been an absolute pleasure," Priscilla told her. "And Gail's got to be ready for Uncle Hugh, and Trudy and Dan are heading south..."

"Which leaves me, I believe, and I do happen to have tomorrow off," Gerald told her.

"I'm dropping Joan off at eight, so can we meet at the coffee shop and head out from there?"

"Coffee with you, first thing in the morning?" He smiled. "I can't think of a nicer way to start the day."

She met his gaze and couldn't hold back the smile.

Neither could he, it seemed.

And when he held her coat for her after dinner, and walked her and Joan to Priscilla's car, it felt good to have him there.

"Jake is tucked in at your house. He was a wonderful guest at our place, and Sammy was more like her old self, playing with him."

"Have you thought about getting her a playmate?" Priscilla asked. It wasn't snowing, and the temperatures had moderated somewhat.

"I have and I decided against it," he told her. "I'm going to be facing choices before too long. I've been at this station a long time, more than is generally allowed, and I'm pretty sure retirement is looming."

Retirement for Gerald...meant what? She almost couldn't get herself to form the question. "I know. And that's a big change for you. It opens up doors of opportunity," she added brightly, and it was true. Those opportunities might lead him away from Martha's Vineyard, and she wasn't real fond of that idea. But then, it wasn't her choice to make.

"A lot to think about. Talk about. Not now," he told her as he opened her door. Joan was hurrying their way as Priscilla slid into the driver's seat. "It's too cold. I'll mull the options. See what's what. Good night, Joan."

"Good night, Gerald." She buckled herself in as Priscilla backed the car onto the road. "I'm going to think of every possible avenue we can explore when I get out of work tomorrow," she declared.

"There's got to be something we've missed. Nobody can do something this complicated without messing up somewhere. Can they?"

"Most don't. But some do." Priscilla tapped the wheel as she came to a turn. "Let's find out more about Howard."

"Shouldn't be hard. He likes to talk."

"And we need to talk with Dee Dee again too."

"Dee Dee?" Joan frowned. "You think she knows something?"

"There is a tiny possibility she might be involved."

"With the theft?" Joan sounded incredulous. "You can't be serious."

"I'm probably wrong. I hope I'm wrong," admitted Priscilla, because she'd gotten to like the quirky, self-made reporter. And respect her diligence. "But there's something going on with her, and I'm not sure what it is."

"Really?" Joan drew a breath as Priscilla pulled into her driveway. "All right we'll check it out. And, Cousin?" She leaned back into the car once she'd stepped out and grabbed her small overnight bag. "Have fun working with Gerald in the morning." She winked and hurried up the short walk to her quaint cottage.

Gerald...

Such a good man. Kind, hardworking, valiant. There was no denying her growing feelings for him.

But she had a lot on her plate right now. First and foremost, Rachel's peace and well-being over this wedding. And getting poor Sonya back to her life, the life she worked so hard for.

Jake greeted her at the door. He wagged everything he could possibly wag, dashed outdoors to take care of necessities, then hurried back in, wagging again. "Good boy! It's good to see you too, my friend. So good! And oh. What's this?" She spotted a pretty, cheerful flower arrangement on the table. Not big, but just enough to add bright color to the leaden January days. "What a grand surprise," she told Jake, and she hurried to call Gerald and thank him. When he answered, there was no way she could restrain the joy in her voice. "Gerald, thank you so much. Jake looks wonderful, and the flowers were an added touch. You shouldn't have done it, but what a treat they were when I walked in the door."

"Priscilla—"

"And bright colors. Full of spring," she went on. "Thank you."

"I'll be right there."

"Gerald, no, I—"

"Priscilla take Jake and get in the car. Right now. And lock the car doors."

Her heart began pounding in her chest. A chill coursed through her body from stem to stern. And she couldn't even speak the words around the lump of fear in her throat because she knew—she knew!—what Gerald was going to say next and it struck a dagger of fear into her.

"I didn't bring them, Priscilla."

She grabbed Jake, took him to the car, started it, and then pulled away. She wasn't going to sit in the driveway, waiting to be attacked. She drove down the road, past Rebekah Alden's pretty place, and waited until she saw Gerald's dark SUV and a police cruiser pull into her driveway. Only then did she go back to her house.

CHAPTER FOURTEEN

So these flowers weren't here when you left on Friday?" Brian Denton asked Priscilla a few minutes later.

They sure weren't. She scowled at the flowers even though none of this was their fault. "No."

"And were they here when you dropped off the dog, Captain?"

Gerald nodded. "I didn't think anything of it. Priscilla loves flowers. I assumed she'd gotten an arrangement to brighten up the winter days."

"So that means they were brought in sometime over the weekend," Brian surmised. "Priscilla, who knew you were going away?"

"Just a handful of people. My neighbor Rebekah and her caretaker. I told them I'd be gone and asked them to keep an eye on things."

Brian nodded as he jotted that down.

"And my family here, although Joan went with me and Gail was on the mainland because Uncle Hugh had a heart attack last week. And Sonya Fleming."

Brian raised a brow. "Sonya knew you were going to be out of town?"

"Yes, I told her about it myself. I'm trying to unravel how the money went missing. I'm certain Sonya didn't take it, and I intend to find out who did."

"Could she have left the flowers as a thank-you for helping?"

"There's no card, and any sensible person would have left a card. The question is, how did they get in here? Into my house? Brian, this is the second time someone's gotten in," she reminded him. "The first time I thought I'd forgotten to lock the door, but what if I didn't forget? What if someone has a key to my home?"

"There are no signs of a break-in or forced entry and that dead-bolt is secure," noted Gerald. "No one can get through that without leaving a mark of some sort, and there's nothing there. Which leads me to think that someone does have a key."

A key to her house.

The shiver that chased down Priscilla's spine was real and understandably exaggerated.

"Did you have the locks changed after you inherited the lighthouse, Priscilla?"

She shook her head. "I didn't see a need, because Aunt Marjorie was the only owner for so long and she'd died. I never gave it a thought."

"Did your aunt have a custodian, or a friend, or anyone with a key?" Brian asked, and the minute he said the words, Priscilla snapped her fingers.

"Gerald, this could be the break we've been waiting for."

He put a hand to his face, then sighed. "Priscilla, this is serious."

"Immensely serious," she agreed, "but if someone has a key to my house and it was given to him or her by Aunt Marjorie, this could narrow the suspect playing field. If this person is trying to scare me off of Sonya's case, then he or she is clearly involved somehow. And I'm willing to bet that Aunt Marjorie didn't have all that many people she'd trust with a key."

"True, although isn't it odd that the person didn't give the key to you as the new owner?" asked Brian. "Most people would do that, wouldn't they?"

"If they thought of it. But with the property being vacant for months, maybe they just forgot they had it until now."

Brian jotted a few notes. "My first suggestion, and I'm going to insist you take it, is to go somewhere else and sleep tonight and get the locks changed tomorrow."

Priscilla started to argue, then clamped her mouth shut. "You're right, of course. If someone can get in here anytime they want, I can't be here sleeping. Jake and I can go bunk at Joan's for the night."

"And I'll text Tommy that we need these locks changed ASAP," noted Gerald.

And then he did it again. He hugged her. He pulled her into his arms, against that nice, broad chest, and held her. "I'm glad you called me right away, Scilla."

Scilla?

No one had ever nicknamed her before. Her old-fashioned New England-sounding name had raised a few eyebrows back in Wheatfield, and she wasn't a nickname kind of woman.

But this…Scilla…from Gerald…

She liked it. "Me too. And now I'm getting out of here and disturbing Joan and wondering how on earth I get myself into these things. But this latest move"—she watched as Brian slipped a plastic bag around the flowers and removed them—"could be the thief's fatal flaw. Trying so hard to scare me off the case means we're either closer than we thought or the culprit is skittish and has a lot to lose. That makes a big difference when we're narrowing the field."

"I'll see you in the morning, as planned?" asked Gerald once she'd grabbed the few things she'd need to bunk at Joan's. Again.

She locked the door for all the good it would do, then whistled for Jake to hop into the car. "Absolutely."

"And, Priscilla?"

She turned to Gerald as Brian set the flowers into his squad car. "Yes?"

"I should have been the one to send you flowers. It would have been a nice thing to do."

"Well, there's always next week. Or next month." She smiled at him over the car, then climbed in. She'd texted Joan, who'd probably been tucked into bed, enjoying a well-deserved rest. But when Joan opened the door a few minutes later, she didn't look one bit tired. "Come in, and tell me what happened. I know we've got to get to bed soon, but let's sort out what we can. Because if that stinkin' thief thinks he can get away with scaring a Latham, well..." Joan shut the door firmly and folded her arms. "He's got another think coming!"

Gerald was waiting in the coffee shop when Priscilla pulled up to the curb out front, something that wouldn't happen during the busy season. She tugged her scarf closer around her neck and hurried inside. The warmth of the gas fireplace came not just from the generated heat, but the image of dancing flames.

"I ordered you a caramel macchiato. Sound good?"

"It sounds wonderful."

"How did Joan take the news of someone getting into your house?" he asked softly.

"About as well as she took having her car wrecked and being inconvenienced for a week," she told him. "But the good thing about Joan is that her memory is sharp, and she was very involved with Aunt Marjorie. All three of the gals were, and she said that Aunt Marjorie left a key for her handyman a long time back."

"Left it for him? As in under the mat?" Gerald frowned. "Please tell me people don't do that sort of thing anymore."

"Well, Aunt Marjorie did, and here's the thing. The handyman she left it for was Berto, the elderly Portuguese fisherman I met at the church supper last week."

Gerald shook his head. "I don't know him, and I know most of the fishermen on the island."

"I should have said former fisherman," she corrected herself. She thanked the middle-aged barista who delivered her coffee and set it down. "He said he never did get proper sea legs under him, but he worked for several of my late relatives in his time. He and his wife moved to New Bedford for a while but came back here to retire. He said New Bedford was almost as special. But not quite."

"The Vineyard gets in a person's blood, that's for sure." He sipped his coffee. "So you think this elderly gentleman brought you flowers? Should I be jealous?"

"No," she told him with amused sincerity. "Just go on being obtuse. That's plenty for one day." When he laughed, she went on. "If Berto worked for Aunt Marjorie, he may have kept the key and someone took it from him. Or he may have blurted out where she kept it because he's a born storyteller, Gerald. And a sweet old man."

"So whoever took the money might have stumbled onto this information about the key. Do you think they left you flowers to be nice? Or to thoroughly creep you out?"

"Well, Dee Dee told me straight out she came to the house, so she wasn't after a scare factor. She was more straightforward. Whether I left the door unlocked that day or not, I don't know. But someone released the dog, and I don't think it was her. That was bad enough, to have that sweet dog running around in wretched temperatures, but to randomly sneak into someone's home and leave flowers on the table with no card is way too *Fatal Attraction* for my taste. Did Tommy say when he was coming by to do the locks?"

"One o'clock. Then he's going to Gail's. He wants to be there when your uncle arrives. He figured strong arms and a good back might be a welcome addition."

"Where Gail is concerned, Tommy's help is always a welcome addition. I just hope my formerly crotchety uncle realizes his own unrequited love, thereby opening the door for Tommy and Gail's romance to blossom."

"Tommy? And Gail?" He sat back, then smiled. "Well, you Latham women are setting hearts aflutter all over the place, aren't you?"

She batted his arm. "Stop it. So where shall we start?"

"With your friend Berto. What's his last name?"

"Santiago."

Gerald consulted his smartphone, then nodded. "Alberto H. Santiago, early eighties."

"I would assume Berto is short for Alberto, so yes, that could be him. The age is right too."

"He's in Oak Bluffs, not far from the hospital. Let's drop by and see what he knows."

"And then let's pay Dee Dee a quick visit."

"Dee Dee the *Daily Dither* lady?" he asked as they moved to the door.

"Yes." Priscilla made sure to keep her voice low. "Something's amiss there. I'm not sure what, but she's a little too close to this case for my comfort. And she's right across from the hospital, with a good ear for news."

Gerald made a skeptical face. "You think she's a suspect because she's nosy?"

"I think there's something gone awry in her world. Whether or not that makes her a suspect is something else again. Do we want to take both cars?"

He shook his head. "Just mine. We've got to pick up Joan at noon and you gals can get home in time to meet Tommy at your place."

They pulled up in front of a compact house that needed more tender loving care than old Berto could give it. The weathered shingles needed cleaning and painting, the roof patches had come loose, and the porch railings listed to the left. Six solid steps led the way down, but the freezing and thawing mix of rain and snow had glazed them with ice.

"Gerald, this is a death sentence for someone Berto's age," Priscilla said as they approached the house.

"It is." He sounded grim. "Let's try the side door." A short concrete walk led the way. A sprinkling of rock salt helped dispel some of the ice glaze but not all. Gerald rapped on the door with a firm hand.

It took a couple of minutes before a window slid open with a groan. "Who's here?"

"That's him," she told Gerald, then she raised her voice. "It's me, Berto. Marjorie Latham's niece, Priscilla. And Captain O'Bannon from the Coast Guard."

"A captain's come to visit me?" Surprise heightened the old-timer's tone. "Well, I'd have put on the dog if I'd known. Come on in, save me doin' the stairs. Door's open."

The door opened easily, and they stepped inside. A narrow stairway led four steps up to the first floor and seven steps down to a musty basement.

The door above them opened, flooding the small entry with light. "There you are, come on up. It's not often folks stop by to see me these days. Not with it bein' just me and all."

Gerald let Priscilla precede him. She stepped into a small box-like kitchen. One small window looked out over the backyard, but plain, worn brown cabinets with no hardware gave a cardboard appearance to the room.

"What a nice surprise, Miss Priscilla." He beamed a smile at her, a smile that indicated he didn't much care about the drab surroundings. "Have a seat here." He shooed a cat off a chair and slid it out for Priscilla. The cat gave a short yowl of protest but scooted off to another room.

"And you, sir." Berto gave Gerald a quick salute. "Thank you for the honor of a visit. I can't say the last time I got to entertain a man in uniform."

"Well, no uniform today, but most days." Gerald saluted him back, then took a seat next to Priscilla. "It's a pleasure to meet you."

"Berto Santiago," the old fellow told him. "I'm fresh out of coffee, but can I get you some water?"

"No, we had coffee just a short while ago and we're good for now," Priscilla told him. "Berto, when you and I talked last week, you said you worked for Aunt Marjorie now and again."

"I sure did. Before I went to New Bedford."

"That long ago?" Priscilla had to fight the disappointment in her voice.

"Well, yes, by the time the missus and I moved back here, Marjorie and I had both gotten old. She had Tommy and Ida Jones helping out as needed. I made sure Tommy knew where the spare key was kept just in case Marjorie was sleeping or out at the doctor or something."

"A spare key?" Priscilla could barely hold back her excitement. "Where did she keep it?"

"There's a loose brick under the ivy alongside the door. It's not full loose but chinked out enough along the edge to hold a key. A place no one would think of looking, and I made sure Tommy knew about it when I ran into him at Candy's bakery several years back."

"How nice of you to tell him about the key," said Gerald. "Was it a quiet day at the bakery?" he asked then. He tried to sound casual but the old fellow perked right up.

"There's a problem with that key, ain't there?" He sighed and shook his head. "I probably shouldn't have opened my trap about it in a crowded place, but who'd have thought anyone cared where Miss Marjorie kept her spare key? Not me, that's for certain."

"Maybe it's not that key causing the problem," Priscilla told him. "Maybe there's another key."

He shook his head firmly. "She told me plain out years back that the locks came with two keys, and that's all a body needs. One to have. And one to hide, in case of emergency. And that's what she did. But I'm sorry to hear there might be shenanigans going on over at the lighthouse. Seeing that bad news about young Sonya and then hearing this makes me wonder what's going on here these days. Was a time everyone could leave their doors open and keys in their car and not worry a lick. It's different now."

"We've got some problems," Gerald agreed, "but nothing like they do in mainland cities and towns. We've still got the best of the best, just a whole lot of crazy that goes on for seven months of the year."

"With those middle three being the worst of the lot. And the best," Berto admitted. "You sure I can't get you anything?" he said again, but Priscilla shook her head.

"Nothing at all. You've been a big help. How long have you lived here, Berto?"

"In this house, about nine years now. We came back here, the wife got sick and went home to Jesus, and I've been gettin' by ever since. Some days it's lonely. But the two cats keep me moving and give me something to jaw at."

"Pets are great company and great therapy, aren't they?" Priscilla stood and smiled at him. "Thank you for talking with us. I'm grateful. I'm going to go home and see if that key is still tucked in there."

"Twelfth brick from the ground, upper left corner. Notched out just enough to hold the key, but not let the rain in."

"A superb hiding place," she agreed. Then she paused. "Berto, do you happen to remember any locals who were in the bakery when you and Tommy were talking?"

"It was crowded, and I expect some of the usuals were there, in their favorite spots doin' too much people watchin' and not enough honest work. Idle hands seem to promote yakkin' mouths in the bakery a little too often for my liking. Ms. Quimby was there. I saw her talkin' with this one and that one. The woman married to the soup guy, why can't I think of his name?" Berto fretted.

"Mr. Pennington, the man who owns Pennington Chowder Company?" suggested Gerald.

"Yes, but not him. His missus, tall, nice lady, but she doesn't like the bakery here in the Bluffs and always makes the drive to Candy's place. She told me once that quality was worth the trip."

The woman whose office linked to Sonya's. Her administrative assistant. Which made Priscilla wonder why a rich woman was working in the hospital. But then Berto's next words offered a sad explanation.

"I think she avoids some places on purpose, like. Places that remind her of her boy. It's a hard thing on a parent's heart to lose a child, especially their only child. I think havin' that job keeps her busy. A body likes to stay busy when everything goes wrong, you know?"

Priscilla knew the truth in that. What a heartbreaking tragedy.

"Candy's place is a bear for parking in the summer," noted Gerald, but Berto waved that off.

"Someone drives her, drops her off during the busy season and she walks straight in, grabs the order she phoned in, and walks back out. Now there's a body that makes good use of her time. Other than that, I don't recall particulars of that day. And Tommy, of course. He might remember better, being more of a youngster."

Priscilla bit back a grin because that youngster was in his midsixties. "Thank you, Berto."

"It was my pleasure. And do come again, anytime."

There was no mistaking the loneliness in his voice. Priscilla gave him a quick hug. "We will. I promise." When they got back to the car, she faced Gerald straight on. "We know where the key is! Now it's just a matter of catching him."

"Or her," Gerald said.

"In the act. And that will be that."

CHAPTER FIFTEEN

Gerald didn't seem quite so certain. "We know where the key was," he corrected her. "If the perp replaced it both times, it's there. If not, it's on someone's kitchen shelf. Or in a car."

"Either way, we have amazingly valuable information. Dee Dee's house is just up there, a stone's throw from the hospital."

"If you have an NFL quarterback's arm," he quipped. "Obviously 'close' is a relative term."

They pulled up by Dee Dee's house where a brand-new For Sale sign was hammered into the front lawn. "She's selling?"

"A bad time of year to be listing. It's few and far between looking to move on-island in January." Gerald climbed out of the car. "This wasn't here last week?"

"No."

"But you thought something was out of whack," he said.

"An intuition is all, because she mentioned money, but this is a major step."

Gerald kept his voice low. "Possibly understandable if she's involved in the embezzlement."

She couldn't be, could she? She'd seemed eager to help, and for all her odd ways, she was developing her online paper into quite a tidy, readable newspaper with real reporting. And while she was skilled with Word files, there was no way her flip phone accessed Sonya's computer. Priscilla led the way to the door and knocked.

No one answered.

She looked around the corner. "No car, although she told me she does a lot of walking."

"We can try her later. Or tomorrow."

She peeked in the window. "It looks quiet in there, and more organized than it was last week."

"Normal when people aren't at home," he told her. "You're not really going to peek in all of her windows, are you?"

She wanted to, but she resisted. "No. Let's stop by police head-quarters and ask if they've looked into the remote access idea. My guess would be no."

The officer on the case looked at her funny when she posed the question ten minutes later. "Why would we do that? We have the perpetrator booked and ready to prosecute, Mrs. Grant." The way he said her name made the collar of Priscilla's cotton turtleneck feel tight.

"So you're discounting the possibility that someone could have remotely accessed her work computer?"

He sighed as if being patient with her was taxing him. "We followed the money exchange straight back to Selectwoman Fleming's computer. That makes this fairly cut-and-dried. Captain, you understand the constraints of a small-town police department, even if your girlfriend finds herself unaware."

"Oh, she's pretty aware," Gerald assured him. "And she's cor-rect. If you don't have the staff to properly do the job then we'll call in the FBI to examine the computer. Even a reasonably good tech will be able to go inside and find out if the computer has been accessed via other means."

"We don't need the feds. We've got this."

Priscilla shook her head. "Unfortunately, I disagree. While this theft was found fairly quickly by comparison to other pension fraud cases throughout the country, and the amount is significantly less, most have been prosecuted in federal courts. If our local government can't provide due diligence for Selectwoman Fleming, a person who is to be presumed innocent until proven guilty by virtue of the US Constitution"—she paused, waiting for him to acknowledge the innocent until proven guilty mandate—"then it is our goal to make sure that the people investigating this theft are willing to explore all avenues, especially because your current one is erroneous. I'm willing to bet that when you examine Mrs. Fleming's work computer, you'll find that someone has accessed it from outside, thereby clearing her name."

"You think Sonya Fleming didn't think of that?" The officer rolled his eyes. "That removing herself a few physical degrees from the crime makes her look innocent? I can guarantee, if anyone got into her computer remotely, it was her. But we'll call the Duke County Sheriff's Department and have their IT department run a scan."

"And I'll make sure the feds know you're investigating the case with the full intent of wanting to find the truth." Priscilla kept her tone level, even though this guy had made fun of her sleuthing skills back at the hospital.

"You be sure and do that." The man had lost all pretense of respect.

"I'll have the FBI get in touch with you," she finished, and if she was hot under the collar when they began the conversation, it was nothing compared to how she felt now.

He glared at her.

She glared right back.

Then she turned on her heel and walked out the door, down the steps, and to the car.

Gerald hadn't locked it, so she didn't have to wait in the damp wind to climb in, and when he settled into the driver's seat, he turned the car on and pulled away. He said nothing until they were parked in the hospital parking lot, waiting for Joan. "Have you cooled off yet?"

She hit Send on her text to A.J. and straightened up. "No."

He waited about ten seconds. "Now?"

She sighed and batted his arm. "Still no, but patronizing people don't just annoy me. They incite me to do better. Go further."

"To prove them wrong."

Now she smiled. "Well, there's that." Her phone dinged. "There's A.J.'s answer."

"What does he say?"

She picked up the phone, read the text, and nodded, satisfied. "The regional office will be calling the Oak Bluffs Police Department today."

"Even if they don't take over the case, the phone call might be enough to inspire further investigation."

"Except we shouldn't need threats from the new girl on the block to instigate that," she told him. "Shouldn't that just be how it's done?"

"In a perfect world, everyone does their job to the best of their ability. Unfortunately..."

"We live in an imperfect world. Gerald, hang here for a minute. I see Dee Dee." But before she could reach the other woman across the parking lot, Dee Dee had climbed into her car and driven away.

Joan met her as she returned to Gerald's car. "What were you chasing?"

"The wind, it seems."

Joan climbed in the back as Priscilla took her place in the front. "My last day for being chauffeured, and I can't say I'm sorry," Joan exclaimed. "I love your generosity, but I don't like putting people out all the time," she went on. "Gerald, Priscilla, thank you for picking me up. I just got word that my car's not in Woods Hole, they actually brought it across for me."

"How nice is that?" Priscilla turned and smiled her way.

"If you can drop me off at the ferry stop, I'll drive to Priscilla's on my own. After I grab Sister, of course."

"I've enjoyed our time together, Joan," Priscilla said. "It might have made you feel indebted, but it made *me* quite happy. Hey. Wait," she said as Gerald made the turn for the ferry landing in Vineyard Haven. "Isn't that Dee Dee's car over there? In line for the ferry?"

"It's her, all right." Gerald pulled to a quiet spot so Joan could meet the dealer representative and claim her car. He frowned at

Priscilla. "You're not going to accost her when she's waiting to board, are you? She'll be back, Scilla."

The new nickname made Joan flash her a smile from behind Gerald's back.

"No, of course not. I'm curious why she's going across in this weather, but obviously folks do it all the time, judging from the cars. I rarely think of going across this time of year."

"Some folks cross regularly, regardless of the season," said Gerald. "Shopping. Appointments. Visiting."

"And a few just get plain claustrophobic on the island mid-winter because it closes in on you. Maybe Dee Dee's like that," said Joan.

Dee Dee steered her car onto the ferry, but her profile didn't look happy or anticipatory. In fact she looked kind of sad. "I'll stop by soon and chat with her."

"About?"

Gerald arched a single brow toward Joan, and she shifted her attention to Priscilla. "You can't think Dee Dee had anything to do with this case."

"Let's just say she's been in the right place at the right time a little too often."

"No." Joan looked across as Dee Dee's car disappeared from sight.

"It's unlikely, but it's something that needs to be checked. Although I'm feeling guilty even thinking such a thing about her. Did you know she's listed her house?"

"She's put it up for sale at this time of year?" Joan arched both brows as the car representative came her way. "We'll talk at your place in a little bit. And I'll stop at Candy's because I'm feeling like an unhealthy lunch is of the highest order today."

"I'll have coffee ready and a fire burning."

"Wonderful."

Within a few minutes Gerald pulled up and parked behind Priscilla's car. They both climbed out. He moved forward and chivalrously opened her door, one of those little things that meant so much in the moment. "Thanks for letting me tag along this morning."

"Tag along?" She pushed her scarf aside and gazed up at him, smiling. "I didn't consider you a tagalong, Gerald."

"No?" He smiled right back at her, looking strong and capable and dear.

"I was thinking we made a good team," she told him, and when his smile turned into a grin, she knew she'd made her point.

"I'm a big fan of teamwork," he teased. His broad smile didn't fade. "Talk to you later."

"Will do." She got home before Tommy arrived, and the first thing she did was hunt for that key. She found it, the twelfth brick up, tucked in a notch. She started to remove it, then reconsidered.

Let the culprit go for the key and try to get in with new locks. She'd have Gerald bring his hunting camera by like he'd done last summer when her door was being vandalized by a wandering goat. Maybe they'd catch the person in the act. She'd be okay with that.

Tommy and Joan arrived together. Sister dashed from Joan's new car, whirling in circles, then barked for Jake to join her. The women gave them time outdoors while Tommy changed the locks, and when he was done, he walked into the kitchen. "We're all set here."

"That was quick. Do you have time for coffee, Tommy?"

He shook his head and tipped his aged baseball cap back. "I'm heading over to Gail's to see if she needs help. Hugh's due back on the 4:10 ferry, so we need to have everything ready for him."

"And he's invited you and your mother to supper on Friday, I hear." Priscilla tried to sound nonchalant.

"Finally!" Joan said. "You two are getting together?"

Priscilla turned to her in surprise, and Joan laughed.

"Really? You think I haven't known for years that this one"— she motioned to Tommy—"and my cousin were doing the whole star-crossed lovers thing, pining away for each other while true love was being thwarted by two grumpy, set-in-their-ways old folks?"

"You know?" asked Priscilla. "Gail said no one knew."

"Well we pretend not to know because she didn't want us to know," Joan said, "and we've done a pretty good job of it. It took the fear of death to knock some sense into that uncle of mine," she told Tommy. "I hope you don't put life on hold until the same thing happens to you. You and Gail deserve a chance at happiness. I know your mother gets crotchety and Uncle Hugh is a real curmudgeon, but if ever there were two people made for each other, it's you and Gail. And quite possibly the two of them," she added, laughing again. "Don't mess this up." She thrust a bakery box into his surprised hands. "Enjoy these before Uncle Hugh gets home. He's going to want all his old favorites, but most of them are off-limits now. I'm hoping that having Marigold around will keep his mind off what he's giving up to stay healthy."

"It's always better to look at what we've gained than what we've lost," Tommy told them. "Joan, thank you. And I suspected you knew right along, but I'd never do anything to embarrass Gail."

Joan's look softened. "You're a good guy, Tommy. Tell Gail we'll be by tomorrow."

"I will."

Joan turned back toward Priscilla once Tommy was gone. "What?"

"You kept that secret all along. I'm so proud of you!"

Joan laughed. "Well, they thought they were so good at hiding it, and maybe they were for the first two years." She rolled her eyes. "But after a while it became sadly obvious, and if they don't take this God-given chance to make something of it, I'll be sad for both of them. But here, we've got to talk about two things. Two very important things. First, this." She slid another box toward Priscilla, and when Priscilla spotted four éclairs inside, her eyes widened.

"From Candy, who is certifiably over the top, fretting about her wedding. She's so worried that everything won't be perfect if she doesn't do it all herself, that she's driving herself to distraction, and she's such an easygoing sort normally."

"I blame cable TV and the Internet," Priscilla said. "Because if everything isn't properly themed and totally adorable and praise-worthy, your wedding is deemed ho-hum by the world. And who can call the union of two people in love, before God and family and friends, ho-hum? Poor Candy," she finished, getting plates for the éclairs. And they weren't the midget puff éclairs, either. They were the big, thick, jam-packed with filling variety. "How can we help?"

"Short of putting the two of them before a minister and being done with it, I don't know, but I hate seeing her all in a dither over this. And that brings me to point number two."

"Which is?"

Joan looked worried. "*Dither* and Dee Dee. I pulled up the town and county rosters online and Dee Dee hasn't paid her taxes for this past year. That means you're right, there are money problems. And there shouldn't be, because Dee Dee was left a solid inheritance from her husband. She's not a spendthrift, so I can't imagine why she's in money trouble now, but it appears she is."

"She knows everyone in the area, and she'd know that Sonya was overseeing the fund, because it was common knowledge, and she's just quiet enough that she might overhear things that could facilitate the money grab."

"Except can you imagine Dee Dee slipping into Sonya's office and not being noticed?"

Priscilla pictured the oddly dressed, layered-up woman with her signature green shoes and shook her head. "Dee Dee is a caricature by design, so no. Maybe you can access remotely without downloading the information into the computer."

"Well, that would be a pretty sophisticated maneuver and probably beyond Dee Dee's technological capabilities."

"I say we table this discussion on Dee Dee because it's going to break my heart if she's guilty," Priscilla confessed. "I've gotten into the habit of reading my devotionals in bed, but once I'm up it's coffee and the *Daily Dither* first thing every morning, and that's saying something right there. We haven't gone toe-to-toe with Howard Hoffman, and he's mad as a hornet at Sonya for voting against his oyster farm."

"If he hadn't wasted time, he could have landed that aquaculture farm approval, which means maybe the better man got the nod. Should we go see Sonya?"

"Not yet." Priscilla wanted to reassure Sonya, but they really didn't have anything reassuring to say as yet. "I want something firmer than suppositions, and she's got to be upset over this latest turn of events. Oh, wait." She picked up her phone as it signaled a text, then smiled. "A.J. says the county sheriff's office has picked up the computers in question and their IT team is going to examine them to rule out suspicious access from outside."

"You'd have thought that would be protocol, wouldn't you?" griped Joan.

"You'd think so, but when the local detective is so sure of himself that simple things like facts get in the way of discovery, why follow protocol? Today I'm eating this éclair, no regrets. And tomorrow…" She sent Joan a rueful look. "I'm going to start an exercise routine, because I need to look good in a dress this summer, and sitting around eating éclair and pizza isn't going to get me there."

"Nothing like a wedding to put us back on the path to single-digit clothing—"

Priscilla snort-laughed at that.

"Or at least toned muscles," Joan finished.

Priscilla wasn't about to scoff, because living on the island in the dregs of winter meant even toned muscles sounded like an impossible goal to reach.

"Let's finish this and pay Howard a visit. And what about that other fellow, the one who was away last week?"

Joan's brows went up. "Frank Ripley? The other pension overseer who had absolutely no reason to do this, no need for money, and no influx of cash that we could see?"

It was probably nothing, but he was the next in line to access the pension funds, and if anything happened to Sonya, he became the fiduciary of the fund. "Yes. Just to be sure of our facts, because sometimes it actually *is* the most obvious person, and he's the second in command. As for Howard, if he thinks we suspect him he might make some kind of grievous error to make our job easier."

"Because neither one of us wants it to be Sonya or Dee Dee," Joan admitted.

"True. And on my way back home I'm going to drive by that cute little gym in town."

"And sign up for a membership?" asked Joan.

"Nope, I'm going to drive right on by and remind myself that I can save thirty-nine dollars a month by working out at home. Incentive is a wonderful thing."

"Agreed. I'm going to drop Sister back off at my house, then I'll meet you in the Bluffs."

"Sounds good." Priscilla locked up with the new key and drove straight into Tisbury.

CHAPTER SIXTEEN

Howard and his wife lived on the busier side of Oak Bluffs. The Ripley family lived right in Tisbury in a well-maintained older home in a neighborhood that breathed classic New England in winter. She pulled up a few houses down from the Ripley house and waited for Joan.

A commotion from the house drew her attention. A man and woman stood face-to-face, arguing through the door. Not just a regular argument, either, but the kind that seemed like it could get ugly. She double-checked the address and cringed. That was Frank Ripley, all right, in a loud shouting match with a very angry woman. Suddenly the pristine home didn't look all that classic.

She slunk down in her seat. The last thing she needed was to have them think she was spying on them. Which she was, but only if he'd done something wrong, and nothing in her research indicated that. But, this...A major blowout fight on the front porch of a town official...This was something.

The door slammed.

Frank Ripley stood on the porch, all alone, staring at the door. Then he turned, chin down, and walked down the steps. He started coming her way.

Priscilla slid farther down the seat, hoping to go unnoticed, but Joan pulled up behind her right then. She heard Joan's car stop, then the door shut with a solid *thunk*. Then Joan was at her car, staring quizzically through the slightly steamed windows. "Priscilla? Are you in there?"

Priscilla sat up because there wasn't much point in slinking around now. She got out of the car and stood by her open door as Ripley charged their way.

"What are you two doing here? I heard you were snooping around, asking questions all over the place. This is my home," he barked at them. "This has nothing to do with you, so get out of here. Off of my street and away from my house. Away from my family!"

Priscilla didn't want to make him angrier. She backed up a step. "No problem. We thought you were Sonya's friend and that you wanted to help her, so we were coming to talk to you, Mr. Ripley. You are her daughter's godfather, after all. But if you don't want to talk to us, fine. Although being the second in command of a pension fund that's suddenly come up short means that once Sonya is cleared, you're in the crosshairs by default. But that's your concern, not ours." She shrugged lightly. "Might I make a suggestion, though?" She shifted her eyes toward his house, then back to him. "If there is a problem you don't want folks to know about, the best way to keep it quiet is to get help. Come clean. Do what needs to be done, because maybe half of your neighbors didn't hear that little back-and-forth on your front porch just now, but I'm willing to bet the other half did. Which means nothing's really a secret anymore."

His expression changed. "You don't know anything about any-thing. Leave me alone. Leave my family alone. And don't lecture me about needing help. I've done nothing illegal. Ever. So don't come around here with your bossy mainland ways and think you know anything. Because you don't."

Priscilla got back into her car. So did Joan. They both pulled away, but Priscilla watched Frank through her rearview mirror. He stared after them, but when he looked back at his house, he slumped, dejected.

She'd fill Joan in later. For the moment, she sent a quiet prayer up for the Ripley family. After what she'd just witnessed, she knew they were going to need it.

"Can I help you?" A woman in her late forties answered the door at Howard Hoffman's Oak Bluffs home about fifteen minutes later.

Priscilla introduced herself and Joan. "We're actually here to see Howard, to ask him a few questions."

"First that *Dither* woman, now two others?" The woman made a funny face. "This will most likely go to his head, not that my husband needs anything else to give him a big head. Come on in, I'm dying to see what this is about."

Howard met them before they got halfway through the entry. "What do you want? You want me to wave a magic wand and make your friend not guilty? The entire Fishermen's Council is convinced that Fleming did it. Like it wasn't enough that our pension was going under on its own, she had to sneak in there and embezzle funds to keep up her glitzy lifestyle."

"You're convinced of her guilt?" Joan regarded him with cool eyes. "Because we're pretty sure someone accessed the pension remotely, through her computer, and that opens up a whole wide list of suspects, Howard." She stretched out the phrase "whole wide list" on purpose. "Where were you the night the hospital offices were vandalized?"

"That's none of your business," he told them brusquely. "Get out."

"Two witnesses saw you in the administrative wing of the hospital," Priscilla said. She kept her voice soft and even. "After everyone was gone. They wondered what you were doing down that hall with the offices all closed for the day."

"Were they all closed for the day, Howard?" His wife folded her arms and tapped her foot, and it was a fairly ominous tap-tap-tap. Priscilla was impressed.

"Leigh, I was nowhere near the place."

"Hospital cameras say otherwise, and being flu season, we thought it might be that. But when we checked the ER records, there was nothing about you in the files. If you weren't sick, if you were in the administrative wing to vandalize Sonya Fleming's window, that would explain a whole lot. She did vote against you when all you needed was one more vote to get approval on your aquaculture proposal."

"And she blocked it. She blocked my petition to launch a new business as if any of this matters to her." He stormed the words, unleashing a tidal wave of emotion, but Priscilla was pretty sure he came unleashed on a regular basis. And maybe some of that was needed, when standing up for a shrinking fishermen economy. "None of this matters to her. Not this town. Or this island. It never could, not like what it means to us old-timers. The families who slogged and fished and dealt with storms for generations."

Joan nailed him with a cold look. "You do realize that her family has been here for four generations now. Counting her children."

"And that your proposal was months after the other guys'," his wife mentioned. "Which means they'd be approving competition for a business they'd just approved eight months before. That's not their fault, or Sonya's fault. That was totally on you because you didn't follow through on things. I believe your mind was elsewhere, Howard. Like maybe on that administrative wing of the hospital you like so well."

"Leigh, can we drop that? Please? How many times do I have to apologize?" She blasted him with a woman-scorned kind of look, and Priscilla was pretty sure that Leigh Hoffman had more than a little practice with that expression.

"You've been blaming Sonya for the negative results of your proposal," his wife continued. "Were you angry enough to set her up by bleeding funds from the pension account yourself?"

"Why would I do that? I don't need money." He stared at his wife, incredulous. "And as much as I dislike her and the board, I wouldn't risk prison to get even."

"But you'd risk your marriage and your family with the director of nursing," his wife said. "Please tell me that's not why you were at the hospital, Howard." Her voice broke and her face shadowed, and Priscilla wished they hadn't accidentally stumbled into such personal waters.

"Leigh, no." He turned toward her. "I promised you I wouldn't see Adele again, and I've kept that promise. Wait. I can prove it!" He hurried upstairs, then came back down. "Here, on my shoe. I tried getting it out with turpentine, and then gas, but there's a stain, still. Red paint, the same paint I used on the windows. And I knew it would wash off the glass," he told Priscilla bluntly. "I checked first, on our windows here. But I don't want her getting away with this embezzlement, because the men who risked their lives on those boats, the men who went out day after day to provide food for the East Coast, deserve better than to have their money stolen. I just wanted to make sure the police took it seriously. A missing million might not seem like much to some of the rich folks on this island now, but it represents a lot of hard work. And I couldn't stand by and let it go unnoticed."

"There's no room for vigilante justice. Or for throwing accusations at innocent people. I expect you to tell the police about your part in this, but I actually understand how you feel," Joan told him.

He turned toward her, surprised.

"My husband's pension went under about eight years before he passed away," she said. "Allan was a union guy. The pension fund was underfunded and mishandled, and after the stock market losses following 9/11, his union pension never recovered. The insurance guaranty program gives me thirty cents on the dollar. If it wasn't for my family inheritance and being able to invest the funds myself, I'd be penniless. So I do understand what you're saying. I'm the last person who wants retired fishermen to suffer because of this, but I can tell you one thing absolutely. Sonya Fleming did not do this. And my cousin and I will not rest until we find out who did."

Joan turned to go, but Howard's wife stopped her. "Do you girls want coffee?"

Howard looked surprised by the offer, but then shrugged. "It's probably a good idea. We should talk this out. If you're so sure Sonya didn't do it, then we need to find out who did. If it wasn't her and it wasn't me, then Ripley is the next closest thing. He wasn't supposed to have withdrawal privileges, but he could have figured out how to access Sonya's code or sign in or whatever it is."

"Coffee would be lovely," said Priscilla. "And I agree, we need to focus on finding the culprit. Not banging heads."

"Come on through," said his wife. "I'm Leigh, by the way."

As they passed through the short hall into the kitchen, Priscilla paused. "Is this you with a bunch of fishermen?" she asked Howard. "It's a great shot. Classic Vineyard."

"It's me and some fishermen and some industry professionals when North Country Fisheries came on-scene to purchase fishing rights," Howard explained. "Little did we know that the big companies had a lot of friends in high places. Within a handful of years they were muscling smaller fishing boats out of the water. We didn't stand a chance after that."

Once they were seated at the kitchen table, Joan said, "We stopped by the Ripleys'. Frank wasn't happy to see us."

"But he also didn't look like he was personally underfunded," noted Priscilla. "Leigh, thank you." She smiled up at Howard's wife as she accepted the big thick mug of coffee. Big thick mugs were an island trademark.

Howard sipped his own coffee. "There's lots of reasons folks need money, though. And not all of them apparent."

Priscilla met Howard's gaze. "How well do you know Ripley?"

"Not well. But there's talk."

"There's always talk in small towns."

He accepted that as his wife took a seat. "True. And it might not be easy to check out. A friend told me he's gone through a lot of cash the past two years."

"The friend knows him?"

Howard grimaced. "Let's say the friend shouldn't have said anything and leave it at that."

"Someone from the bank," Priscilla surmised, and when Howard nodded, she went on. "Count on small towns to share what shouldn't be shared. Did your friend speculate why money was being drained?"

"No, just that it seemed unusual for an official to be pulling that kind of money out of accounts . . . unless he's paying for someone else's silence."

"Blackmail?" Joan's eyebrows shot up. "Seriously?"

"Or paying someone to do something nefarious. It could be either, I suppose," Howard mused. "Generally if someone's bleeding five thousand a month, there's a reason for it."

Five thousand a month? Priscilla nearly choked. Instead, she turned to Leigh. She didn't want Howard jumping to any more conclusions. "This is great coffee, Leigh."

"Moka Sumatra from Mocha Mott's over in Tisbury."

"Great coffee shop," Priscilla agreed. "And they stay open all year, making them a favorite of mine too. I'd never tried this blend, but I'll make sure to have it on hand now. Well." She finished her coffee and stood. "We've got to get back. Dogs are waiting, and we've taken up enough of your time. Howard, call one of us if you think of anything. Anything at all."

"I will. And I'm sorry I went off like that, that I pushed for Mrs. Fleming to be arrested. If I was wrong—"

"And you were," Joan assured him.

"Then I've made a mess of things for someone who didn't deserve it."

"The best way to fix this is to find the real thief." Priscilla tugged her scarf around her neck. "Nothing like the truth to set us free."

"I believe that too." Leigh followed them to the door. "I'm glad you came by. And I'm equally glad it was only paint that drew my husband to the administrative wing of MVH."

There wasn't much Priscilla or Joan could say to that. They said goodbye and hurried to their cars. The wind hadn't just picked up. It had funneled in from the mainland, bringing an Arctic system of cold air and thick snow, making the drive back to West Chop long and tedious. But when Priscilla got there, Jake's happy greeting lightened the moment.

Howard Hoffman wasn't a nice man in many ways. But she'd witnessed his genuine concern for the fishermen, for the fishing community, and she saw his grief at how things had changed. How what seemed to be a blessing, to have big companies come on board for fishing, turned out to be a major loss instead.

So what about those big fishing companies?

Could they be involved?

She kicked off her boots and let Jake have a quick romp in the snow. When she let him in ten minutes later, he shook big, thick, clumpy snowflakes from his coat before heading to the fire.

Her phone rang just then. Rebekah Alden's number showed up, and she answered the call quickly. "Hey, neighbor. What's up?"

"Priscilla it's Ellie Doyle from next door. I'm just calling to say you had a visitor while you were out. Before the snow began, unfortunately."

"Before the snow began..." Priscilla repeated. "I'm not following you, Ellie."

"Whoever it was kind of rooted around in your ivy."

Looking for the key! And of course she hadn't gotten Gerald's camera yet.

"Then he tried the door, seemed flummoxed that it wouldn't open, and went back to the ivy. Then he left. He kept his car on the road and I couldn't see a bit of it, and just his profile. Tallish. Oldish. But in a hat and coat, who can really tell? Still, he walked oldish. If you know what I mean."

Priscilla knew exactly what she meant, but she rued the order of events. He'd figured out that she'd changed the locks and wouldn't bother with his scare tactics again, at least not that way. But she now knew it was most likely a man and had a narrowing description, especially this time of year when the island was far less populated. "Ellie, thank you for keeping an eye out."

"Well, I had to get the mail and the movement drew my attention. It seemed a little odd, you know, with your car not in the driveway. Although with this snow, you might want to think about clearing out that garage and parking in it. I love that I don't have to scrape and brush and do all that other stuff winter brings us."

She was absolutely right, and Priscilla would tackle that in the spring. Maybe. Except that a girl had to have someplace to keep things. The small cottage on top of a damp basement didn't leave many options, and her narrow attic didn't offer a lot of accessible space. "Thank you, Ellie. For the neighborly care and the advice." She hung up the phone and stared outside.

So he'd come again. Did that mean they were getting closer? Or just that he was old and worried?

It could be either, and for right now she was going to check out all she could about Zoning Commissioner Ripley. He wasn't old, and he wasn't tall, but distance could skew those things.

Zoning boards carried a lot of weight in small towns. Their approval was much sought after by anyone eyeing change or development. Usually that meant money would be flowing into the commissioner's account if someone was buying favors. Frank's money was going the other way, and Priscilla was pretty sure she knew why. She also knew that desperate people were prone to do desperate things. From what she'd seen, Frank Ripley might be the definition of desperate these days.

CHAPTER SEVENTEEN

A t 9:32 the next morning, A.J. called Priscilla. "The select-woman's computer was accessed via cell phone three different times. The first time was simply to access the computer."

"A practice run."

"Probably. The second time was to access the pension fund that was already open."

"After the monthly payments were made."

"Yes." He sounded intrigued. "How did you know that?"

"Because Sonya said she generally only checks the fund to make sure all payments went through, and then at the end of the month to make sure all deposits to the account have been made and to reconcile it. Except she didn't do that in December because of the holidays, and when she went into the account in January, the money was gone."

"So if she told you that, it might be something she'd mention to others in casual conversation," A.J. mused.

"Like 'Wow, this clam dip is great, I'd love the recipe and by the way, I only go into the pension fund at the beginning of the month and the end of the month'?"

He laughed. "Lose the cocktail party mentality and think workload. People talk about their lack of time and their workloads all the time. So now picture her saying, 'Well, the pension fund isn't a big time drain. I check it at the beginning and end of each month, and it practically reconciles itself.'"

"That sounds exactly like something a busy executive would say."

"People talk far too freely these days, and a little hint dropped in the wrong place becomes a window of opportunity. So check with her and see if she talked with anyone specifically about work and timing last summer or fall."

"So the third time the account was accessed was when the funds were taken?"

"Yes. Transferred to an untraceable foreign account which sounds a whole lot more sophisticated than it is. It's all done with numbers, and the computer sends the funds to the right numbers. It's just some countries don't want us spying on their numbers so rich people and corporations can hide taxable funds."

"That's so wrong," Priscilla said.

"Tax collectors have been a thorn in the side of humanity since biblical times," he reminded her. "And people have probably been trying to hide from them just as long."

"Can we trace the phone?" she asked.

"Burner phone, so no. The tech tried. It's a dead end."

"So this person is smart and savvy enough not to leave a trail, and to slip into a computer invisibly. This puzzle just got distinctly tougher, A.J."

"Except that probably ninety-five percent of the people on the island can't do these things. So in some ways, your job actually just got easier."

He was right.

"Don't make it tougher than it is," he advised. "Usually it's someone so close to the money that they're practically invisible because it's so obvious."

"Obvious, huh?" She made a doubtful noise, and he laughed. "All right, this is all great stuff. Thank you for putting the pressure on, or thank whoever in the regional office did it. This gives me a new perspective, and I hope it teaches that detective a lesson or two."

"I'm sure it will." She laughed because A.J.'s words said one thing and his tone another.

She put the phone down, took Jake out for a brisk, snowy walk along the hill's edge, and when the young dog eyed the ice-crusted steps, she said, "No."

He looked back, dejected, and she understood the emotion quite well. "It's not safe. It's icy, and we don't have time in any case. I'm going to make a nice vegetable salad to take to Uncle Hugh and Gail this afternoon, but first Joan and I are going to visit Sonya."

He studied the steps, then her, and then walked toward the house, nose down, tail tucked as if she'd just ruined his day.

"You're killing me," she told him when they got back to the house. She grabbed her phone and put a quick call in to Gerald. When he answered she dove right in. "I have a neglected dog here that would like to meet your dog for a nice, if somewhat cold, walk in the dog park later this week. Do you think we can arrange that, Captain?"

Gerald hesitated, surprising her. "Priscilla, I'd love it," he finally said, "but I don't think Sammy's up for it. Not until the weather breaks. She doesn't go outside for anything but to take care of business and then comes right back in. She used to love the snow." He sighed, and Priscilla imagined him watching the old red dog with more than a little gray and white in her muzzle. "Now she barely tolerates it. But I can go with you and Jake on my next day off. I'd like that."

"No." She didn't know why, but going to the dog park with Gerald and not Sammy seemed wrong. "Let's do something else. Something that won't tax her. How about we have supper together and I bring Jake over there or you bring Sammy here."

"A double date. I like the sound of that, Scilla."

"You know I'm not a nickname person…"

"And yet, it fits. If you don't mind, that is."

She didn't. Was that because the shortened name was sweet? Or because it was Gerald using it?

Both, she decided. "I don't mind at all, actually."

"Good. How about tomorrow night for a supper date? Come on over here and we can cook together."

"Sounds wonderful. Oh, and Gerald, I almost forgot." Where was her head? She had information to share and it all went out of her head talking about double dates and beloved dogs. "Our mystery visitor showed up here yesterday when I was in town."

"How do you know?"

"Ellie saw him from next door. She's pretty sure it was a man, tallish and oldish. He messed with the ivy, then went to the door, then ivy again, then he left. She was walking out to get the mail and a breath of fresh air, saw movement, and watched."

"Did she see his car?"

"No, it was parked on the bend and she couldn't see it."

"Well it's a beginning, and at least he knows we're taking action."

"And…" She drew out the word purposely.

"Yes?"

"Sonya's computer was accessed by an outside burner phone. Untraceable, but it shows that whoever stole those funds did it via a remote connection."

"How do you know this?"

"FBI pressure on the local police, so they let the county sheriff's IT specialist examine the hard drive."

"Is this confidential information?" he asked. "Because it sure sounds like it."

"Hopefully it's information that will get charges dropped for Sonya. But we can keep it confidential, of course. You. Me. Joan. Gail."

He laughed but then cautioned her. "In all seriousness, here's the thing. If we find the real solution, this becomes a non-issue, but if Sonya ends up going to trial, we don't want to taint evidence that might be in her favor."

"All the more reason to solve this swiftly and give Sonya her life back."

"Somehow I knew you'd say that. Call me if you need me. And I'm looking forward to tomorrow night."

So was she. She smiled. "Me too. Bye." She picked Joan up an hour later, and they headed to the Fleming house. When Sonya

answered the door, she didn't look like the poised business professional Priscilla had met the week before. A worn expression and
red-rimmed eyes indicated an anguished lack of rest. That made
Priscilla more determined to fix things for her.

Sonya led them into the living room. It was nicely propor-
tioned and un-themed, which made Priscilla like her even more.
"Timeless taste." She took a seat. "This room looks like you, Sonya."

"I glanced in the mirror this morning, and I'm pretty sure the
room looks far better than I do at present. But thank you."

"Sonya, I'm sorry the police jumped to conclusions on this so
quickly," Joan told her. "It's rash on their part and they should
have known better. Anyone who knows you understands the
impossibility of you being involved."

"Bless you, Joan." Sonya smiled at her, but she dabbed her eyes
with a clutch of tissues. "I know I'm innocent, but I was also naive.
By leaving files open, even for a few minutes, I was putting funds
at risk. It never occurred to me that someone might steal pension
money. Or that someone would see it on my computer and put a
plan in motion. There are so few people who would even have the
chance—"

"Exactly the point a law enforcement friend of mine made this
morning," Priscilla told her. "He said the culprit is generally someone close to the crime, and we overlook them because they're so
obvious."

"You said you didn't think my girls were involved," Sonya
reminded her. "You thought the culprit might be whoever vandalized the office windows. Are you changing your mind? Because I

can't imagine either of the girls would even think of something like that, much less do it. But when your office is close to the ER, life's unexpected tragedies come by in full swing. I've witnessed a lot of heartbroken and surprised parents in my time."

"No, I don't think the girls are involved, but I'm pretty sure the thief wasn't the spray painter, either," Priscilla explained. "What about your husband? Or any family that might have stumbled on you working here?"

She made a face of doubt. "Jon is as honest as they come. He's more of a worrier than I am, but even though his family has lost a share of real estate value this generation, he's never cared about that. We do well, we work hard, we're not greedy people. And it's not like I have a family gathering and pause to work on the pension in the middle of it, you know?"

"That makes perfect sense." And it helped frame Priscilla's next question. "What about casual conversation? About work, about time, about ambition? The kind of back-and-forth we have all the time without considering the surroundings."

Sonya shook her head. "I don't know what you mean. We all talk about work, don't we?"

Priscilla and Joan both nodded. "Absolutely," said Joan. "I've heard it said that hospitals and school systems are the worst when it comes to loose talk because you have so many people in an integrated and somewhat unstructured setting."

"People talk, that's for sure, but around me it's generally innocent conversation. I don't gossip, it's not something I would ever allow in the office."

"So—" Priscilla began.

"Although," Sonya interrupted Priscilla. "We did have that open meeting with the Fishermen's Council last fall. They held it at St. Augustine's Church, in the hall. I was asked if I needed help with the pension fund or if I felt confident in handling it with Frank as backup. I told the group that once we got it established with direct deposit and withdrawal, my job was much easier. That I access it around the third of the month for withdrawals to make sure everyone got their money. And then around the thirtieth to make certain the deposits were all recorded correctly." She paused and stared at Priscilla. "I told that entire room that there was about four weeks of time to pull off a crime, didn't I?"

Priscilla didn't hedge. "Yes, but that's only a problem if there's a criminal mind in the room. Or someone who got the idea based on your timeline. Sonya, you were asked a question," Priscilla reminded her. "You answered it. That doesn't make it all right for someone to break into your computer, use your login, and steal money. The crime is on them. Not on you. If you leave your keys in the car, that doesn't make it okay for someone to steal it, does it?"

"No, but it does label one careless. And how did they get into my office, unnoticed, during the day?"

"They didn't have to," Priscilla told her. "They may have accessed it long enough to download permission for a remote application to be installed, but that only takes a few seconds of time. We've discovered that the thief used a remote burner phone to access your computer, go to the pension fund and, because the equities company allowed passwords to be remembered, the computer helpfully let this person into the account."

"You know this? That someone got in from outside?" For the first time during their talk, a ray of hope brightened Sonya's face. "I can't believe it."

"It's fact, and facts are hard to dispute, but because it was an untraceable phone, we don't know who. Do you remember who was in the room the night of the Fishermen's Council meeting?"

"We actually have a sign-in log," Sonya told Priscilla. "Wait, I'll text it to you." She moved to her smartphone, drew up a page, then texted the image of it to Priscilla's phone. "Now you have it. Of course I can't be sure that everyone signed in. It's not like a rule or anything. It's more to make sure everyone stays informed."

"We'll check it out." Priscilla stood, and Joan followed. "We'll keep digging," she promised.

"And we won't stop until we figure this out," added Joan. "We were furious to see that you'd been arrested while we were in Boston."

"It was an experience I hope to never have again," Sonya said. "Luckily Maura's brother is a defense attorney across the bay and he came right over to help, so I wasn't locked up for long. But it was a wretched feeling, to have my freedom wrenched away from me. I never want to repeat that experience, so if we can find the real thief, I can handle everything else. The loss of my job, the loss of stature, whatever. But I never want to see a jail cell from inside the bars again."

"An innocent person shouldn't have to suffer like that," Priscilla told her. "Being accused of a crime you didn't commit shouldn't have residual effects. Unfortunately that's exactly what's happening. We'll have to figure that out as we go, because it's wrong, Sonya."

Joan hugged her old friend. "We'll be in touch."

"Thank you. Thank you both." Sonya gripped Priscilla's hand like a near-drowning victim clings to her rescuer. "Whatever you're able to do, I'm grateful."

They left the Fleming house. Priscilla drove straight to the Oak Bluffs police station, and when her nemesis saw her coming, he looked pained. But then he did the right thing and restored her faith in the office when he came forward and extended a hand. "You were right, Mrs. Grant."

Priscilla tried her best not to preen.

"We should have had IT do the internal exam on the computer before we made judgments, and it's not a mistake I'll make again."

"Are you dropping all charges against Sonya Fleming?" Joan faced him with quiet determination. "Because we all know she's innocent."

He hedged then. "We will drop the charges but not the investigation into Mrs. Fleming." When Joan bristled, he held up a hand. "Hear me out. I think you ladies are correct, I no longer think she did it, but the fact that she could buy a burner phone as easily as anyone else, then access the funds, means she's not fully in the clear yet."

"Except that if she did that, she wouldn't have to go remotely through her computer," Priscilla said. "It's her sign-in and password.

If she wanted to take the money via a burner, she could have done it and there would be no trace on her computer at all."

"Unless she was trying to make it look like someone else accessed it," he told her. "I don't think that's the case, and I commend you because your instincts were spot-on."

"It's hardly instinct when it's a simple matter of connecting the dots," Priscilla told him. "The baser elements of human nature are often the best clues. Whoever did this needs money."

"That applies to at least fifty percent of the population in winter," he reminded her.

"The guilty party is also probably male, middle-aged or above, on the tall side."

"Where is that information coming from?" He looked from her to Joan and back.

"Someone's been trying to scare us off the case," Priscilla told him. "Someone has been breaking into my house, letting me know I'm not as safe as I thought. My neighbor saw him, and she said he was tall and looked like an older man. He doesn't want us digging around, but I don't think he wants to hurt us. Just scare us off the trail."

"Is this information verifiable?"

"The Tisbury police have been called each time," she assured him. "You can check with them. Ellie Doyle, living in the Alden house up the road, spotted the man when she was getting the mail."

"Did she see his car?"

"It was out of sight from her angle."

"This could be coincidental," he began. "But probably not. No prints in the snow?"

"He showed up before the snow began," she told him. "This might be able to narrow it down further." She drew up the picture of the sign-in sheet. "This is the sign-in sheet from the annual fall meeting of the Fishermen's Council where Sonya mentioned that she only accesses the pension fund twice a month. On the third, when funds go out. And on the thirtieth, to make sure all funds came in."

"So everyone at that meeting realized there's a significant window of time to take funds and go unnoticed."

"Yes. And then, because of the busy holidays and the flu, she didn't go back into the fund until the second week of January, and that's when she discovered the missing funds."

"Well, no one should lose their job and their reputation for spending a little time with faith, family, and friends at Christmas," he said. "Everybody takes some time off then. They hold war-time ceasefires for Christmas, so I think it's all right that Sonya Fleming took a few days to celebrate with her family. Can you send me that list?" He gave her his number, and she texted it to him.

"There's no guarantee that everyone signed in," Joan told him. "Sonya said it wasn't mandatory."

"The ones who were there might be able to fill in any missing pieces. Thank you, ladies. And at the risk of sounding repetitive, let me apologize again. I let assumptions color my approach to this case, and that was wrong. It won't be repeated."

They left the police station, and Joan waited until they were in the car before she high-fived Priscilla. "Humble pie is topping the menu at the police station today. And I'm pretty sure it's not tasting all that good."

CHAPTER EIGHTEEN

We need to check out that list, Joan." Priscilla nudged her phone Joan's way. "Can you open it up and see who's on it? See if there's anyone we know who might be able to tell us who else could have been at that meeting?"

It took several seconds, then Joan said, "Bingo. Bertie was there. And Frank Ripley was there too, so that could be interesting."

"What about Dee Dee?" Priscilla asked.

"There's no way that—oh." Joan swallowed hard. "Dee Dee was there. She's signed in."

Was the feisty little reporter part of this mess? "Who sells burner phones on the island?"

"The apothecary with the little coffee shop sells them," said Joan. "He keeps them in stock because people drop their phones in the water all the time, and he said it became easy money because today's people don't know how to exist without a phone in their pocket."

Priscilla glanced down at her watch. "Let's swing by there. We can talk to him and still have plenty of time to cook for Uncle Hugh and Gail."

"Gail texted that Uncle Hugh is sleeping after his morning cardio therapy at the hospital."

"Bless his heart." She was so glad to have him back. "I'd be okay with no funerals for a while. You know?"

"I hear you."

Priscilla pulled along the curb opposite the old-fashioned drugstore, and they walked in together. The aroma of freshly brewed coffee filled the air. "Isn't it amazing how a smell like that warms the day, even though the clouds and wind are wretchedly inhospitable?"

"Like a gift," declared Joan. "I'm going to order us coffees, then we'll find the manager." She put the order in before they moved toward the small pharmaceutical section to the right. "Mr. Hutchins?"

"Joan, how nice!" The more-than-middle-aged man came around a corner from the one-step-raised pharmacy area. "And Mrs. Grant, how are you? What can I do for you ladies?"

"Joan said you sell burner phones here."

"A lot of them during the season." He walked up two aisles and turned right. "I've got models right here, but I started keeping the stock behind the counter because these were disappearing last summer and no business can swallow shoplifting like that."

"So people have to ask you for them?" Joan asked.

"Yes, it's a pain for them and us, but it's proven to be necessary, unfortunately. What kind did you need?" he asked.

"We don't need one," Priscilla said. "But thank you. Mr. Hutchins. Do you remember who you might have sold them to in the past few months? Locals, I mean. Not tourists."

"I barely sell any after October," he told her. "Islanders aren't nearly so careless with their electronics and there's a lesson to be learned there, I expect. Let me see." He tapped his jaw with one finger, thinking. "There was a fellow from Chilmark that came over for a project and dropped a piece of equipment on his phone and didn't have time to go to the phone store up-island. Then there was that charming little woman with the big smile, Ms. Quimby. She writes that online newspaper that's starting to pick up steam. She was the only other person I sold one to, but our stock is down by five, so that means three others were sold by one of the clerks when I wasn't here."

Dee Dee Quimby bought a burner phone last fall.

Dee Dee Quimby was selling her house.

Dee Dee Quimby knew a lot about the hospital comings and goings, but was it from her window, like she said? Or was it because she was a quiet neighbor, silently accessing funds for some reason?

Priscilla didn't dare look at Joan. "Thank you, Mr. Hutchins. We're going to get our coffees and head out to get some work done. You have a great day."

"I will. You too."

Joan gathered the coffees, then ordered one more.

Priscilla heard the order and nodded.

They would take all three coffees back over the beach road and visit Dee Dee now. She carried her coffee to the car and when Joan had settled the two others in the back seat cup holder, Priscilla started the engine. "I don't want her to be guilty, Cousin."

Joan winced. "I know. Me neither. But we need to find out, one way or another. And I'm clinging to the fact that it can't be her if Ellie saw a man at your place."

"I'm clinging to the same thing." Priscilla steered the car back toward Oak Bluffs. "Let's hope we're both right."

Dee Dee opened her door a few minutes later. She looked surprised and pleased to see them, not a typical thief-like reaction. "You ladies look like you're hot on the case, so I'm hoping that means you'll give me an exclusive for the *Daily Dither*. Come in, it's cold out there."

Joan handed her the coffee once they got inside. "Caramel, extra hot, foam, no whip."

"How did you know?" Dee Dee lifted both brows, surprised and delighted. "Kick your boots off and come on in. I hate to ask you to do that, but when you're selling a place you have to be ready to show it at a moment's notice, and that's not exactly how I live my life. But now..." She indicated the room with a wave of her arm. "I look quite normal, and that's a sorry state of affairs."

"I was surprised to see the For Sale sign," Priscilla said. "When I was here before, you didn't mention anything about selling."

"Well, most old-time islanders play their hands with caution," she told Priscilla. "We don't talk about money like today's young people do."

"It's tough getting by on the island without a solid source of income from somewhere." Joan sipped her coffee, then set it down as Dee Dee's phone rang.

A flip phone, like she'd been carrying all along. Did that mean she'd tossed the internet-accessible burner phone?

Priscilla and Joan exchanged looks as Dee Dee stood. "I have to take this. I'll be right back." She moved to the small kitchen and dining area behind the living room.

Priscilla wanted to move closer and eavesdrop on the call, but her conscience wouldn't let her. She waited until Dee Dee returned, and one look at Dee Dee's expression tipped her into compassion mode.

"Dee Dee, what's wrong? What's happened?"

Dee Dee sank onto the sofa. She clutched the phone as if her life depended on it, then threw it onto the adjacent chair. "Have you ever been at the end of your rope?"

Joan sat on the sofa next to her and took her hand. "More than once."

"I'm at my wit's end," Dee Dee said. "I'm in such a sad state of affairs that I've done things I never thought I'd do. I've only made things worse, and now I have to live with the consequences of my choices. But I'll manage." She lifted a stoic chin as she faced the women, but the look in her eyes showed fear and sorrow. "I always manage, but this isn't how I saw this playing out."

"It rarely is," Joan assured her, while Priscilla waited to hear the confession she didn't want to hear. "How can we help?"

"Well, if you've got a whole lot of money in your pocket—"

Priscilla barely breathed. The missing money. Mystery solved. Game over.

"I don't." Joan squeezed her hand. "What do you need money for, Dee Dee?"

"The house." She swept the funny cottage-style home a fond look. "Not that I have any regrets," she went on.

"None?" Priscilla couldn't hide the note of surprise in her voice.

"No, not one," Dee Dee told them firmly. "It was worth every penny, and I'd do it again if necessary, but things are looking better now. And I haven't mentioned one word about selling the house, that wouldn't sit well. This is one time where the end truly does justify the means."

"Do you want to tell us how you did it?" Priscilla asked.

Dee Dee frowned. "That part was simple. I went to a loan company and signed the papers."

Priscilla looked at Joan.

Joan looked back. "And then what?"

"I just assumed I'd have enough money coming in between my monthly check and the sale of Randolph's paintings, only that deal hasn't closed, the original buyer backed out, and now the art studio is shut until March for needed repairs, so they're not doing any business, which means no one will see the Quimby collection and no money will be coming in and the bank's about to take my house."

"So that's why you took the pension money?" Joan asked. "Oh, Dee Dee, what a spot to be in."

"Pension money?" Dee Dee's eyes widened with surprise. "You can't honestly think I'd do something like that, can you?"

"Didn't you just say you did? With all that regret and choices talk and needing money?" Priscilla had leaned forward. Now she sat more upright.

"Oh, no, no, no." Dee Dee rolled her eyes at Priscilla. "Nothing like that, what is the matter with you two? After all the help I've given you too." She shook her finger first at Joan, then Priscilla. "Michael has cancer. Had cancer," she corrected herself.

"Michael is Dee Dee's oldest son," Joan explained.

"They'd done all kinds of treatments, but it came roaring back, so we sent him to Philly for one of those new treatments that goes right into the body and goes to war with the bad cells."

"How's he doing?" The thought of waging war for a child's life...Priscilla's heart squeezed tight.

"The treatment worked. They're considering him cured, and that's the greatest gift of all, but his insurance only covered a portion of the treatment. I covered the rest." She folded her hands in her lap. "I was upset and not as cautious as I should have been. I took out a mortgage on the house, with one of those balloon payment plans. I figured it was an easy fix because we already had an offer on several seascapes, but then that deal fell through, the art studio closed for renovations, and the balloon payment is due by the end of January. Or I lose my house."

"Oh, Dee Dee." Joan reached over and hugged her, then turned to Priscilla. "Dee Dee's husband was Randolph Quimby."

"The artist made famous for his hauntingly beautiful seascapes featuring an undisclosed presence of light."

"Yes. Randolph was such a faith-filled man, and he used light to represent God and faith in all of his work. It's there, in the darkest storm or the most raging sea...It's there in the calm before dawn. In the homes along the shore. And in your light-house too," she told Priscilla.

"Your husband painted Misty Harbor?"

"Twice, from different angles. One has a glimpse of the cottage and Marjorie's gardens. The other shows the tower with the marshy woods beyond it, at night."

"It's like the perfect mix of light in the darkness," Joan told her.

"You've never mentioned these," Priscilla said to Joan. "Why not?"

"Well, I refused to sell for a long time," Dee Dee told her. "Randolph was a private artist. When he died, it was all I could do not to curl up and waste away from the sadness of it. He didn't see the boys grow up. Get their degrees. Start their businesses. He didn't get to see that Michael got his talent and now has a gallery showing of his own, and that Peter teaches art in a Boston high school, inspiring kids to see beyond the obvious. But I'd do anything to save my son's life. And I believe that God kept me from selling the pictures off before so I'd have them to fund Michael's treatment now. But timing is against me."

"You bought a burner phone."

"What?" The out-of-the-blue statement surprised Dee Dee, then she made a face. "Ah, I see. You think the burner phone was used in the pension crime."

"*A* burner phone," said Joan. "And I'm probably not supposed to say that, so don't use it in the paper, okay?"

"You have my word, but did you really think I might have taken that money?"

"Well, you mentioned money problems last time I was here," Priscilla told her. "And you have the proximity to the hospital. And you said you had trouble sleeping, and then the house went up for sale, and we saw you heading to the ferry looking very sad..."

"I was going to appeal to the bank's softer side. Turns out they don't have one, by the way. And I bought that phone in case I needed to use it as a reporter. Sometimes you need to access the internet, and I didn't want that traced back to me. And I didn't want to pay the monthly costs of a smartphone when it's more an occasional use kind of thing."

"A frugal choice."

"That put you right in our crosshairs." Joan sighed in exasperation. "But we knew it couldn't be you, Dee Dee, even with so many things pointing us in your direction. The thing is, how are we going to help you now?"

"There is no help," she answered. "The bank will extend the loan after January for a huge sum of money—"

"Stinkin' pirates."

"My thoughts exactly," she told Priscilla. "And I can't in good conscience waste that kind of money even though I don't want to lose my home. I hate to leave here. But I made a rash gamble, and now it's time to pay the piper. Honestly, as long as Michael's going to be okay, I can handle whatever happens. I prayed for a miracle, and this new treatment was kind of like that, so I'll be all right. I just know he's going to feel dreadful when he realizes what happened."

"He doesn't know about the mortgage."

"No. I told him I was selling some of Dad's work, and he felt bad enough about that. I didn't think the mortgage would become an issue."

But it had. Priscilla stood up. "We've got to go, Dee Dee, because we need to make food for Uncle Hugh and Gail, but I'm going to think on this because if you had one solid offer on the work, we know there will be others. It's just a question of timing."

"So is the contract I have with the Boston gallery. They just never mentioned that they'd be closing for two full months and that leaves Randolph's work in gallery limbo, doesn't it?"

An idea hit Priscilla. The gallery might be closed, but the internet was wide open. She gave Dee Dee a hug. "Let's see what we can do. I've seen two of your husband's works, one in the library and one in Mildred's museum."

"And there's one in the whaling museum as well," Dee Dee told her. "He did that one as a tribute to the New England Coastal history, how whaling and fishing built so much of this region. He knew there was bad that went along with the good, but Randolph was man enough to see both and not hate anyone. He had a good heart." She stood, then crossed to a bookcase and took down a framed picture. "This is us the year before Randolph passed away."

A happy family smiled for the camera. A younger Dee Dee, still sporting her own unique look of crazy layers, two handsome boys, and just behind her, with his arms resting lightly around his wife, was a handsome dark-skinned man, smiling as if he had everything he could ever want, right here in the picture.

"Beautiful," Priscilla said.

"It was. It is," Dee Dee corrected herself. "Like I said, as long as Michael's fine, the rest is just stuff. And stuff can be replaced. Eventually. So." She folded her arms and faced Joan and Priscilla as they tugged on their coats. "Am I in the clear? I hope?"

"Yes, and I'm sorry you made the suspect list at all. But wait. Dee Dee." Priscilla pulled out her phone and brought up the attendance sheet for the fateful November meeting. "Can you look at this and tell us who might have attended the meeting but didn't sign in? Sonya said there was quite a crowd but that people weren't required to sign in."

Dee Dee saw the list then crossed to her desk, which was actually a very nice desk that had been hidden under stacks of magazines and books when Priscilla had visited before. "I'll go one better. I made a list of everyone who was there because we can all see that the changes to fishing rights aren't in the little guys' favor. The official list is here." She handed Joan a hard copy of the attendance list Sonya had texted them. "And then this is my list." She handed them another. "When you look at this one, you can see that people with money didn't feel the need to sign in."

Priscilla scanned the list. "This is like a Who's Who of all the major Massachusetts area fishing businesses. Reed's Fisheries, Waldron Tuna, East Shore Tuna, Caldon Fish Company, Fresh Catch, Pennington Chowder, Haddock & More..." She whistled. "That meeting attracted some deep pockets."

"They have a legal right to be there," Dee Dee said. "But they come to get a feel for the current climate. If the small fishermen are going to rile up the state senate, the bigwigs want to know about it."

"Wow. So that's how it is, huh?" Priscilla wrapped her scarf around her neck. "May we keep these?"

"Of course. I can print them off as needed. And thank you both for coming around. I know I thwarted your original purpose of throwing me in jail…"

Priscilla and Joan both winced.

Dee Dee smiled, satisfied. "Good. I like that you're feeling guilty for even thinking such a thing. But I'd have thought the same if the circumstances were reversed, and I'd have been knocking at your door. Keep me in the loop, okay? And if that exclusive does come my way, I would be okay with that too."

They hugged her goodbye, then hurried to the car. Once inside, Priscilla faced Joan. "We have to figure out a way to help her, Joan. We absolutely, positively have to. If nothing else good comes from all this, helping a widow whose kid is fighting cancer is a win in my book. Now we just have to make it happen."

Joan fastened her seat belt. "I know, but how? It's not like we're sitting on that kind of money."

"I agree." Priscilla pulled out onto the side road. "But we're talking about a cache of one of America's most beloved artists, sitting unseen in a closed-up studio, with technology that offers a world of options." She noted her smartphone with a quick tap. "That's unacceptable. I'm taking Jake to have supper with Sammy and Gerald tonight, so I won't be home. Could you get a folder of those seascape images put together? Let's see what can be done with an internet platform."

"But she's contracted with the studio, and it's closed," Joan reminded her.

"When our little Kansas town faced a water crisis after a storm, Pete Gentry stopped his remodeling and threw open the doors of his store. He sold four thousand cases of water at bargain prices. He made money. We had water. I expect that gallery owner will open her doors for guaranteed sales."

"So we look for the buyer!" Joan laughed. "Do you think it could work?"

"It can't hurt. And if the gallery is doing major upgrades, a percentage of multiple sales wouldn't be a bad thing."

She dropped Joan off at her house, hurried home, and put together two salads. One for Uncle Hugh and Gail and one for her supper with Gerald. She dropped off the salad and two fresh dressings at Gail's house. She didn't want to tire Uncle Hugh out, but when he barked at her to come in, she crossed the room and hugged him gently. "It's good to have you back home," she told him softly. "So stop yelling, don't stress those new link-ups they spent so much time building, and enjoy your salad. And your time with us."

He grinned and gripped her hand in his. "Bird and bush, that's my future. But I've *got* a future, and hopefully time enough to fix some old wrongs. Thanks for the prayers. And for coming by. We love you."

"I love you too." She hurried back to her car, pleased. He looked good. Maybe better than before the surgical interventions, even. And he seemed truly determined to be a kinder version of himself, and that could be a big plus for his gentle-hearted daughter.

She closed her car door as her phone rang. Gerald's number came up in the display. She hit the Bluetooth connection and answered brightly. "Hey, I'm on my way, I just had to drop food off for Uncle Hugh." Jake woofed from the back seat, and she laughed. "Jake's saying hi! We'll be right there."

"Priscilla."

Gerald's voice sounded wrong. Very wrong.

Jake woofed again, but she shushed him with a hand command. "Gerald, what's wrong? Are you all right?"

He drew a strangled breath, sounding nothing like himself. "No." A pause followed. A long one, as if the big, strong Coast Guard captain was having a hard time finding words. "It's Sammy, Priscilla."

Oh, no.

Priscilla's heart raced. A cold shiver chased down her spine. Her own air caught crosswise, hearing the pain in his voice. "Gerald, no."

"I walked in after work and found her. I can't—" He choked up again.

"I'll be right there," she promised, but there was no way she could take Jake to Gerald's house. Not now. She hung up the phone, got Jake out of the car, and ran up the steps to Gail's door. "Can I leave Jake here for a bit?" she asked when Gail opened the door. Gail and Uncle Hugh didn't have any pets, but the old fellow loved Jake. "Gerald's dog just died, and I was going over there with Jake and—"

"Go." Gail took the leash. "Jake's always welcome here."

"Thank you."

She hurried back to the car, started it up, and choked back emotion. Gerald needed her to be strong. She pulled out of the driveway and headed toward his house, praying for the right words. As she pulled into his driveway, he appeared at the side yard. He set the garden shovel down and came toward her.

She went to him just as quickly, and when she wrapped her arms around him...

And he held her just the same...

They both cried. They cried for the loss of a good friend, the loss of a heart, so loving and true. And when they'd wrapped the sweet red dog in her favorite quilted throw, and laid her to rest, they sat in Gerald's front room, barely lit, with a woodstove fire chasing the cold.

And they cried again.

CHAPTER NINETEEN

Okay if I come by for coffee?

Priscilla answered Gerald's text quickly the next morning. *Absolutely.* She ran a comb through her hair, tucked the laptop aside, and had his coffee waiting for him when he walked in the door ten minutes later. "Hey." She pulled the door wide. "Rough night."

"To be expected, and when the newest nor'easter charges in it's going to be a rougher time yet." He frowned, took off his jacket, and slung it over the chair, then half-smiled, half-grimaced when Jake hurried his way. "Hey, boy."

"I can put him in the bedroom."

"No." Gerald took a seat at the table and gave Jake a good petting. "He's good therapy. It's not like I didn't know this was coming, you know?"

Priscilla nodded.

"I just didn't expect it to be like this. To walk in and find her. And yet, how much better to cross that rainbow bridge thing people talk about on her own, with no suffering, than to string it out."

"You're a good-hearted man, Gerald." She leaned down and put a tender kiss on his forehead. "I've been praying for you all night. Between naps."

"I'm grateful. And I wanted to thank you for coming right over last night. You never did get supper."

"Which will help my goal of looking good for this wedding," she replied. She brought the coffees over and took the seat next to him.

He took the coffee, then covered her hand with his. "You don't have to change a thing, Priscilla. You're beautiful just the way you are."

Oh, those words. His expression. The affectionate appreciation in his gaze. "You're sleep deprived, so I'm going to take all that with a grain of salt."

"True on the first part. Not the second." Jake nosed up, under Gerald's arm, and settled his snout along Gerald's thigh. Just that. Not begging to be petted like usual. Not whining. Just offering his presence. "It's like he knows something's wrong."

"I think he does. You're sad. I'm sad. He's not used to that from either of us. Are you working today?"

He sipped his coffee and nodded, gruff. "Of course."

She made an "oh, really?" type face at him.

He shrugged his shoulder. "It's easier to work, actually, than to stay home. I called Aggie and told her last night after you left. She explained it to Max."

"Never an easy conversation."

"Well, he called me this morning and said it was all right that Sammy went to heaven, but could he play with her when she gets back?" He sighed. "So then I mopped my stupid eyes and explained that you can't come back from heaven, and he got all upset."

"Oh, Gerald." She got up and hugged him, then grabbed tissues from the countertop. "He's too little to understand the full meaning."

"I know. I just hated to hear him cry because Grandpa's been able to do pretty much anything up to this point, and that's felt pretty darned good. But I can't bring Sammy back."

He wiped a couple of tissues over his eyes, then drank his coffee quickly and stood. "Duty calls."

"It always does." She hugged him again, and Jake rubbed his doggy cheek along Gerald's nice, neat pants, leaving a hint of red-and-white fur behind. "Let me get my adhesive roller," she said. "We'll get rid of that fur."

"I've got one at work. Dog hair was a daily occurrence with Sammy." He reached down and scratched Jake's ears, making the young dog smile. "Thanks, pal."

Jake wagged his tail. He smiled up at Gerald, and that tail wagged so hard he looked like one of those funny little animated dogs for a moment.

"I'll call you later."

"Good."

He left. No whistling today. No hands shoved into his pockets, the way he usually did. Just a quiet man, chin down, going to his car.

"Loss is a terrible thing," she explained to Jake as she set up her computer. "It leaves a hole inside us, just gaping open, and we go around, wondering how to fill it up. And then God and time fill it up for you, and you realize you're going to be okay. At last."

Jake gazed up, attentive, and when he tapped his tail against the kitchen floor, she was sure he understood. She pulled up the pages Joan had sent her.

Oh, those seascapes.

Dee Dee had said her husband was inspired by Winslow Homer's work, but where Homer painted stark realism in his paintings, Quimby layered hope in the darkest of storms, the highest of waves. When he tucked fishermen into the setting, they weren't always the tall, square-chested rugged Viking-types of commercial lore. They looked more like Berto. Smaller. Leaner. Darker.

He'd captured the flare and flash of the sea at its best and worst, and made the most of each brushstroke.

She called Rachel and explained what she was doing to promote the sales, and her amazingly smart, gifted daughter hit her with an even better idea.

"Mom, that all sounds great, but has anyone talked to Mrs. Quimby about reproductions for the masses?" Rachel asked. "It's fine to sell the originals for big bucks, but what about the everyday folks like you and me? Reproductions, calendars, puzzles, wall art. I think she needs a licensing firm, like the one Kim works for near Sacramento."

"You mean like my Charles Wysocki prints." Gary had given those to her nearly ten years before. She'd framed the four seasonal prints and now they hung on the far wall, overlooking the table, near the precious photo Gerald had framed last fall. The four cousins, totally at ease, being themselves.

"Exactly like that. Kim has connections. Let me call her and see what she thinks. Can you email me that file?"

"Done."

"Perfect. I'll get back to you later."

Licensing. Trademarks. What would Dee Dee think? She'd kept her husband's legacy of unsold work tucked away for years. Would she be open to letting the world embrace his gift? She put the question to Joan when they met midday.

"I'd wait and see what Rachel's friend has to say, then go from there. Reproductions are all the rage and it makes perfect sense, but I'd hate to get her hopes up and have them dashed."

"What if she doesn't like the idea?" Priscilla saw the sense in it, but maybe she was a little more mercenary than the eccentric newsletter reporter.

"Then we help her sell the originals. But Dee Dee's regular people." Joan used the New England saying easily. "I think she'll like the idea of getting Randolph's work into people's hands and on their walls. Just imagine some of those seascapes with scripture inlays. There's some sweet inspiration for a lot of folks, isn't there? Now, what are we going to do about Ripley?"

Priscilla frowned. "Here's my take on him. I didn't want Dee Dee to be guilty because she's such a fun, unique personality. So although things pointed in her direction, I wanted her to be innocent."

"And she is."

"Now, this Ripley guy is the opposite," Priscilla told her. They'd pulled up to Candy's bakery but stayed in the car so their conversation wouldn't be overheard. "I'd love for him to be guilty, because he's annoying. He's a hard-talking know-it-all type who does parts of his job for the zoning commission well, but then he tends to go overboard like a mini-dictator. He annoys me, so I want him to be guilty, but I don't think he is."

"Because?"

"My house and your car. He doesn't match the description Ellie gave, and she's one sharp cookie. And even though I know the person who crashed your car and cut my wires isn't necessarily the same person who used Marjorie's key, it certainly could be. When I was checking things out online, I found an article about Frank. He used to drive chartered buses for Misty Harbor tours. He earned money through college that way, and then to make extra money on weekends during the season while he taught school and before he retired and went into financial advising part-time. A guy who has an advanced license and has driven tour buses for years isn't likely to crash a car into a tree because of a little snow."

"Then who?" Joan raised her hands. "I don't know if you realize this but we're fresh out of suspects, my dear."

"I know." Priscilla gave the steering wheel a little slap. "It's infuriating, isn't it? I keep coming back to what A.J. told me, that it's usually someone in the circle. Someone obvious."

"Well, I'd like to talk to Ripley before we write him off the list, because if it turns out to be him, we'd look downright foolish and I am never a fan of looking foolish."

"After muffins and whatever else looks good," said Priscilla. "I want to leave a box of treats on Gerald's porch this afternoon.

He knew Sammy was getting frail, but he still felt blindsided yesterday."

"It's like that," Joan agreed. "We're never quite as ready to say goodbye as we think we are." She got out of the car and breathed deeply. "Only in January does a thirty-six degree day feel balmy!"

"And no wind yet, so that's an unusual relief." They went into the bakery, and Joan noted another winter difference.

"The short lines are a respite, but those crazy summer lines pay the winter bills. Luckily, Candy does a solid business even off-season."

There were only four people in front of them today. Harper, one of Candy's employees, took care of the first woman as Candy smiled at the man who moved forward behind her. "Good morning, Mr. P. Are you picking up for your wife or here on your own this morning?"

"A little of both," the distinguished-looking man answered. "I'm picking up her order, but I have an executive assistant going out on maternity leave over at the office, so we're doing a send-off thing."

"Like a baby shower?"

"Yes, that's exactly right." He smiled at her. "I should have ordered beforehand, but it's been busy."

"Busy is good," declared Candy as she moved to the side so he could see both display cases. "Were you thinking cake? Or handheld treats?"

"Both." He picked out a lovely quarter sheet cake done in pinks and mauves. "She's having a girl, so that one's nice, don't you think?"

"It is." Candy handed the cake off to one of the other employees. "What would you like her to write on it?"

"Whatever one customarily writes on such things," he told her.

"'Congratulations' is short and simple."

"That's fine. Her name is Lisa. And then can you fill a box with a dozen of those tart things?"

"They'll love them," she assured him. "Those tarts have rocketed up the popularity list, but as much as folks love them, I don't think they're right for a wedding, do you?"

The man looked blank.

"I'm getting married and trying to find what to make for the most delectable pastry table ever made, and it's driving me a bit bonkers."

Harper cleared her throat, which meant it might be more than a bit.

Candy sighed. "The expectations for weddings these days are unbearably high. Okay, cake is done." She sealed and taped the box. "And here are the tarts. Anything else today?"

"Not as long as we don't forget the wife's order," he told her and Candy flushed.

"Where is my head? Of course!" She removed a white box from the "Pick Up" shelf and settled it on the counter. "Harper will help you to the car with these."

"I'd be grateful. It would be the one day I'd slip and fall, wouldn't it?"

"Let's hope not." Harper smiled at him, completed the purchase, and walked outside. She didn't grab a sweater, so when she hurried back in, her cheeks were flushed with cold. "Why don't I remember to hang my sweater near the door?" It was a rhetorical question, and she faced Priscilla with a smile. "But it's fun to see Mr. Pennington's sweet ride. He was driving his BMW today, and when a BMW is your winter car, that says money, money, and more money."

"That's who that was." Priscilla snapped her fingers. "He was in the picture at Howard's house, remember?"

Joan nodded as she gave Harper her order. "I haven't seen him in years. They're a little more upper echelon than my usual crowd. His grandfather started Pennington Chowders early in the last century, and it's been the baseline for canned soup for generations."

"I love chowder," said Candy. "I'm partial to white but I've been known to feast on red too. We don't say the *M* word around here," she told Priscilla. "We decided a long time ago that while New York likes to poke its nose into just about everything, chowder is off limits. Mr. P.'s father used to say that one of his employees developed the red chowder recipe years before it started showing up along the shore. Now some say it started over in Rhode Island because of the Portuguese fishermen there, and that's an all right story, but we've had a lot of Portuguese influence here too, so we are not giving up the claim to red chowder. And that's that."

"Who would think soup would have such a volatile history?" mused Priscilla as she recalled the tomato-based broth of the Manhattan clam chowder she'd eaten off-island.

"Well there's soup and then there's chowder," noted Candy. "I guarantee that anyone in New England will tell you there's a world of difference."

"And since I love both, I'm happy to be part of a culture that embraces them heartily. Candy, can you pack me up a box with six of your signature chocolate chip cookies, and a crème horn? And then in my sack can you give me my traditional cranberry-nut muffin and two cookies?"

"Only two today?" Candy asked.

"We can't eat them at Uncle Hugh's because that would be mean, and I have to look good for my daughter's wedding this summer, therefore I should start paying attention to things now."

"They're offering a winter sale at the Workout Haven," Candy shared as she packaged up the box for Gerald. "I'm so tempted to sign up, but with designing new recipes and planning a wedding and running a business, who has time? The whole thing has me in a crazy state."

"Candy, dear." Joan had finished with Harper, and she moved over to Priscilla's side. "You don't have to come up with one new thing for this wedding to impress your family or friends. Don't let the current craze of Best Wedding Ever nonsense steer you away from the important things. Marrying your beloved, the sacred church setting you've picked, taking vows in front of family and God. I was married for well over thirty years, dear, and I can promise you. The rest is enjoyed and soon forgotten, but the marriage. Those vows. Well, my sweet friend, those are meant to last forever."

Candy burst into tears. She came right around the counter and hugged Joan, and while she cried, sweet Harper pretended it was all business as usual and finished Priscilla's order, then the rest of the line. By the time Joan had comforted Candy so she could return to work, it was time for them to go.

"Oh, now you don't have time to have your coffee here." Candy brought her hand to her mouth, embarrassed.

"Coffee is good anywhere," Joan declared. "But a heart-to-heart with a friend should always take precedence."

"I totally agree," Priscilla added. "Thank you for all you do, Candy. All you do for this sweet town, and the people, and the nice place of respite you provide through all four seasons. Folks around here don't take that lightly."

"You're so welcome," Candy told them. She took Priscilla's free hand. "It is absolutely done with love. Love for baking and love for this town."

Joan carried the coffees and her bag while Priscilla balanced her bag, Gerald's box, and her purse. Once in the car, she turned toward Joan. "Weddings have become ridiculous. These sweet gals are putting way too much pressure on themselves and your advice was perfect. Keep it simple. Keep your eyes on the Lord to guide you through. When did we lose track of that, Joan?"

"When people have too much, the longing for more can grow inside them." Joan snapped her seat belt into place. "It's gotten the same for big events. It's like we lost track of what is enough. My wedding was a coffee, cake, and punch reception in the church hall, and it started off thirty-plus mostly happy years. Now that's not a bad record from where I'm standing."

"Same here, although we had a very nice selection of cold cuts and fresh rolls. Farmers like to eat," Priscilla added, and Joan laughed.

"I expect they do. Okay, off to see Frank Ripley, correct?"

"Yes. I'm going to text Gerald first." She quickly typed a "thinking of you" text and hit Send. "I know how hard it is to walk into an empty house that wasn't empty the day before. So do you." She made a face of sympathy and tucked the phone aside. "I'll call him after we've talked with Ripley. Hopefully Mr. Ripley has had time to cool off since our last abbreviated meeting."

She pulled into the small parking area abutting the professional building not far from the town hall on Spring Street. She hiked her purse up over her shoulder and fell into step with Joan as they approached the building, a mix of doctor's offices and professional consultants. Frank Ripley was listed on the second floor, left.

"My aching knee says elevator, my urge to be healthier says take the stairs."

"Stairs it is."

They climbed the stairs and walked through the fire door leading to the second-floor offices. When they got to Ripley's door, Priscilla paused. "Knock or just walk in?"

Joan answered by opening the door and stepping inside. Priscilla followed.

"May I help you?" A woman about their age turned from a printer. She had a sheaf of papers in her hand and looked surprised to see them.

"We'd like to see Mr. Ripley, please."

"Uh...I'm afraid he's busy at the moment," the woman said. She moved forward, set the papers down, and took a seat herself. "If you'd like to make an appointment..."

Priscilla waved her off. She had a feeling Mr. Ripley was not quite as busy as his receptionist would have them believe. "No problem. We'll just wait right here until he can see us. No worries, none at all. I've got time on my side. How about you, Joan?"

Joan gave a spritely nod. "Same here. I have a book I'm just dying to read, so I can wait a couple of hours, at least."

The two of them didn't hesitate. They sat down on a luxurious brown leather sofa, and Joan pulled her Kindle out of her bag. Priscilla took out her cell phone and settled back as if she had all the time and battery power in the world.

In less than fifteen seconds, the woman was on the phone, Ripley's door popped open, and the man himself stood there. "You wanted to see me? What is it with you two? Isn't it bad enough that my friend is being brought to justice over this whole mess? Why do you keep hounding me?"

"I'd hardly call a pair of visits *hounding*." Priscilla kept her voice and expression wry. "But we do have some matters to discuss with you. Unless you'd rather we go to the police with our concerns first."

"Come in here." He sighed as he stepped back to allow them entrance to his office. "Ladies, let's get this done, once and for all."

CHAPTER TWENTY

appy to oblige," Joan told him.

They moved into a nice but not overly done room. He shut the door, rounded his desk, and sat, then steepled his hands. "What is it that you so desperately want to know?"

"Did you bilk the funds from the fishermen's pension fund, Mr. Ripley?"

He jerked back. "No, of course not. And if I did, were you expecting me to say yes and that's it?" He almost smiled, and it was almost attractive. "No, I don't steal. I've never stolen anything in my life. And I don't misappropriate funds because if I did, I wouldn't be in business long, would I?"

"Sometimes people are pushed too far." Priscilla made the observation softly. "We know that Sonya is innocent. We have proof, and the police realize they made a grave mistake by arresting her. Now they're going to look deeper, and your name is second on the oversight list. You were also at a meeting last fall—"

"With the Fishermen's Council," added Joan.

"A meeting that discussed the problems with the pension and the virtually nonexistent potential ways to solve them..."

"It's in a self-depletion cycle," he told them. "Sonya and I saw that several years ago, but no one wanted to listen. And even though it's backed by a guaranty corporation, the collapse of pension funds across the country is going to bankrupt the insurance in the not-too-distant future. So if someone has a 401(k) or is with a company that will give a lump sum distribution, that person has a shot at doing all right. But in an unfortunate number of these union pensions, the employee has no option but to sit and watch the money run down the drain. It's amazing how the fallout of decreased jobs and employment plays out in an arena governed by numbers."

"There were a lot of big-name companies at that meeting," Priscilla said.

"And some of them are struggling," he told them. "The sale of fresh fish products has skyrocketed with the current push for fresh overprocessed goods, but there are only a specific number of shoreline companies equipped to handle fresh product for resale. My guess is that canneries are under duress with surplus goods while fresh fish markets across the Northeast run out of product regularly, thereby pushing for bigger catches even if they run on the outside edge of legal."

"So if it wasn't Sonya, and it wasn't you, who did this?" Priscilla locked eyes with him. "Who needed money and would access this account right after a meeting where Sonya revealed that she only checked the account at the beginning and end of the month?"

"I forgot about that." Ripley appeared genuinely distraught. "The council asked us if she needed help after she gave them the grim report and she pointed out that even though the fund was diminishing, it was operating smoothly and needed little oversight. Did she tell you that she's never taken a dime of the oversight salary?"

"We'd heard that," said Joan.

"She's got the best heart and the strongest spirit. She said she was making enough to live on from the hospital, and she wouldn't take money from a struggling fund she didn't have the means to fix."

"And did you refuse your salary, Mr. Ripley?" asked Priscilla quietly.

He met her gaze. "No, I didn't. I've never stolen anything, but I have exercised very poor judgment with my personal funds." He worked his jaw, then frowned. "I have a gambling problem. I joined Gamblers Anonymous this last weekend when I realized that my life is spinning out of control. I don't know how anonymous it will be in a small town on an island, but that's my problem for messing up so badly. And how bad does it look for a financial advisor, handling other people's funds, to have a gambling addiction?"

"Really bad." Priscilla kept it to the point. "But how strong it is when we admit our failures and get help, Mr. Ripley. That's the mark of strength any person or investor wants to see. We all fall down. It's the people who get back up and keep on going that plot the way for others."

"I hope folks see it that way," he told them. "You're expecting the police force to dig up that information, aren't you, Mrs. Grant?"

She nodded.

"I'll pay them a visit and stay a step ahead of the game."

"It looks much better to be self-disclosed than to be discovered while under investigation."

"I agree. You said that Sonya has been proven innocent?"

"We brought some technological information that indicates outside involvement to the detectives overseeing the case. Information they were happy to receive."

He followed her track right away. "You think it was someone at that meeting."

"We think it's a distinct possibility," Joan said.

"Well, you've got a lot of angry fishermen who paid into a fund that's drying up, so that's never a good thing," he told them. "They were assured they could count on this money as they aged. If the fund fails, the few cents on the dollar that the guaranty corporation will offer won't pay the bills or put food on the table for them."

"It's a rook deal," Joan agreed.

"But then there were all the major players there, as you already know," he went on. "There were a dozen representatives from local fish-canning industries, and as I said, they're all probably hurting. I can't name names, but I've been called in on consult audits for a few, and the money going out is outpacing the cash coming in."

Money going out is outpacing cash coming in.

Fresh fish beats processed.

Maura Pennington's husband runs a chowder company and has access to Sonya's office through his wife and was at the meeting in question.

Priscilla stood quickly. "Mr. Ripley, thank you for your time."

He looked surprised, but then so did Joan. "We're leaving?"

"We've got a nagging chore to take care of, so yes." She met Joan's gaze and tried to send a silent message with her eyes.

"Are you all right?" asked Joan. "Did you get something in your eye?"

Clearly the silent eye message maneuver needed practice. "No, but I realized that we've got a few loose ends to tie up, so we should let Mr. Ripley get back to work…"

Now Joan got it. "Of course." She nodded briskly, then extended her hand across his desk. "Thank you for seeing us, and I'm wishing you well. And keeping you in prayer," she went on. "I see your wife going in and out of St. Augustine's with your grandchildren. It's a lovely church with a great staff. It might be something worth checking out yourself."

He gripped her hand. "You're right. It's time to shift my priorities. Hopefully it's not too late."

"Then that will be the focus of my prayer," she told him. She followed Priscilla out the door.

There was no question about taking the elevator this time. Priscilla dashed down the stairs, then almost dragged Joan to the car. Once in, she turned Joan's way, excited. "Mr. Pennington," she told Joan.

"Huh?"

"The guy in the bakery, with a car collection that rivals Jay Leno's, right?"

"The owner and CEO of Pennington Chowder Company, yes." Joan stared at her, then her eyes widened. "You think he did it."

"I think every arrow is now pointing in his direction," Priscilla said. "His wife works near Sonya, so it wouldn't be unusual to see him in the offices. He's got motive if the canned soup industry is crashing down around him, and he can't protect the lifestyle he's accustomed to, and as a major business owner, the sad truth is he probably already has offshore accounts to avoid state and federal taxes."

"Godfrey Pennington?" Dismay darkened Joan's face. "Godfrey is one of the town leaders. A true philanthropist. He and Maura have always helped folks. The towns, the causes. I can't imagine him doing something like this. His house alone is worth millions."

"Well, for a town leader he's kept himself under cover since I've moved onto the island."

"You know, you're right." Joan's frown deepened. "I hadn't thought much about it, we've been so busy, but he and Maura used to be at everything. They would sponsor this, that, and the other thing on a regular basis. If there was charity afoot, they were right there, doling out money."

"And yet she works at the hospital. Doesn't anyone find that curious?"

"No." Joan's voice dropped. "No, they lost a son, their only child, about eight years ago and Maura began working shortly after that. He was such a delightful boy, midteens, and like so many teenagers, he thought himself indestructible. He and his best friend took out a boat without permission. One of those freak mini-thunderstorms came up late afternoon. They were lost at sea, and the entire island mourned for them. Maura told Sonya she couldn't bear to be at home, thinking. Because thinking got her nothing but grief."

Priscilla understood that. "So she didn't start working because money was growing tight."

"Godfrey's a proud, hardworking man. If the company is floundering, he probably wouldn't let on. You can be sure it's not common knowledge around town or we'd have heard about it."

"Well we can't just pop in on him and accuse him. Or can we?" Priscilla put the car into gear.

"But we'll be interrupting his assistant's baby shower."

Priscilla frowned but stopped the car. "Well, let's check out his car history. If he's sliding downhill, maybe he's sold a car or two to keep things afloat."

Joan typed the words *vintage auto sales Godfrey Pennington* into her smartphone.

The three top hits were from Bontrager's Car Auction. Bontrager's was an online service based just outside of Boston, overseeing the sale of pricey autos, the best of the best. Their records pinged three cars previously listed to R.M. Pennington. "They're discreet about numbers, but according to the internet rating scale, he netted nearly two million from those sales."

"From old cars?" Priscilla couldn't believe such a thing. The closest she'd ever come to a pricey antique car was the Model T old Mr. Loomis used to pull out from under the dust covers every year for their short but sweet Memorial Day parade back in Wheatfield. "So why steal? Why not just keep selling the cars?"

Joan shook her head. "I don't know, but baby shower or not, let's pay Mr. P. a visit, shall we?" She didn't sound one bit pleased about the choice, but in typical Joan fashion she sounded absolutely determined.

CHAPTER TWENTY-ONE

The soup baron's factory was on the mainland, but he had offices overlooking the water in Oak Bluffs. Priscilla knew this because the building sported the Pennington Chowder Company logo along the wall facing the road. "Where do he and Maura live?"

"They have a mansion on Paul's Point that actually started as a small farm to grow vegetables for the soups. All of his great-grandfather's kids worked the farm, growing carrots, potatoes, and peas. He said in an interview that it was a shame celery wouldn't grow well here and that mainland pork was better than island pork, but other than that, he tried to produce as much as he could here on the island, giving work to others. They've been voted one of the top New England employers for over ten years in a row, so if he's guilty, this could be a game-changer for a lot of people."

"I'll say." Priscilla pulled into the parking lot adjacent to the corporate office building. The strengthening wind bent the leafless trees into slim, curved models of themselves, bobbing and weaving in nature's choreography. The stately structure looked more like a gracious waterfront home than a corporation. The building reflected the coastal look favored by the town. When they went through the hardwood colonial door, it was like stepping into someone's home. A long foyer comprised the reception area, and to the right, folks were enjoying the afternoon with cake and pastries while one very expectant young woman opened gifts.

"He cares about his employees. He cares about this town. He loves his company," Joan whispered.

A woman spotted them and came their way. "I'm so sorry, we're having a little send-off for one of our employees. May I help you?"

"We need to see Mr. Pennington," Priscilla told her.

"Do you have an appointment?" the woman inquired. She moved to the reception desk. "Mr. P. knew we were celebrating today and kept his calendar cleared for the bulk of the afternoon, I believe."

"We might be unexpected, but I think he'll see us. Tell him we're here about the pension fund."

"The pension fund," the woman repeated, then she shrugged. "I'll be right back." She walked up the flight of stairs and disappeared. She came back shortly and motioned them to the left. "Mr. Pennington will see you in the Littleneck room." She took them to a midsize conference room. "Would you like something while you wait? Coffee? Tea? Water?"

"We're fine, thank you," Joan replied. The woman went back to the party area. A few curious looks came their way, but then it seemed like they were forgotten—literally—for twenty minutes.

Joan looked at Priscilla.

Priscilla made a face.

Then they crossed the room to interrupt the party once again. "Is Mr. Pennington available or not? We're still waiting."

"Of course you know he's a very busy man," a youngish man told them. "I'm sure he'll get to you when he can."

Now the whole group was watching Priscilla and Joan. Quiet descended as they listened.

When no one moved, Priscilla made her way to the stairs, Joan close behind. "Or we'll just go up there ourselves. Come on, Joan."

"No, wait, I—"

The original woman tried to intervene, but Priscilla and Joan went up the stairs quickly. They approached the upstairs hallway. Two doors stood open. One was closed. She moved to that one, knocked briskly, and thrust it open. "Mr. Pennington?"

No one answered.

She stepped in farther and tried again. "Mr. Pennington? Are you here?"

Silence.

Joan looked around, then slapped a hand to the hardwood desk. "Priscilla. Oh, no, Priscilla. Look at this." She lifted a sheet of paper from the center of the old wooden desk, a desk that had seen more than one generation of work, Priscilla was sure.

Priscilla looked at the note and felt the blood drain from her face. "'Tell Maura I decided to go fishing,'" she whispered. "Oh, Joan, no. You don't think?"

Joan's phone dinged a weather alert. So did Priscilla's. "I do, and that nor'easter's imminent. We might run out of time, Priscilla."

"Well, we can't."

They hurried out of the office, tore down the stairs, and Joan barked out a question. "Where would Mr. Pennington go if he went fishing?"

"Fishing?" The employees were hurriedly packing up leftovers, eager to beat the storm. They looked at one another, then Priscilla and Joan, wasting valuable time.

All but the pregnant woman. "He would take a boat right out of Vineyard Haven, near Owen Park. But no one in his right mind would take a boat out today." Her mouth dropped open as she faced Priscilla and Joan, then she brought a hand to her chest. "You've got to find him." She came forward hurriedly. "Don't let this happen, tell him nothing matters this much. Ever," she stressed, and from the intensity of her voice, Priscilla figured that Lisa knew more than most about the man's money problems.

"We'll find him." Joan and Priscilla hurried out the door.

The pregnant woman grabbed a hooded coat and followed them down the walk and to their car. Priscilla turned when she realized Lisa was standing right behind her.

"What are you doing?" The rising wind whipped through Priscilla's hair, wrapping it around her face as she struggled to open the car door. "Get back inside where you're safe."

"I'm coming." The pregnant woman climbed into the back seat and shut her door. "You can either waste time arguing or get going. Your choice. I'm not getting out of this car."

"You're risking your baby's safety." Priscilla met her gaze through the window, then took her seat in the car. "Think about what you're doing."

"I'm trying to save my father's life." She spoke calmly as she scooted to the middle of the seat and fastened the seat belt. "See? I'm in the safest spot in the car. Let's go before they shut Beach Road down."

Her father…

Priscilla didn't dare look at Joan. She had all she could do to fight the wind to get out of the small lot and onto the road.

The wind had been building steam while they were inside.

Now it was gale force, and the sound of the wind and the surf pounding the nearby beaches didn't make hearing difficult. It made it almost impossible. "Will we make it across Beach Road?" Priscilla yelled to Joan as she thrust the car into gear.

"We don't have a choice," Joan yelled back. "We have to. I tried to contact the Tisbury police, to tell them what's going on, but the call didn't go through. It's either us…or no one."

They'd had nor'easters before. The Atlantic coast braced for them regularly, but this one was rolling in with grave intensity.

Transformers sparked above them. Trees thrashed to and fro, leafless dancers, bending in the wind as water poured across the narrow road connecting Oak Bluffs to the Haven. "They'll close this quickly," Joan told her. "It's not safe in these conditions."

Priscilla kept her eyes on the road. "Text Gerald, okay? Tell him what's happening. A text might go through when a call can't. He might be able to connect with the police."

Joan's thumbs danced across the small letter pad.

The strong gusts shoved Priscilla's car into the opposite lane. On this narrow stretch of road, there was nothing to block the onslaught of almost hurricane-force winds and drenching rain, piling tidal waters in its path. "Will this road wash away, Joan?" She didn't want to ask the question, but she had to.

"Hasn't yet," shouted Joan, with a spark of her old self shining through. "But then the day ain't over."

It was a ridiculous thing to say, but it was enough to lighten Priscilla's angst as she held the car in check the best she could. "That's for certain." She yelled over her shoulder, "How are you doing, Lisa?"

"Praying."

"Best defensive move we've got," shouted Joan as the full force of the winter storm barreled toward the New England mainland. Unfortunately for them, they lay between the storm and the coast with not much to block the onslaught.

The wind didn't just shove them.

It battered.

The tires slipped in the rising water, and Priscilla refused to think about all the warnings she'd seen on TV over the years, how a few inches of rushing water was enough to sweep a car off the road. She refused to think about it, because she was facing a lot more than a few inches of water…The massive winds and the pulsing tide added their own levels of insanity to the drive. "It should be better once we get across," she reasoned as she battled the tires and the steering wheel to stay the course. "Right?"

The bright flash of an electrical transformer jarring loose made Priscilla jump just as a large tree limb slammed down to their left.

"Or not," Joan said. She turned around to speak to their unexpected passenger. "Lisa, this is too dangerous." Joan put on her strong mother voice. "Let us drop you off at one of the shops here."

"I'm not getting out of the car and at this size, you don't want to get into a wrestling match with me. Trust me on that."

Priscilla couldn't help but like her spunk. A tree limb and downed power lines sparked ahead of them as they approached Center Street. Downed wires and a hefty tree lay between them and the turnoff for Owen Park. "Main Street is blocked."

"Take Center Street up to William Street, then," Joan directed. "Lisa, give me your phone. I'm going to put our numbers in it in case we get separated."

"Good idea."

Flashing lights dotted the area as police and firemen began responding to the rapidly growing damage. "Should they be out in this?" Priscilla asked.

"Should we?" Joan shot back. "William Street is blocked with tree limbs too. Keep going to Franklin, and Lisa, you pray this one isn't blocked, because once a cop gets close enough to stop us, they're not going to let us continue through."

"They think they'll stop us." Lisa stayed calm, hands folded. "But they won't. Guaranteed."

"Good heavens, child, are you packing heat?" Priscilla asked brusquely. "Are you carrying a gun?"

"Better. I'm packing the best weapon ever. Faith." She'd fastened her cloak-style coat over her sizable belly. "Franklin Street looks clear."

"So far," declared Priscilla as she made the turn under horrific conditions.

Poles sparked all around them. As they passed Church Street, a string of light poles began to tip their way.

"Incoming!" shouted Joan.

Priscilla hit the gas and cleared the string of seven poles in the nick of time.

"'The Lord is my shepherd. I shall not want.'" Joan's voice came through like a beacon.

"'He maketh me to lie down in green pastures: he leadeth me beside the still waters.'" Lisa chimed in. "'He restoreth my soul. He leadeth me in the paths of righteousness for his name's sake...'"

"'Yea, though I walk through the valley of the shadow of death, I will fear no evil,'" whispered Priscilla as the turn for Colonial Lane appeared through the sheeting rain. "'For thou are with me,'" they prayed as she turned left onto Main, just shy of Owen Park Way. "'Thy rod and thy staff, they comfort me.'" She turned down the road and there, to the left, was a silver BMW.

"That's it. That's his car."

Priscilla pulled in behind the car, blocking it in. If he somehow got back to the vehicle, she didn't want him to take them on another chase in dreadful conditions.

"Smart." Joan noted the positioning as she tied her scarf around her head. "Let's go."

CHAPTER TWENTY-TWO

The wind beat them back as they exited the car.

Priscilla turned to Lisa. "If you do something that hurts this baby you will never forgive yourself. Get back in the car," she told her, handing her the keys. She'd have said it softly and nicely, but the conditions didn't allow for soft and nice, so she kind of yelled it. "Let us save him. You save that baby. Keep the car nice and warm because your father's going to be soaked and frozen."

Lisa hesitated, then gave in. "Tell him the contract came through during the party. The money's been released. Tell him everything is going to be all right. He'll know what you mean."

"I will."

Lisa got back into the car and started the engine.

Joan and Priscilla fought through the slashing wind and rain, searching for a visual on the elongated narrow stretch of beach.

A large boat had washed ashore to the south of them, then they spotted an equally large sailboat that had been ripped from its moorings. Listing right, the tall masts stuck up over the shore like long, skinny sticks.

Joan put her hand to her forehead to shield her eyes. She peered to their left, then grabbed Priscilla's arm. "That way!" They took off up the beach, but the slippery wet sand and harsh weather slowed them considerably.

Priscilla couldn't see Godfrey. Despite her hat and scarf, the wind kept whipping her hair into a mat across her face, making the thought of a crisp, clean cut like Joan's seem mighty attractive about now.

Then she saw him. He'd wrestled loose one of the small boats people kept along the sand dunes. Most people stowed them away for the winter, but there was always an odd boat or two lying against the piled sand. "Godfrey!"

She shouted his name, but the wind snatched the words away.

"Godfrey!" Joan did the same with similar results.

They'd never make it to him before he hit the water with that boat. He was nearly there already. And while Priscilla wouldn't have the strength to row a boat out through the waves, Godfrey Pennington was no lightweight. He tugged the boat against the wind and rain and appeared to be winning the battle.

"God help us." Priscilla uttered the prayer as the time/distance ratio became clearer. He'd just reached the water and they were hundreds of feet away, fighting for every step they took. "Please, Lord. Please."

A monster wave rolled up, driven by the back-thrust of the one before it. It raced into shore just as Godfrey got the boat righted and tried to get in.

The wave hit.

The force of it shoved the boat and Godfrey a good thirty feet back up the sand. Enough to get them closer. Maybe enough to save a man's life.

"Godfrey!" Joan was closer. She shouted again. "Godfrey Pennington. Don't you dare do this!"

He looked up. Spotted Joan. Then Priscilla. With a mighty shove he began pushing the boat with superhuman strength back toward the water, but the increased force of the wind stymied him as the boat dug into the wet sand.

"Get away!" he shouted when he realized they were approaching faster than he was getting away. "What are you, nuts? This is a terrible storm. Go home. Get out of here. Be safe."

His words touched Priscilla. She'd have liked them better if she wasn't soaked and frozen, but she understood Joan's respect for this man, because even now he was looking out for them. For their well-being. Their safety. They'd caught up to him now, and she laid a hand on his arm. "Not without you. We promised Lisa."

His head jerked her way. "What do you mean?"

"Your daughter," shouted Joan. "She's back there, in the car. She wouldn't let us leave without her, even though her baby is due in a few weeks."

"You let Lisa get into a car in this storm?" He stood frozen, as if the boat and suicide didn't matter much compared to Lisa's safety. "Are you insane?"

"Possibly!" Priscilla shouted. "Can we talk about this somewhere else, maybe? Where death is less imminent? Please?"

"No." He seemed to suddenly remember his goal. His cause. "No, you need to go. I'm going to drop a line in for a while. That's what you tell Maura, all right? Gone fishing."

"We won't tell her any such thing." Joan's scarf had come loose. She tightened it as she plopped herself right into the boat, her back to the wind, and faced him. "Let's see how far you get with an extra hundred-and-twenty-eight pounds on board."

"Make that an extra two-seventy-five," said Priscilla. She followed Joan's example and got into the boat. "If you thought it was tough to push before, I expect it's tougher now," she shouted.

Pennington put his hands to his head as Priscilla moved to his end of the boat. "Lisa sent a message."

For brief seconds the wind calmed, allowing her to speak. "She said the contract came through in the middle of the party. The money's been deposited. She said everything will be all right."

He stared at her, then Joan, then her again. "It came through?"

"That's what she said."

"Oh, thank God." He dropped to his knees, hands folded, face down.

The wind roared again, ending the momentary reprieve. Priscilla climbed out of the boat and took his arm. "Let's go back to the car and figure all this out. No matter what you've done, it's not worth your life, Mr. Pennington."

"Come on." Joan took his other arm. "Let's get warm and dry and talk about this rationally. If Lisa is your daughter, then you've got a granddaughter on the way, and she's going to need a grandpa who will push her through the parks and along the sidewalks..."

"Get her an ice cream."

"Teach her to whistle."

"Teach her to fish."

As they walked back, the wind started dying down and it took less time to get to the cars. Priscilla opened the back door. "We've got him."

"Dad, you're soaked through." Lisa got out of the driver's seat and joined him in the back. She tugged at his long raincoat.

"Pretty wet," he agreed as Priscilla and Joan climbed into the front seat. "What are you doing here? What were you thinking, Lisa Ann?"

"I was thinking that Danny and I want this baby to have a proper grandfather. I was thinking there's no way I can run that company without your advice and counsel, especially now that *Fresh To You!* has offered us a multimillion-dollar contract to supply the East Coast and Mid-Atlantic states with our fresh chowders and soups in a merge with the New England Bread Company."

"That's better-than-perfect food," breathed Priscilla. "Their bread and your chowders? That's like the best combination ever!"

"It is," Godfrey agreed. He'd gotten the wet coat off and with Lisa's help, he stowed it in the back of the SUV. "But I was running low on cash to get the production lines changed over, and no one wanted to loan a fading enterprise any money. I have holdings, I have a house worth plenty and paid for, and I have the cars, but I needed one more temporary million to upgrade the factory to a fresh chowder packaging and shipping center. I knew the contract was coming. We'd made the deal back in November, but I didn't expect it to take so long and we had to go into renovations to be able to launch in February. Our value ratio had tanked the past two years and, despite my worth, no one wanted to loan us business money without putting a lien on the house, and I was trying to keep Maura from worrying. She's already had to endure too much, being married to me."

"So you took the million from the pension fund to tide you over."

"I figured I'd have it back in there before Sonya checked the books at the end of the month, but then the contract was delayed, folks were on vacation, and I'd already sold three cars. I would've sold more, but no one wants to buy and transport beautiful cars in December and January."

"Winter curbs sales on a bunch of things, I guess." Priscilla couldn't help but sympathize with him. "So you did this to save your company?"

"I did it to save jobs," he told her, sounding like the executive he was. "All those folks working at the factory, at the office, would be let go if we bellied up. I can live without working. I have investments and equity in a lot of things, but the regular person who lives paycheck to paycheck doesn't have any of that. They'd be crushed by a bankruptcy or total shutdown, and I was this close to having everything go right when the delays hit. I'm sorry." He faced Lisa. "I shouldn't have taken the money from the pension fund, but I was in a hard spot right then, and I never dreamed I wouldn't have that money back in the account by Christmas."

"That's why you were so sad at Christmas," she said. "Oh, Dad, I wish you'd told me."

She hugged him. Then she pulled back. "We'll figure this out. We'll get it all taken care of, and whatever happens, the most important thing is that we've got family."

Joan cleared her throat, and when Joan cleared her throat like that, it meant she expected the other person to fill in the blank.

"So Godfrey," she said. "About my car...and Priscilla's wires being cut...and her dog being left out in the cold...and the flowers...?"

Godfrey drew a long breath. "Yes. I wasn't thinking very clearly. After I overheard Jon Fleming say he'd asked Priscilla to work her magic on the case, I panicked. I knew from the grapevine that once you gals sink your teeth into something, you don't let go. I just meant to scare you a little, to get you to stop asking questions. Now, the car—I didn't mean to wreck it, of course. And your dog—" He turned to Priscilla. "He got out when I opened the door, and I couldn't catch him. I felt so badly, and I tried and tried to herd him back in." He shook his head. "I hope you both can forgive me for what I did."

Priscilla couldn't bring herself to make the man feel worse than he already did. "I'm too busy being glad that Sonya's name is cleared and you're alive and Lisa didn't give birth in my car to hold any grudges," she told him. "Now can you please fill us in on...this?" She pointed back and forth between Godfrey and Lisa and raised her eyebrows.

Godfrey drew a breath. "Lisa is my daughter. Her mother and I had a relationship thirty-two years ago, before I met Maura. Lisa's mother broke it off with me and went back to Providence and never said she was pregnant at the time. Lisa found me three years ago."

"Does Maura know?"

He grimaced. "Yes, but after losing Stevie, to have a child show up out of the blue, my child from before, it made her relive the loss of our son all over again. So we've kept things quiet."

"They'll come out now," Priscilla said as a flashing light came their way. "You know how reporters are."

"Wretched scavengers," he said bluntly.

"Well, there's one who isn't," Joan cut in. "Dee Dee Quimby. She runs that little online paper, Godfrey, and I bet she'd do your story proud. When you're both ready to tell it, that is."

"Is she that funny little woman with the cockeyed hat and green boots?" asked Lisa.

"That's her. Although in the summer she chooses to wear lime-green sneakers instead."

"We'll talk." She took her father's hand as the flashing light pulled up alongside them.

A police officer climbed out of one car.

Gerald climbed out of the other.

He crossed to her car and tapped on the door, and when Priscilla rolled down the window, he sighed. "First, I'm glad that you're all right. Second, I see that the rescue has been achieved."

She nodded.

"And third." He leaned down and planted a sweet kiss to her very surprised lips. "Could you please stop scaring me like this? Maybe?"

She smiled up at him as the officer came around to Joan's side of the car. "I'll do my best, Gerald. I promise."

"Everything's okay now?" the officer inquired.

"It's fine," Joan assured him. "I expect we can't get back to Oak Bluffs, correct?"

"We're going to shelter in St. Augustine's hall for now," Gerald told her. "Give the storm time to wind down and get the roads cleared."

Joan sent Priscilla a worried look, but said nothing. Neither did Priscilla.

"And don't worry about the dogs."

Clearly he read their minds.

"Tommy was up that way doing a job for Rebekah so he gathered up Jake and Sister and has them at his place. He'll keep them as long as you need him to."

"Oh, Gerald, thank you. You do think of everything."

Gerald half-grinned, half-grimaced as the officer hurried back to his patrol car, then drew his rain slicker tighter. "Priscilla, when it comes to you, my dear, I consider it a requirement. I'll follow you back to the church."

The parking lot was full when they arrived. The storm had beaten a nasty path, particularly along the shoreline. Here, a little more inland, there wasn't as much tree and pole damage.

"Before we go in."

The three women waited for Godfrey to continue.

"When we can get through, I'm going to turn myself in to the Oak Bluffs police. I will tell them honestly what I did, and I'll take whatever comes my way."

"Dad."

He covered Lisa's hand with his. "And whatever happens, I expect you to rise to the occasion of running the company. You've been at my side for three years, watching and learning. You're young, but no younger than I was when my dad's heart forced him to an early retirement. We can do this, Lisa. With Danny on board to work on the cash flow end—"

"My husband's a CPA and investor with Mainland Securities and Equities," Lisa explained.

"We can still make a difference. And maybe help that ailing pension fund too. No man in his late fifties needs fourteen classic cars when one is all you can drive. You pick out your favorite, and we'll liquidate the rest. Heaven knows Maura's been after me to do that very thing for long enough. Why sit on things when people are so much more important?"

"The Ford Phaeton," Lisa said instantly. "That's the perfect American classic for driving your granddaughter to prom in seventeen years."

"I should be out of prison by then," he said, only partially joking.

She laid her head against his shoulder. "Did my brother have a favorite, Dad?"

His eyes misted. "Stevie was a truck man," he told her. "He loved that two-tone 1965 Ford F-100. Not worth so much."

"But priceless now." She hugged his arm. "Keep those two. Sell the rest. And we all move on."

Gerald got out of his car and came to theirs.

Priscilla and Joan climbed out. So did Godfrey and Lisa. As they moved toward the shelter of the church hall, Joan touched Priscilla's arm. "Do you suppose there's a nurse nearby? Or a doctor? In case she goes into labor?"

"We'll check inside," Priscilla whispered. "But I did hear that our friend Gerald here delivered a baby with not much help from a panicked father about a dozen years back."

"That's right." Joan grinned at Gerald as he held the heavy door to the church open. "I'd forgotten."

"I'm pretty sure there's someone far more qualified in this hall," he told them, and he didn't look all that amused. "At least I'm hoping there is. Furthermore, she's had enough stress for one day, so let's hope that baby gets born in the hospital like most babies do. Frankly, all I want right now is to know you two are safe, and that Godfrey's in good hands. And food."

"Then we're all set because it looks like the good people of St. Augustine's have outdone themselves. Again."

A group of people began bringing out hot dishes of food. The scents of soup and pasta mingled with the yeasty aroma of fresh bread.

"Bread and chowder," declared Gerald. "Two of my favorites."

"And after today," Priscilla told him once she'd exchanged a smile with Joan, "they're two of our favorites too."

CHAPTER TWENTY-THREE

They stayed in the shelter for two long days, and then it was another two days before power was restored across the island. Uncle Hugh's "date" with Marigold had to be postponed, Sister and Jake were thoroughly spoiled by Tommy Townsend, and for a few days the sun shone bright, always a welcome sight.

Gerald arrived at the lighthouse with a sizable pot of beef and vegetable soup the following week.

Priscilla opened the door when she heard his car. "Come on in, you're early."

"I wanted to get here before the others," he told her.

Jake jumped up and dashed across the carpet as soon as he heard Gerald's voice. He panted at Gerald's feet, gazing up, waiting for attention in a much more appropriate way than he had a year ago. Gerald handed Priscilla the pot and gave Jake a good petting. "Hey, boy."

Jake's tail beat a steady rhythm against the kitchen floor.

"I miss Sammy." Gerald's voice didn't sound depressed, but it sure did sound sad.

"I know." Priscilla set the pot down. "It's got to feel very different, I expect."

"It does." He kept petting Jake. "There are moments when I forget, and I expect her to come walking out. Tuck her head beneath my arm and look up at me with those big brown eyes. It's been a long time since she had the energy to do this," he went on, noting Jake's happy excitement. "But that was all right. It just feels odd to have the house so quiet. Not like she added a lot of noise." He shook his head as if that made little sense. "Maybe it just *feels* quieter. Emptier."

"I expect it does." She crossed the kitchen and laid an arm around his shoulders. "I'm sorry you have to go through this."

He shrugged and stood up. "It's life. I know that. Still miss her, though. And it looks like this year is going to mark a lot of change. I'm looking at retirement this fall. I'd thought I'd hold out a year or two. But now..."

"Looking at it?" Priscilla lifted one brow. "You mean you're considering it? Or doing it?"

"The time has probably come," he told her. "I'm not one-hundred percent on board," he went on as the crunch of tires on gravel announced another arrival. "But a part of me thinks it might be the right choice."

"Now there's something to pray about," she said softly. "More time with those two grandkids would be a wonderful thing."

He looked at her. And then he laid one big, strong hand against her cheek. "More time in general would be a wonderful thing," he said softly.

Her heart melted.

Not really, because that would be a disastrous experience, but it kind of did. She leaned her head in.

He kissed her forehead with sweet tenderness. Then he stepped back as footsteps rushed the door. "The crew has arrived."

She met his smile and matched it with one of her own. "Indeed they have."

Gail came in first, fussing at Uncle Hugh. "Take it easy, Pop, we're not running a race. Are we?"

"I've been pushed like a Kentucky racehorse the past week, so you can't tell it by me," he shot back. "Work on this machine, now on that one, breathe in, breathe out, keep on walking, go a little faster, now." He rolled his eyes at Gerald and Priscilla. "After all that, I think I'm okay to walk from the car to the cottage. In fact, I can't believe how much better I really do feel," he announced as Joan came in behind them. Ellie Doyle's car pulled into the drive as he talked. She and Rebekah were coming to celebrate with them, a wonderful rounding out of family and friends, and when Mildred pulled in at the last minute, Priscilla welcomed her with open arms.

"We are a great crew," she announced as Gail fussed over what food should go where. She left that in Gail's very capable hands and hugged Rebekah and Ellie as they came in one door and Mildred slipped in through the other. "Let me take coats. I'm tossing them on the bed for the afternoon."

"And what an afternoon it is!" Rebekah's eyes lit up as she motioned to the bright, sunny day. "I thought it would take us months to clean up after that storm, but the people on this island have done an amazing job of working together."

"Who'd have thought we'd be without electric in January?" said Joan. "And so many people jumping in to help one another. Including Tommy, taking in the dogs while we were tucked in the church hall for two days. Are he and his mom coming today?" she asked Gail.

Gail shook her head. "He's too busy with repairs all over the island. The storm made him and his mom miss our original supper date, so we rescheduled it for this past Friday."

Priscilla and Joan knew that. They nodded.

"Well, it was quite the outing, as I'm sure you both know, and after Marigold thought the invitation to this gathering over quite seriously, she said it wouldn't be seemly to appear too eager."

"I said at our age, we have to be eager," bellowed Uncle Hugh from Priscilla's living room. "But she just laughed and told me to cool my jets. That woman always was a pistol!"

Priscilla ducked her chin.

Joan turned her back.

They didn't dare exchange looks because laughing at the aged romancers would be rude, especially when they were so absolutely cute.

Gail rolled her eyes. "Shall we eat now or do you want to fill us in on everything first, then eat? Because I've been dying to hear the details. Dee Dee did the nicest feature story today, all about the Penningtons and his long-lost daughter and how she's going to run the firm for as long as needed."

"Once she recovers from having that beautiful baby girl," noted Joan with a smile. "I stopped by the nursery to peek in on

Friday, and she's just a total doll-baby. A little bit of hair, big blue Pennington eyes, and the sweetest face, just like her mother."

"Did they name her?"

Joan nodded as she settled into a chair with a mug of coffee in hand. "Sophia Ruth after Godfrey's mother and grandmother. And she's perfect."

"As is every child born," declared Rebekah, and they all smiled.

"So, Priscilla, tell us what happened? How did you know it was Godfrey?" Ellie wondered.

"When he left no trace?" noted Gail.

"And he deliberately stooped over when he was here," Ellie went on, "because if he'd walked tall and strong like always, I'd have known him straight off. Godfrey Pennington carries himself like an English aristocrat, and I've said that for years."

"He does," Priscilla agreed. "Well, it wasn't one bit obvious until we managed to exhaust our prime suspects."

"Which left us wondering if we had any chance at all," Joan cut in.

"But then came a quest for cookies and a crème horn." Priscilla smiled at Gerald, and he smiled back. "That led us from Candy's, where we saw Mr. Pennington, to Frank Ripley's office, and when he started talking about fresh fish being more in demand than processed and the fish industry being low on cash..."

"That's when we knew," said Priscilla.

"She knew." Joan pointed to Priscilla. "It made sense once she filled me in..."

"So then we checked to see if Mr. P. had sold any of those amazingly upscale classic cars he's got in that big barn-like garage."

"And he had," revealed Joan. "Three of them, it turns out, but not because he was doing anything illicit with the money."

"I'm so glad to hear that," said Mildred. "I've liked him and Maura for a long time, and respected their philanthropy for not only Tisbury and the Haven, but the island in general. Why did he need the money? Is someone sick?"

"To change the soup company fittings to become a fresh chowder and soup company, not canned. But that meant he had to reoutfit everything to nab the New England Bread Company deal."

Rebekah frowned. "Back it up, ladies. What deal?"

"New England Bread had extended an offer to carry the Pennington soups and chowders at all their restaurants and stores up and down the East Coast," Joan explained.

"But that meant a full changeover, which he was trying to do quietly," added Priscilla. "He ran low on money, the contract check hadn't come through, and he was in a dreadful bind at a time of year when no one wants to transport old cars or monkey around, and he didn't want to mortgage the house and put Maura at risk."

"Most people aren't looking at big ticket buying like that in December," Joan said.

"The restaurant chain said the contract would be closed and payment issued before Christmas, so he borrowed money from the pension fund, figuring to replace it once the funds were in his account."

"Only December being what it is, *i*'s didn't get dotted and *t*'s didn't get crossed, and the payment ended up coming the day of the storm. But by then the missing funds had been discovered, Sonya was a prime suspect and put on leave, and the whole thing spiraled out of control."

"Oh my word." Rebekah drew her lacy ivory shawl more snugly around her shoulders. "Would he have truly taken his own life, do you suppose? Over something as replaceable as money?"

"Replaceable if you have it, I suppose," noted Priscilla. She sipped her coffee, then set it down. "He was caught in an impossible spot. He had this beautiful daughter who'd shown up out of the blue—"

"You don't think she's a carpetbagger or sandbagger or whatever they call it when folks just show up pretending to be one thing when they're really quite another to get another person's money, do you?" asked Gail.

"She's the real deal," said Gerald. "While Godfrey believed her from the beginning, he was savvy enough to have a DNA test done."

"That being so easy these days. It's an amazing thing, isn't it?" Rebekah sighed. "A long-lost child and a new business venture. But I can't imagine how Maura took all of this. She's never been the same since Stevie's and Caleb's deaths. Caleb Bennett was the boy who went out on the boat with Stevie on that wretched day. Caleb's family tried to sue the Penningtons for a lot of money, but the judge, being a sensible sort, said sometimes tragedy strikes and it's not about money. It's about opportunity and fate and good choices and each boy had the chance to make a different choice and didn't. But then I heard that Godfrey paid the lawyer fees and court costs for the Bennetts because they'd already been slammed once."

"Will the court go easy on him?" Gail wondered.

"They should," grumped Uncle Hugh. "And everyone in this town knows it. And shame on the bank that they didn't just ante up the money when he needed the loan."

"The canned soup business did look pretty shaky, Uncle Hugh." Priscilla thought about sampling the plate of peanut butter fudge cookies, but thoughts of a summery dress worn in front of a lot of people held her back.

"It may have, but Godfrey wasn't shaky. I expect pride got in the way of him telling them the whole tale."

"And he was sworn to secrecy until the deal was finalized," added Joan. "New England Bread stocks would have gone up if someone leaked the news of a merger, so he couldn't even tell the bank what was pending."

"How *is* Maura doing?" wondered Ellie. "She's got such a kind heart, but she's been angry over losing her son for a long time."

Joan and Priscilla exchanged looks before Priscilla answered. "I don't know. We didn't want to pry, and there's really no reason to invade her privacy, but this is a lot to handle. An old flame's daughter, her husband's grandchild, the crime. Now it's all out in the open. And she's such a private woman."

"She needs our prayers," said Gail sensibly. "As does Godfrey. And the judge. I know it sounds simple to equate borrowing or stealing a million dollars from a fund as a small error of judgment, but he didn't intend to keep the money. And we all know he'd have sold things to repay it, and that's got to weigh in his favor, don't you think?"

Priscilla had no idea. "I've found that things are a little different here than in Kansas," she told them, and they all laughed. They knew the truth in that. "But I think it all comes down to the judge and if he believes Godfrey's intent. We'll have to wait and see. For now, that food smells awfully good. Let's eat. You go first, Uncle Hugh, and don't think for one minute we won't be watching your choices. Not because we're mean," she added. "Because we want you around for a while, yet."

"Our goals are simpatico," declared the old man. "A courting fellow wants to look his very best for his intended, so I'm set to behave myself. Once spring arrives, Marigold Townsend won't be able to resist my charms."

"Oh, Pop, you crack me up." Gail reached around from his side and hugged him. "No sane woman would be able to say no."

Gerald had come up alongside Priscilla in the living room. "So a courting fellow should look his best for his intended?" He whispered the words as he gazed forward, then he grinned.

"Indubitably," she whispered back, but then she added just as softly, "Fortunately, you already look amazing, Gerald." Then she smiled at him.

And Captain Gerald O'Bannon smiled right back.

CHAPTER TWENTY-FOUR

Priscilla planned to meet Joan in the village three days later. She wanted to drop off Mildred's washed and dried casserole dish, see Candy about Rachel's wedding cake, and swing by the hospital to meet Joan. Then they would both stop by and see Sonya.

She hurried up the walk to the museum and knocked on the kitchen door.

"Priscilla!" Mildred looked happy to see her. "I am so glad to see another human being that I need to give you a hug, and we both know I am not a hugger by nature." She hugged Priscilla and then huffed a breath. "I've found that the long days of winter make me pine for summer. And then the insanity of our busy summers makes me long for the quiet of winter. Both stretch too long in my opinion. Have you got time for coffee?"

"Not today, but I'll come by Friday," Priscilla told her. "And I can grab cookies from Candy's place," she offered.

"No need, I'll make cookies tomorrow. It will feel good to do something. And if Joan or Gail would like to come along, feel free to make it a group meeting."

"I'll do that." She handed Mildred the 13 × 9–inch pan. pan. "And thank you for that potato casserole. It was marvelous! I'll see you on Friday, my friend."

"Perfect." Mildred shut the door, and Priscilla hurried over to the bakery.

It was fairly quiet. Midday, midweek, and in the off-season. She bustled in, ordered a dozen cookies because she felt like it, dress or no dress, and then she cornered Candy. "We need to talk, my friend."

"About a certain wedding cake?" asked Candy.

"That is my chosen topic of conversation." Priscilla laughed. "Can we contract you to do Rachel's wedding cake this summer? I know how busy you are."

Candy made a face. "Summers are insane."

"And I know you don't like to take on extra work."

"Except for the very nicest of friends," Candy allowed.

"So what do you think?" Priscilla wouldn't press her, but there was no one on the island that would do a better cake for Rachel's upcoming nuptials than the funny young woman standing in front of her.

"Absolutely. I'm putting it on the calendar right now," she told Priscilla. She pulled out her phone, brought up her Google calendar, and added Rachel's date into the bakery listing. "I need Rachel to come see me to finalize the arrangements, and I need that to happen before we get busy. Before the end of April. Once May hits, I don't have time for meetings."

Priscilla texted that to Rachel on the spot. A few seconds later she received a reply. "She'll be happy to come meet with you," Priscilla said. "Probably not until March because they're swamped for the next four weeks, but she'll call you and set it up."

"Perfect."

Harper had bagged the cookies, but then Priscilla had another idea. "Do you ladies know what Maura Pennington likes?"

"Sure do, we pack it up a few times a week."

Priscilla turned back to Harper. "Can you pack me a Maura box, please? I'd like to drop it off to her. I'm going right by the hospital to see Joan."

"Of course." Within a couple of minutes Priscilla had both boxes in hand, and another errand done. And now...

On to see Sonya.

She parked in the hospital visitors' lot and walked in. Joan was coming down the hall. She hailed Priscilla, and they fell into step as they moved toward the administrative wing. They both smiled to see Sonya back at her desk, right where she belonged.

"Joan! Priscilla!" She rounded the desk and came their way. "Oh, this is such a pleasure, to see my two favorite sleuths! I can't begin to thank you both for all you've done. I honestly don't know if anyone would have realized the truth about what happened if you two hadn't gotten involved."

"Well thank that husband of yours," Priscilla reminded her. "If he hadn't come to Joan, we might not have gotten a good jump on things. How's everything going? And how is Maura doing?" She darted a glance to the empty cubicle to their left. "I brought her a box of her favorites. It's awfully hard to be the innocent bystander in a situation like this."

"I'm just leaving to go see her on my lunch. Come with me."

"Oh, we shouldn't. Should we?" Joan looked doubtful. "I mean, with all that's gone on?"

"She'll want to thank you. Both of you," said Sonya. "Hop in my car. We can be there in a few minutes and back by one thirty."

They climbed into Sonya's SUV, and when they pulled into the Pennington driveway on Paul's Point, Joan sighed. "I can't even imagine something like this." She got out of the car and surveyed the sprawling sea-gray home. Trimmed in white and with cranberry red doors, the vintage-style home blended old and new in absolute perfection.

"Come on, it's cold out here." Sonya led the way.

At the last minute, Priscilla was tempted to dash back to the car and hide out, but then the door opened and Maura stood there.

Chance over.

"Maura." Sonya motioned Priscilla and Joan in before her, then she stepped in and hugged Maura. "Oh, I miss you, my friend. The office isn't the same without you, but of course you know that." She stepped back. "Priscilla and Joan stopped by, and I absolutely forced them to come with me to see you."

Maura turned their way, and Priscilla wasn't sure what to expect. She and Joan had uncovered her husband as the thief who quietly secreted a million dollars from an investment fund. Most women wouldn't take that favorably. "I'm so glad you came," she told them.

Joan looked at Priscilla and Priscilla looked right back at her, surprised. "Really?"

"Yes. Come on in here and have a seat, ladies." She led the way into a gorgeously appointed living room. Broad. Deep. Filled with comfortable sprawling furniture.

Priscilla started to sit, then handed Maura the box. "I was by Candy's and I wasn't sure if you'd been able to make it into town since the power came back on..."

"Or do I have the nerve to show my face in town, is more likely," Maura said. She accepted the box and set it on the nearby table. "Priscilla, thank you. Both of you. That's so very kind, but mostly, thank you for giving me my husband back."

Priscilla raised a hand to her chin, like she always did when life didn't compute. Then she dropped it back into her lap. "I don't get it," she told Maura. "I am officially confused."

"We'd drifted apart," she told them in a calm, measured voice. "When our son died, it took the light out of both of us. We were never able to have more than one child. We tried. The health professionals tried. It didn't happen, and they didn't have all the crazy miraculous things they've got in their reproductive arsenals now back then. So Stevie was our life. When he was gone, it was like we didn't know how to go on as a couple anymore. Godfrey went his way. I went mine. And we smiled for the cameras as needed. I had no idea the company was in such dire straits. He couldn't talk to me, and I couldn't talk to him. So much time wasted." Regret deepened her expression. "And when Lisa showed up, I wanted to leave. I can't believe I'm admitting that now, because it's such a hateful thing to resent another person's joy like that, but it's true.

"I didn't leave. I just worked hard. Godfrey would come by the office, bringing me this and that. My order at Candy's. Chocolates. Flowers. I made that good man feel guilty that his daughter had found him, because I couldn't have what I wanted. Our son." She looked at Sonya as if for help. "What was I thinking? Where did my Christian charity go?"

"Grief is a hard housemate, my friend." Sonya laid her hand over Maura's.

"It is, but when does grief become an excuse to be mean? To keep yourself separate? Because that's what I did, as if I was the only person in the world to suffer. While I'm ashamed of my actions, I'm myself again, and ready to move on. With my husband, good man that he is, and luckily, a forgiving one."

"Are you going back to work?" Priscilla asked.

"I'm actually beginning a new job in a few weeks' time," Maura told them. "I think a new career path is the best thing at this point, don't you?"

"I do," Sonya agreed, "but only because it's the best possible change you could make."

Priscilla was about to inquire about the new job when a distinctly familiar sound echoed from the adjoining room.

"And there's my new boss right now." Maura's smile lit her face. She got up, crossed the room, and came back carrying an amazingly perfect newborn baby. "Miss Sophia is going to run her Grammy ragged, I expect, and once she's walking and talking I'm pretty sure I won't need trips to the gym. Trips to the playground will take their place, won't they, sweet thing?"

She held little Sophia Ruth up for them to see.

Joan wiped more than one tear from her face. So did Priscilla as Sonya passed them each a tissue. "You've come to terms with Lisa, then?"

"I've erased my former foolishness off the slate for good," Maura declared. A young woman in a housekeeper's smock came in with a bottle.

"Here you go, Miss Maura."

"Thank you, Ana." Maura settled herself into a broad, wing-back chair and tipped the nipple toward the hungry infant's mouth. "Lisa's catching a nap upstairs, so this is the grandparent feeding. Godfrey's overseeing things at the plant, Lisa's husband is at the local office, and I get to feed my precious granddaughter. I'm thrilled that the fishermen's council has dropped the charges by citing an internal oversight error and that the judge happily restored things to order. Godfrey has replaced the funds and donated an additional three million to the fund. He still feels terrible for letting Sonya take the blame for so long, but she's been very gracious. I don't think life could get any better than that. Do you?"

"I do not." Priscilla had to fight down the emotion rising within her. "In fact, I think this is our happiest ending ever. Isn't it, Joan?"

Joan smiled at Maura, Sonya, then Priscilla. "Without a doubt. We've got a lot to thank God for on this island. That storm showed us that reality firsthand. But this"—she regarded the poignant image of grandparent and child as the wee girl nuzzled her bottle like her life depended on it—"this is absolutely the best ever."

It was, Priscilla decided as Ana brought mugs of fresh coffee to the living room. They'd won and lost in these past few weeks. They'd buried a trusty friend and celebrated Uncle Hugh's home-coming. They'd cleared one name and helped a quirky newspaper woman add some serious credentials to her résumé. And while four of the Quimby paintings had seriously good offers, a California licensing firm had advanced payment for Randolph's work, a deal that would keep Dee Dee in her home and comfortable shoes for the rest of her life. And a man at risk of losing it all had joined Gambler's Anonymous, hopefully creating a new life plan.

It was the best ending ever, she agreed, but she knew one thing. When something ended, something else began, and February on the island loomed long and cold for a relatively short month.

It didn't matter. Whatever it held, they'd be ready for it with faith, hope, and love. She smiled at the newborn baby in Maura's arms. Yes, love as their mainstay.

AUTHOR LETTER

Dear Readers,

I am thoroughly enjoying my "time" in Martha's Vineyard with you! This book was so much fun to write for a variety of reasons. First, I love these characters! Priscilla and the cousins.... Gerald.... the dogs! (*grin*) And while our beloved Sammy crossed the rainbow bridge in this beautiful story, our love for dogs and cats and our fur babies continues. Even though we know it's for a limited time.

I love how Priscilla and Joan put their heads together to fix things for Sonya...and that the collateral impact helped one man own his mistakes and take a much-needed right turn, another man get over a grudge, and pushed Dee Dee to get the help she needed. God surely does work in ways mysterious, and He uses us to be the hands and feet of Christ. Isn't it glorious how that happens? As long as we're willing to walk the walk!

Thank you so much for reading *Catch of the Day*. I hope you loved reading it as much as I enjoyed crafting it with the help of the wonderful editors at Guideposts. Feel free to contact me at loganherne@gmail.com or friend me on Facebook. Or stop by my website http://ruthloganherne.com You're always welcome!

In God's love,
Ruthy

ABOUT THE AUTHOR

Multi-published, award-winning author Ruth Logan Herne loves God, her family, her country, chocolate, coffee, dogs, miniature donkeys (she owns three, and one might be expecting!) and stinkin' cute kids. Author of over forty novels and novellas, Ruthy lives on a pumpkin farm in Western New York. She's married with six kids, a borrowed/stolen daughter of her heart, fourteen grandkids, and a love for storytelling. She occasionally has Fritos for breakfast and alleges that they are merely a salty, crispy form of breakfast cereal. And she'll stand by that statement. While crunching!

AN ARMCHAIR TOUR OF MARTHA'S VINEYARD

Traveling to Owen Beach Park in Vineyard Haven

Located in Tisbury, this out-of-the-way beach is a true gem on Martha's Vineyard. Owen Beach, named for William Barry Owen, was gifted to the town by his wife in 1922. The bandstand and the seats surrounding it were all built by volunteers. Local women provided the workers with a free supper each night. In that same spirit of generosity, talented visitors to the island have been pressed into the gift of their services, providing band concerts, fireworks, and entertainment.

The sandy beach edges a shallow, warm-water cove. That makes it a great place to bring children. Because it's tucked away, it tends to avoid the seasonal mayhem that provides crucial tourism dollars for local businesses. It's also a lovely spot to sit and watch the sunrise over the water, a quiet place of contemplation.

Located at the end of Owen Park Way off of Main Street, there's not much parking space, but it's in easy walking distance from Vineyard Haven. Dinghies often dot the shore in milder months, ready to be rowed to larger vessels. In 2015 the town declared Owen Beach to be one of its finest treasures. While a master plan for upkeep and renovation is being designed, volunteers are following in the footsteps of their forbearers. They've repaired the flagpole, planted new gardens, repainted the grandstand, and leveled and moved the existing benches. This quiet corner wasn't just a gift to the town back in 1922. It's become a gift to all who love the Vineyard.

SOMETHING DELICIOUS FROM OUR SEASIDE FRIENDS

Joan is understandably proud of her bread pudding, and with good reason! Bread pudding is one of those New England staples, a hearty, filling dessert that makes good use of stale bread and fresh eggs from country hens. Wise cooks like Joan realize it bakes better when immersed in a "water bath," so they set the pudding pan into a larger pan filled with about an inch of hot water, letting the water "ease" the sides of the pudding (to avoid hard crusts) and keep the moisture level even in the oven. Joan bakes it at 350 degrees until the pudding is firm on top and lightly browned or dark gold. This is her apple version, a sure winter pleasing variety. And note she uses NO RAISINS, but if you choose to, well...we won't tell! Just add about ½ cup to the mix before you bake it!

Joan's Apple Bread Pudding

Six large eggs, beaten

2 teaspoons vanilla

1 teaspoon cinnamon

½ teaspoon nutmeg

¾ cup sugar

1¾ cup milk

1 apple peeled, cored, chopped, and microwaved for about 2 minutes

Enough stale or crusty bread, cut or broken into small pieces, to add to the custard. (Usually 8–10 slices or bagel halves. I use whatever is left over in the bread drawer... with the exception of onion or garlic or everything bagels! ☺)

Preheat oven to 350 degrees. Depending on the size of the pan you're using, put a larger pan (Doesn't matter what kind, a big ol' frying pan will do. Doesn't have to be fancy, just serviceable!) filled with about 1 inch of water into the oven. Your pudding will sit in this pan of water while it bakes.

Whisk eggs thoroughly. Add sugar, vanilla, cinnamon, nutmeg. Mix. Add milk. Mix thoroughly. Add chopped apples. Pour into lightly greased 8" square pan (deep) or 13 × 9-inch. Add broken bread until it pretty much soaks up all the custard. Place this pan into the heated water pan in oven. Bake at 350 degrees until the pudding looks "dry" on top, a kind of golden-brown appearance. (Length of time depends on depth of pan. The deeper the pan, the longer the baking time). Pudding will puff up some as it cooks.

Serve warm with ice cream or whipped cream or my mother's standby: butter balls! Butterballs were an easy way of sweetening the pudding by mixing 1 part butter with 3 parts sugar. Here's how you make this old-fashioned treat:

½ cup soft butter

1½ cups granulated sugar.

Mix thoroughly... form into tablespoon size balls. Tuck one butterball into each serving of hot pudding.

Read on for a sneak peek of another exciting book
in the series Mysteries of Martha's Vineyard!

Beyond the Sea
by Janice Thompson

E liza Jamison bought a...what?"

Priscilla shifted her cell phone to her left ear to answer her cousin Trudy's question. "A 1957 powder blue Bel Air convertible. I can't believe I'm telling you this. It's supposed to be top secret. But I'm going to bust if I don't tell someone."

"My goodness." Trudy's pause felt elongated, and Priscilla wondered what she might be thinking. "I know she loves classic cars. She and that fiancé of hers both do. I've seen them up and down the island, struttin' their stuff, Carson in that blue Jaguar and Eliza in her red Corvette. But why get a new one this close to the wedding date? They both already own classics, after all."

"Right." Priscilla struggled to maintain her hold on Jake's leash as he pulled her along the cliff's edge. "I guess it doesn't make sense when you consider what they already have."

"Right. Then why spring for a new...er, old...convertible?"

Priscilla shivered as she waited for Jake to do his business. Her teeth chattered, and she fought to pull her jacket tighter to ward off February's chill. "It's all part of a big surprise. Eliza's been planning this for ages. They'll drive off into the sunset—rather, to the Harbor View hotel in Edgartown—in this brand-new-to-them car. Carson has no idea she's purchased it, so he's going to be wowed, for sure."

"Happy wedding day, I bought you a car!" Trudy laughed. "That's some present, don't you think?"

"You can say that twice and mean it." Priscilla glanced out over the water, catching a glimpse of the early-morning sun dancing across the ripples. "Anyway, the car arrived yesterday afternoon from the mainland. You wouldn't believe what we had to go through to get it here."

"We?" Trudy's question was laced with curiosity.

"I've been helping," Priscilla explained. "Long story. Don't want Carson to catch on, you know."

"I see. Wow, she's taking this present very seriously."

"Wouldn't you, if you spent that much money on a surprise gift?" Priscilla shifted the phone to her other ear, never releasing her hold on the leash. "Anyway, I've been helping Eliza communicate back and forth with the restoration company in Boston over the past month or so. You wouldn't believe how much work has gone into that vehicle. It was a mess when she bought it, but you should see it now." Priscilla fought the temptation to whistle, though memories of the beautiful vehicle warranted such a response. The car was a real beauty, after all.

"I was wondering how you figured into this story." Trudy laughed. "Then again, you manage to find your way into a great many stories in Misty Harbor, don't you, Priscilla?"

"That seems to be the case, whether I want to or not." She paused to think through her cousin's words. "In this case, I also made all of the arrangements for the transport of the car from Boston to the Vineyard. The driver—a woman named Sally Jenson—arrived on the ferry yesterday with the car."

"And you're hiding it where?"

"In Gerald's garage. Carson never goes to Gerald's place, so it's safely tucked away until the wedding on Saturday. Just three more days. It'll go by fast. I went by last night and admired it again."

"So, Gerald has played a role in this too." Trudy's voice took on a suspicious tone. "Very interesting."

"Just loaned us his garage is all."

"Right. So, how did the car turn out?" Trudy asked. "After the restoration, I mean."

Priscilla paused as memories of the gorgeous vehicle flooded over her. "It looks amazing. I could almost see myself driving along the coast in that gorgeous convertible, my hair whipping in the wind."

"In February?" Her cousin laughed again. "Remember that big winter storm that just blew through?"

"I don't mean I would drive it with the top down in February, silly. Only in the spring or summer. Anyway, I can definitely see the appeal. A car like that would make me feel young again."

"In that case, I'll take one, myself." Trudy chuckled, and Priscilla could almost see her expression. "But I'm really surprised you were able to keep all of this a secret from us, Priscilla. You really are turning out to be quite the sleuth—you know how and when to keep secrets and you're able to solve crimes, to boot."

Priscilla managed to coax Jake back toward the house. "Nah. Just trying to keep Carson from finding out anything, which is why I didn't let you ladies know about the goings-on. It's all top secret as I said, so mum's the word."

"So, now you're a sleuth and a car aficionado?"

"Hardly." Priscilla laughed as she thought through her cousin's choice of words. "For the record, I know zero about old cars. Zip. Nada. But Gerald seems to. I only know what I see with my eyes—a gorgeous old classic."

"Are you calling Gerald O'Bannon a gorgeous old classic?" A girlish giggle escaped from Trudy's end. "My goodness."

"No." Though Priscilla had a hard time not smiling as she thought about how comfortable things had become between the two of them. Of course, it didn't hurt that the man had striking eyes and the perfect laugh lines. Perhaps he could be called a classic after all.

"Did I lose you?" Trudy's voice startled her back to reality.

"Um, no. I'm still here." Priscilla was glad her cousin couldn't see her face over the telephone. Her warm cheeks must be beet red.

"Sure you are. Well, you must admit, he's easy on the eyes, a lot like that car you're describing. And runs well for his age too."

"Trudy, please."

"I do believe Gerald would be there for you, no matter what you might need." Trudy sighed. "Just saying. The two of you are as thick as thieves."

A delightful shiver ran its way up Priscilla's back as she thought through her cousin's words. Or was that just the cold wind off the water? She watched as Jake paused near the garden, coarse and brown from February's chill. "C'mon, Jake. Do your business and let's get back inside. I want to watch the morning news and then get this day started."

"Yes, get inside where it's warm," Trudy echoed. "We're supposed to have another cold snap over the next few days. Reporter on the news said to stay inside."

"If only I could," Priscilla said. "I have plans to help Eliza with last-minute details for the wedding. I sure hope we don't end up with another nor'easter like the one we just went through. Brr."

"Surely not. Anyway, this wedding will happen, good weather or bad. I talked to Eliza just the other day, and she's so excited about having the ceremony and reception at the B&B. She and the owner, Anna, have become good friends."

"Yes, ever since Eliza's mom passed away, Anna has played a motherly role in her life."

Jake tugged at the leash and then took off after a squirrel. Priscilla fought to keep up with him, nearly losing her grip on the leash. "Do you m-mind if I p-put you on speaker, T-Trudy? I'm having a hard time keeping the phone next to my ear. Jake keeps dragging me around the yard."

"Sure. I don't mind being on speaker. There's no one there but you and Jake, right? Not that it would matter. I'm an open book."

"It's just us. I'd just fixed a cup of coffee and turned on the TV to watch the news when Jake decided he couldn't wait one minute longer. I was afraid to let him out without the leash. You know how he likes to wander."

Just as she rounded the side of the house, the crunch of tires against her gravel driveway caught Priscilla's attention.

"Hang on, Trudy. Sounds like someone just pulled into my driveway." Priscilla made her way to the front of the cottage and caught her first glimpse of Gerald O'Bannon's Coast Guard vehicle. As he opened the driver's side door and stepped out, she couldn't help but smile. Fully decked out in his Coast Guard uniform, he looked like a hero from another era.

Unfortunately, the somber expression on his face did little to bolster her enthusiasm.

"Um, Trudy...it's Gerald."

"Ooo-la-la. You two going to drive off into the sunset in that new convertible before Eliza and Carson have a chance? Sounds like fun."

"I'm not so sure he's in the mood for fun, judging from the body language."

"Oh no. Well, keep me on speaker. I'm dying to hear what's going on."

"Trudy, I can't do that. I'll call you back later." Priscilla hastily swiped her finger across the screen of her phone and slid it in the front pocket of her hooded sweatshirt.

Gerald took several steps in her direction, and the pronounced wrinkles in his brow did little to put her at ease. "Everything okay?" she asked him.

He pulled off his hat and waves of hair fell across his forehead. "No. There's something I need to tell you, but it's probably a good idea if you sit down first. Can we go inside?"

"Of course. But, sit down? Why?" Her heart raced. Had something happened to a family member? Uncle Hugh, perhaps? After a recent heart issue, she worried about him.

Priscilla pulled Jake to the front door of her cottage. She opened it and stepped inside. Gerald followed closely behind, then shut the door.

"Is it Uncle Hugh? Please tell me he's okay."

"He's okay. Just do me a favor and sit down, Scilla."

So she sat. Like a compliant child, she dropped down into her favorite living room chair. Priscilla set the cell phone on the end table and faced him.

Gerald paced the room, which only caused her blood pressure to rise even more. When he finally turned her way, she could hardly believe the words that tumbled out of his mouth.

"I hate to be the one to tell you this, but Eliza's newly restored Bel Air convertible...has been stolen."

Sign up for the
Guideposts Fiction Newsletter
and stay up-to-date on the books you love!

You'll get sneak peeks of new releases, recommendations from other Guideposts readers, and special offers just for you . . .
and it's FREE!

Just go to Guideposts.org/Newsletters
today to sign up.

Guideposts®

**Visit Guideposts.org/Shop
or call (800) 932-2145**